Inn Hallowed Ground

by

Rhonda Blackhurst

Spirit Lake Mysteries

Cover Art by *Tina Lynn Stout*

The Wild Rose Press, Inc.
PO Box 708
Adams Basin, NY 14410-0708
Visit us at www.thewildrosepress.com

Publishing History
First Edition, 2025
Trade Paperback Print ISBN 978-1-5092-6372-1
Digital ISBN 978-1-5092-6373-8

Spirit Lake Mysteries
Published in the United States of America

Dedication

To Clint, my One. And to Ben and Alex—being your mama is my greatest blessing.

Acknowledgements

There are so many people to thank that it could consume an entire book on its own. To keep things simple, I would like to thank: My editor, Ally Robertson. You are such a dream to work with. My cover designer, Tina Lynn Stout. Karen Whalen for your wisdom, insight, and honesty in your feedback. My parents, who taught me the love of story at a very young age. My boys, who have taught me from day one about unconditional love. Yvette, for her example of grace and gentleness. For my grandbabies, who teach me the importance of taking time for play. And for my husband, who supports me in all my endeavors, my go-to for police procedural questions, and who puts up with me when I stray from "proper" procedure for the sake of story, something not easy to do for a retired police chief.

Chapter 1

Max Winters was to arrive at my inn this afternoon.

I couldn't decide if what churned in my gut was anticipation or foolishness. Thanks to the wide-reaching reputation of a so-far friendly ghost, Spirit Lake, Minnesota flourished with tourism, so it was a stroke of luck my inn had an available room. From early spring through mid-January the following year, I scarcely had a vacancy, save for the rare last-minute cancellation. As was the case when Max called to schedule for one day during the first week of April. Today.

I glanced at my fitness watch. Twelve thirty. Check-in time wasn't until two, unless guests made prior arrangements. Which Max hadn't done because I'd been peeking at the guest register all morning.

As I kept busy straightening and setting tables in the dining room, I stole frequent glimpses of the lake's spring melt. Whisper Lake, named so because of countless people hearing a woman's faint voice while out on the lake, despite no one else being present. None could decipher words, only that it was a mournful tone.

Today, the ice was eerily dark in places, looking like it was ready and waiting to devour its next victim. Yet, it held such beauty.

What *wasn't* beautiful was my reflection in the wall of windows. I sighed and smoothed my unruly red curls, the inexorable result of Minnesota humidity.

"Andie Rose," Lily, one of the desk gals, said from around the corner to the foyer. "Detective Parker is here to see you."

I swallowed the sudden lump that formed in my throat. Noah Parker was the new detective in Spirit Lake. According to Lily's counterpart at the front desk, Jade, and Izzy, my seventeen-year-old genius sous chef, he was *hot*. I kept my opinion to myself. But his presence here when Max was to arrive at any time spiked my heart rate. Not that I was dating either of them. Even if I wanted to date, the two of them weren't likely, each for his own reason. But their presence here at the same time made me, shall we say, uncomfortable.

"What does he want?" I asked Lily.

"You." She grinned and winked.

"Pfft. Aren't you just a hoot."

"I can be," Noah said as he walked into the room.

I waved my hand forward as I pressed my other hand against one last out-of-control curl, smashing it against my head. "Come on in."

"Thanks, I will." He sidled up beside me and admired the lake. "The lake is stunning. But you wouldn't catch me out there."

"I would hope not." His presence was so close I could nearly feel the heat from his body. I took a step back and faced him again. "What have I done to deserve this visit? I can't remember breaking any laws or getting in the way of one of your investigations." I grinned. "Or did you just miss me?"

"I haven't seen you for a couple of months. That scares me, like a *lot*, so I thought I'd do a welfare check." His eyes danced with amusement.

"Well, lucky for you, I haven't had any murders to

2

solve for you. Not even a murderer to save you from. Again."

He laughed. "Each has their own version of events."

I smiled. I saved his butt from a murderer last winter, and I wasn't about to let him forget it.

"You're right," I said. "Some of us believe the truth and some of you believe what you *wish* was true. I'm keeping it in my back pocket. Just in case."

"It?"

"The knowledge of saving you from death."

He arched his eyebrows. "In case of what?"

"I might need it for leverage someday."

He nodded and laughed again. "I kinda missed this verbal sparring. No one does it better than you."

I gave him a deadpan look. "You must lead a boring life, Detective." He remained quiet, so I spread my arms out. "You came. You saw. I'm alive and well. And yet you linger." Still, he was quiet, so I gave him a sidelong look. "Okay, why are you really here? Need a coaching session?" I couldn't imagine that was the case, but hey, who knew? Besides running the inn, my side hustle is as a life coach. Relationship coaching is part of my coaching specialty. Ironic since I suck at relationships. I live by my dad's favorite phrase, *Those who can, do; those who can't, teach.* I teach.

Noah bit his lower lip as if to stop what he was about to say. "My sister is moving to town. She bought the old bookstore."

My eyes grew wide. "The one that went out of business a long time ago?"

"Is there another one?" He cocked his head.

"Not that I know of."

"Well, yeah, that one then."

"Sister Alice mentioned a couple of weeks ago someone bought the building and was fixing it up, but I haven't checked it out yet."

He shook his head, as if clearing the confusion lodged there. "Now *that* surprises the heck out of me."

"Why are you surprised?"

"Because you make it your business to know literally *everything* in this town."

"How rude." My scowl turned into a grin. "But probably true. Lately, though, except for my meetings in town, I've been busy here. Up Your Game Coaching has really taken off." I thrust out a hand, palm facing him. "I'm not complaining."

"Remind me to refer everyone I come into contact with to you, so it keeps you busy for a long time and out of my hair." He smirked. "Seriously, though, I know how busy you are with the inn and coaching, but I hoped you could give my sister the grand tour of Spirit Lake."

I dropped my chin and looked at him. "After that last dig?"

He smiled sheepishly. "What if I say please?"

"I'll add it to the growing list of things you owe me for."

He tucked his hands in the front pockets of his jeans and rocked back on his heels, blowing through pursed lips. "Well, I—"

I snickered, enjoying his discomfort for a moment, before deciding to put the guy out of his misery. "I'd love to. I don't have any available rooms though, unless there's a cancelation."

"She doesn't need one. She's one of these tiny-home-loving people and applied for a permit to build small living quarters onto the back of the bookstore, which the town approved. Until that part's done, she's staying with me. At least whenever she's not supervising the construction crew." He snickered. "I bet they'd prefer her to stay out from under their feet."

"Speaking from past experience?"

"Not from experience with my sister, no. But I know what it's like to have an amateur detective get under my feet as I'm trying to work."

I gave him *the* look again; once more he snickered and playfully ducked, avoiding the proverbial arrow.

"How old is she?"

"My age. We're twins."

I groaned. "Oh, God. There's two of you?"

"I'm the good twin."

"Ha! I'd be hard-pressed to believe that."

"Well? What do you say?"

I bit back a smile and said nothing, knowing it was driving him crazy.

"Are you gonna make me beg, or what? Because I won't—"

"Of course I will. But it would have been satisfying to hear you beg for my help."

"You're impossible," he muttered.

"As an only child, I always wanted a sister. Give her my number."

"First, you can't have her as your sib. I like her. Most of the time." He smiled. "Her name is Nova, but—"

"Nova and Noah?" I said, face askew. "I can't imagine how difficult it must have been for your folks when you were growing up. Or why they would have done it to begin with."

He nodded. "When they realized their mistake, they

began calling her by her middle name. Quinn. It was my grandmother's name."

"What do *you* call her?"

"Brat."

"She probably calls you the same thing."

He laughed. "Probably worse. I don't know what your schedule looks like today, but I'm sure she'll be at the bookstore until the evening hours."

"I'll make a point of getting away from here. I'm looking forward to meeting her." I tilted my head to the side. "You know, to see what secrets she'll tell me about you."

"There are none. Besides, she'd never betray me, because I've got secrets about her."

I sucked in my lips. "Hmm. Now that right there sounds like one healthy relationship. If you tell, I tell."

"Like you excel at relationships," he quipped.

"Ouch." I grinned. "But true."

"As I said, she'll be at the store. The guys'll probably thank you for getting her out from underfoot."

"No problem. I'll hang out with her there and then they'll have two of us, one under each foot."

He groaned and ran a hand over his face. "Good God, what have I done?" He met my eyes. "The point of this is to get her *out* of the store and see the town. She's not exactly adventurous on her own and could use a little help. You know, to see what she's gotten herself into here in Spirit Lake."

"Maybe she enjoys keeping to herself."

He nodded. "She does. Too much."

"You're trying to change who she is?"

He drew his eyebrows together. "Why are you making something so simple, so difficult?"

I caught my lip between my teeth to restrain a smile. "Because it's you." Reality dawned on me, and I let the smile break through. "I cannot even begin to tell you how thrilled I am about this. The bookstore. From what I know, Spirit Lake has grown exponentially, not to mention the level of tourism we have here. She could probably make a killing in books about ghosts alone. Besides, there's nothing like a good, independent bookstore."

"Please don't say kill. With you, that's a four-letter word."

I shrugged a shoulder. "It's a four-letter word no matter who says it."

"With your dad being a big-name thriller author and all, I'm not surprised you like bookstores."

I gave him a side eye. "How did you know? About my dad. I never told you about him."

"I'm a detective, remember?"

I narrowed an eye. "Yeah, but he uses a pen name."

He nodded. "Chandler Langston, I know. What can I say? I'm good at my job." I waited for more. "Okay, fine. I may have seen his books in your library upstairs last winter when I was staying here. And I may have read the dedication and his note to you on the back page."

I chuckled. "That makes more sense." He stayed still, hands in his pockets, so I said, "Is there something else?"

He shook his head. "Nope."

I looked down at Aspen, my red retriever emotional support animal (ESA) for a panic disorder, lying by my feet. "All right then. I'm looking forward to meeting her. Aspen and I will head into town as soon as I tie up one loose end here." I wiggled my eyebrows. "Maybe we'll even beat you there."

He groaned and tipped his head back. When he was almost at the door, I called after him. "Hey, Noah?"

He pivoted to face me, hands still in his pockets. "Yeah?"

I grinned mischievously. "I'm honored you trust me. That you don't think I'd be a bad influence on her and all. Mind if I get Sister Alice to tag along with us?"

He splayed a hand over his face. "How about you don't scare her off before she opens the store? Good grief," he muttered.

"Our women's detective agency could use a third member. Just sayin'."

He narrowed his eyes and turned toward the door. "Not funny."

"One doesn't need formal education to become a P.I. in Minnesota."

"True. But there are other requirements you do not possess. And there's this thing called ethics."

I chuckled. "Okay then. See you later." Aspen trotted after him through the door and into the foyer.

For the short time I'd lived in Spirit Lake, Sister Alice and I had earned the reputation of being a pain in the butt for the police department, but we'd gotten several accolades from townsfolk appreciating our *help* in solving a couple of murders. Ironically, Sister Alice was also my twelve-step recovery sponsor, which kept things—well, *spirited*. She had thirty-one years of sobriety since all those years ago when she'd moved back to Spirit Lake and my grandparents gave her a room at the inn while she, quote, *got her poop in a group and gave up one habit for another*.

Jade's voice reached me in the dining area, a tone

she reserved only for Noah. "Goodbye, Detective."

I snorted and gave a bemused smile before mirroring Noah's statement from a moment ago. "Good grief."

Aspen trotted through the door and sat on his haunches beside me. I reached down and ruffled his silky fur.

"Jade's goofiness over Noah is too much for you, too, huh, buddy?" He lifted his nose and licked my hand. "Come on. Let's go to the office for a minute."

I led the way to the back of the inn, snatched a favorite red wool sweater from the back of a chair, and slipped my arms into it as we walked. My office was a cozy lamp-lit room that doubled as space for both the inn and Up Your Game Coaching. Since I'd begun offering a free coaching session as part of the package for our guests, my business had flourished by word of mouth alone. It'd reached the point where I had to implement a client waiting list. It sometimes dipped into my income, but the benefits for the inn's business took priority. That said, the past few weeks, I'd entertained implementing a different incentive so I could take on more clients who fall within the parameters of my specialty. It's not like the inn lacked business. It would do fine with or without the free coaching session perk. I tucked it back into the recesses of my mind.

I perched on the edge of my desk chair and reached down to love on Aspen, who sprawled on the floor beside me. He usually stayed with me and went wherever I did, but once in a while he'd wander to the desk to be with Jade, who'd just got back from maternity leave. I'm not sure who missed the other more, Aspen or Jade. In Jade's absence, Frank Flowers, the inn's seventy-nine-year-old gardener, became his alternative choice.

My right arm dangled beside Aspen as I leaned back in my chair and wondered about Noah's sister, Quinn. The inn's library was impressive, but the library in town was open for fewer and fewer hours. I kept hoping the town council would step in and require them to be open more. Instead, I discovered they supported the fewer hours due to funding issues, claiming people didn't read physical books like they used to. You could have knocked me over with a feather quill pen at my shock of their ignorance. Of course, they probably thought those of us diehard physical book fans were ignorant. But I was sticking with my opinion and was certain the bookstore would be a huge draw for the town.

I startled when my phone rang, and I sat upright. Aspen looked up lazily, then laid his head back down. I looked at the caller ID. Sister Alice.

"Yo!"

"Has your new boyfriend arrived yet? I'm itching to meet him."

"When a person in recovery tells her sponsor something personal, it's not to be used against her," I said dryly. "And he's not my boyfriend, nor will he be. You know full well I'm not interested in a boyfriend."

"Yeah, right," she scoffed. "You're definitely interested."

"Not in *that* way," I retorted. "Did you call to harass me or for something important?"

"Both. I haven't heard from you today, so thought I'd check in."

"You should be happy I haven't bothered you yet. Hey guess what?" I said before she could say anything. "I know who bought the bookstore in town."

"You don't say," she said, as if pondering the news.

"Whoever bought it has got it looking better already. The place was in shambles and an eyesore."

"I'm leaving here as soon as we hang up to go check it out."

"Well, who is it? And who did you hear it from, one of our sober members? Not everyone is exactly a reliable source."

"Noah Parker. His twin sister bought it. Quinn. She's even got a permit to build small living quarters on the back of it."

She was quiet for a moment. "You don't say. I asked the workers, but they clammed up as if I'd asked for a confession."

I laughed. "You nuns are so intimidating. Noah asked me if I'd show his sister the town. He specifically said you aren't allowed to go with, though, because he doesn't want her corrupted."

She harrumphed. "He can't be too concerned, given he asked *you*. Now are you going to tell me what time Max is supposed to arrive?"

"If I knew, I'd tell you."

"Yeah, right."

"I swear to—"

"Don't say it, young lady."

I laughed. "All I know is sometime this afternoon. Honest."

"Well, keep me posted. For entertainment, if nothing else."

"Don't you have better things to do? Like prepare for your new job on Monday?"

Despite being sisters at St. Michael's church, each of them, three in all, worked in the community. Sister Ida at Lakes News and Reviews, Sister Eunice took Sister

Alice's role at the hospital, and Sister Alice was set to be a temporary librarian for the Ravenwood Junior and Senior high school.

"I'll be sixty-six at the end of the month. That they want a dinosaur for their librarian makes me prepared enough."

"I pity the kid who antagonizes you. Or even misplaces a book."

She snorted. "I love kids."

"I know. If it was me, I'd have a harder time dealing with the parents than the kids. But I guess as a librarian you won't have to deal with parents, anyway."

"From your lips to God's ears, dear. Now call me when the man shows up."

"Wanna meet me at the bookstore? I'm leaving as soon as I hang up with you."

"I'd love to, but I can't. I have a prayer meeting and another meeting afterwards with Father Vincent."

"What'd you do this time?"

"Someone's a little squirrely for not being *interested*. And by the way," she added quickly before I hung up. "Thought you might like to know I'm starting a journal and hope to turn it into a book some day before I meet my Maker."

I scrunched my face. "You're doing what?"

"I didn't stutter, dear. I said I'm going to keep a journal, dating back to when you first took over the inn, and turn it into a book."

"But—"

"Some things are just too good not to use for the sake of entertainment. That's been life since you've moved here."

"Oh God," I muttered, hand over my face.

Chapter 2

Sister Alice snickered as she hung up the phone. In hindsight, she wished she'd told Andie Rose in person of her idea to write a book. The look on Andie Rose's face alone could probably take up an entire chapter. Oh well, this just meant she'd have to get creative when writing it down. Sprinkle a little fiction into the facts—kind of like watching the news. Sister Alice giggled quietly.

Life in Spirit Lake had never been the same since Andie Rose came to town. She'd known of her when Andie was a child and had seen her from a distance, but had never met her face to face. The stories she'd heard from Honey and Henry, Andie Rose's grandparents who owned the inn prior to Andie, had spoken so lovingly about her. They'd never mentioned Andie Rose's history of alcohol abuse, or any specific issues, for that matter, but Sister Alice got the feeling long ago there were things Honey and Henry didn't talk about, even with her. When Sister Alice first saw Andie Rose at a twelve-step meeting in the basement of St. Michael's Church, it all came together like she'd just won a match on that online video game she used to play early in her own sobriety, where you try to get jigsaw pieces to fall into place. The name escaped her at the moment. Age—the gift that kept on giving.

Sister Alice, known for her own rebellious nature, especially by Sister Ida, the house moderator, thought life was exciting before Andie Rose moved to Spirit Lake. Since then, well, she realized just how dull it had been. Ordinary even, and that was something Sister Alice had never been used to. She was grateful Andie Rose had come along to spice things up, if even just a little. One doesn't notice the routine of comfort one falls into until something shakes up said routine, sending one into what felt like another world. And lately the other world surrounded her.

She smiled, grabbed a pen, a paper towel, and began jotting down a few notes to help jar her out of the blank page syndrome. She pushed her eyeglasses up further on the bridge of her nose with her pointer finger and prepared to write, but her mind was a complete blank. The syndrome made a sneak attack. Finally, she wrote two words: Andie Rose.

"There," she said aloud, put down the pen, and smiled. "This'll surely produce an infinite number of words."

****

When Aspen and I got to the bookstore, four men blocked the sidewalk in front of it as they raised a large, attractive backlit sign. We watched as they hoisted it up against the brick building and above the door. Book Den & Pen. Brilliant name.

One guy, hands on hips, took a few steps back. He motioned with one hand and said, "A little to the right." Then, "Nope, too much." He shook his head. "Still no. It's too high. Bring it down some."

One of the men on the scaffold scowled and shouted some obscenities at the director before he looked at me. "Sorry, ma'am."

"I assure you, I've both heard and said worse."

He grinned. "My kinda lady."

I caught my lower lip between my teeth. "Doubt it."

His grin grew wider. "Feisty. I like it. Whatcha doing Friday night?"

I took a deep breath while I stared at him. Did this guy seriously think he was charming? Finally, I said, "I'm busy Friday night," and began to walk away.

"What about next Friday?"

I shook my head. "Nope. Busy then, too." I made another step.

"What about—"

"Busy."

I glanced up at him in disbelief. People deserved to be treated with dignity and respect, no matter who they were, but at times like this, it was a struggle. He cupped his crotch, adjusting whatever needed adjusting. *Ick*! "They're still there, buddy," I mumbled.

"What?" he said, hand now cupped behind his ear.

I exhaled, shook my head, and glanced down at Aspen. "Come on, buddy." But his posture grew rigid.

I glanced at what had caught his attention. Another furry four-legged kid, this one feline. Its heavily lidded yellow eyes peered at Aspen through the bookstore's front bay window.

I chuckled. "Aspen, that thing looks about as disinterested in you as it will be in the books soon to line the shelves."

Aspen barked, garnering a reaction from the cat, but not one of fear. It stood, stretched, and licked its paw before running it over its ear and face, paused to peek at Aspen, then did it again. A wisp of a woman in a white t-shirt that read *Keep Calm and Read a Book*, blue jeans, and sporting round glasses with blue frames the color of denim stepped in front of the window. She pointed toward the side of the building, swooped up the cat with one arm and pulled her long brown hair back with the other hand.

Aspen and I rounded the building to the side where she was already holding the door open. No way could this be Quinn. She couldn't be more different from Noah. Not to mention she looked at least five years younger.

"Hi! I'm looking for Quinn."

She smiled, showing perfect teeth in an ever-so-slight uneven mouth. "Right here." She raised her hand and put it back down. "You must be Andie Rose." She shook my hand with a grip tighter than any I could remember. The pounding of hammers and shriek of drills muted her voice, and I strained to hear.

She looked down at my furry bestie before patting his head, garnering a poisonous look from her enormous feline. "And this must be Aspen. I've heard so much about the both of you."

I arched an eyebrow. "I'm not sure if I should be flattered or afraid."

She waved her hand in dismissal and turned, motioning for us to follow her. "No need to fear my brother."

She and Noah looked like opposites, but the way they talked was similar and made me think of the color orange—warm, comforting, thoughtful.

We trailed behind her into a large room filled with chaos, but sirens now bellowed, muffling the obnoxious noise of the drills and hammers. Aspen lay down and buried his head beneath his crossed paws.

I winced. "You're going to be deaf by the time you open this store," I said. Loudly.

"To be honest, I usually wear those foam ear plug thingies when I'm here."

She bent over and set down the cat, who then wandered toward Aspen to check him out. I held my breath, waiting for sparks to fly. No other cat I'd known was fond of dogs, and this cat was as large as a dog.

Quinn smiled. "Don't worry. Lord Watson is harmless."

"Lord Watson?" She nodded. "What kind of cat is he? Other than huge. He's almost as big as Aspen."

She laughed. "Lord Watson's a Maine Coon." As if hearing his name, Lord Watson turned and rubbed against her leg as he walked past her, turned and walked back the other way, leaning into her. And back again. "They're enormous, but social. Gentle giants. I'm not even sure he'd hurt a mouse if it stood right in front of him."

She nudged the bottom rim of her glasses up with the side of her forefinger. "So Noah said you're going to show me the town?"

I nodded. "I'm looking forward to it. Did he give you any warnings?" After one last deafening wail, the sirens stopped, and the construction noises once again filled the room.

She tipped her head back and laughed. "He did. He also warned me about someone by the name of Sister Alice. But it was all in jest. If he didn't trust you with me, he definitely wouldn't have chosen you to show me around. He's annoyingly protective." She shook her head and sighed. "I'm afraid one of these days I might come unglued on him."

All ninety-five pounds of you. Now that would be a sight.

"He acts like I'm some helpless female," she continued. "And I'm not. I might be small, but I've learned to stand up for myself. I've had to."

In my business as a life coach, we're trained to ask questions. Not just any questions, but the *right* questions. So I was about to ask her what she meant when my phone vibrated in my pocket and distracted me. I slipped it out and looked at the display. Sister Alice.

I held the phone up, smiled. "Sister Alice must have known we were talking about her." I clicked the button and put it up to my ear. "Hi! I'm in town at—"

"We found a body."

I gave a sharp inhale. "Where?"

"In a coffin in the cemetery."

I squinched my eyebrows and looked at Quinn, who again held Lord Watson.

"Okay," I said, drawing the word out. "That's interesting and all, but I'd be more concerned if it *wasn't* in a cemetery."

"It was on top of the ground on an empty plot."

I blinked rapidly as I processed the information. "Holy wicked whiskey!" Aspen sat and peered up at me. "I'll be right there." I hung up the phone and started for the door. "Wanna come with me to St. Michael's?" I asked Quinn. She nodded. "You're about to meet Sister Alice."

Sensing my urgency, she sat Lord Watson on his bed in front of the big display window, grabbed her jacket, let the workers know she'd be back a bit later, and followed Aspen and me. I thought about Noah and inwardly groaned. He was gonna kill me. But it has always been my motto, *It's better to ask for forgiveness than permission.* Why change that now?

****

We reached St. Michael's, and while the strobing lights continued, I thanked the good Lord the sirens were off. I'd been told my voice *carries*—a term my dad called "speaker's formant," and something I've worked to mitigate most of my life—but after the sirens from earlier and the drills and hammers, it wasn't my voice I was concerned about, but my hearing.

Aspen and I jogged across the snow patches, past the daffodils, a few feet away from where Sister Alice stood huddled with Father Vincent and a uniform; Quinn caught up by my side. Sister Eunice and Sister Ida hovered in the background, but I could tell Sister Eunice was dying—pardon the pun—to get to Sister Alice and closer to the action. But apparently the possibility of Sister Ida's wrath for being too much like Sister Alice was too great a threat.

"What are you doing here?"

I jumped at Noah's voice from behind me and turned to see him scowl. "The first day you meet my sister, and you bring her to a crime scene? And not just any crime scene, a *murder*?"

Quinn stuck out a hand toward her twin. "Easy, Noah. I'm here of my own free will. Not to mention I, not you, am acting like an adult right now."

He scowled once more, but it held less power. "How did you find out about it so quickly?" he asked me. Before I could answer, he tilted his head back and groaned. "Sister Alice."

Sister Alice glanced at us and trotted over. "You rang, Detective?"

"*I* didn't, but apparently *you* did."

Quinn sighed. "Noah, stop being so ornery and work

on solving the murder."

He took a beat and shook his head before he glanced toward the crime scene techs and back at Quinn. "I'm going to regret asking Andie Rose to show you around. I don't know what I was thinking."

I squished my eyebrows together. "It's a small town. You don't think we would have met, anyway? Especially in a bookstore. Heck, I might set up camp there."

He groaned. "God help me."

"Parker!" a woman called from where the body was. "We're taking him out of the coffin."

He faced her, jutted his chin in the air in acknowledgement, and briskly headed her way. So did I, quiet as I could, so he didn't hear me. Aspen stayed back with Sister Alice and Quinn.

Noah ducked under the crime scene tape. I followed, as yet unnoticed—by Noah, at least. Two of the uniforms charged with securing the perimeter of the crime scene were too good at their job. One rushed over toward me and barricaded my path with his arm.

"Sorry, ma'am. You have to stay on the other side of the tape."

"Keep your eye on her," Noah called over his shoulder without turning to look.

Shoot! I had to work on my stealth skills.

Sister Alice, Aspen, and Quinn, holding Aspen's leash in her hand, joined me.

"Is my brother always so grumpy at a scene?"

Sister Alice snorted. "Only when we're in the vicinity of said crime scene."

Quinn dipped her chin and looked at her over the rims of her glasses, and then at me. "This happen often?"

Sister Alice pressed her lips into a flat line and the

corner of mine ticked up before we both said in unison, "Hm."

"More so since Andie Rose has moved here," said Sister Alice.

"Thanks a lot," I scoffed. "Here I thought you'd have my back."

"I do, dear. I do. But truth is truth."

Her choice of eyewear for the day, orange with black stripes, contradicted the ever-present crucifix hanging from around her neck.

"Cat got your tongue, dear?" she asked.

I gave her a deadpan look before I turned toward the body just as several people, hands stuffed into latex gloves, lifted it out of the coffin to place it on a large sheet of plastic spread on the ground. I gave a sharp inhale; my hand flew up to my mouth. Unaware of the uniform standing by us, I lifted the crime scene tape and ducked underneath when the uniform gripped my arm.

"Ma'am, you can't—"

"Let her through, Simmons," Noah said. He glued his attention to my face, as if trying to read what was there. "Your face tells me you know something. Do you know who this is?"

I met his eyes and inched closer to get a better look at the body. *It couldn't be. How?*

I reached for my phone. "I gotta call my dad." My voice quivered.

Noah's hand covered mine and gently lowered my phone.

"Andie Rose, who is this?"

"His name is Beau Banks."

"So the sign says. But how is he connected to your dad?"

I took a deep breath and scanned the entire area, my gaze landing on a crude headstone made of cardboard, anchored by a large rock: *Beau Banks: Deserved to Die*, scrawled in red marker.

"Umm." I clamped my lips shut. I couldn't tell Noah the truth. Clearly, someone murdered the man, and given what I knew, it could implicate my dad.

"Um what?" he asked.

I shook my head and licked my lips. "They're old friends. Writing buddies."

"When is the last time they've seen each other?"

I turned back toward Quinn, patted my leg for Aspen, and she unclipped his leash, freeing him to come to my side. I squatted beside him and wrapped an arm around his neck, burying my hand in his silky red fur. He leaned into me.

"Andie?"

His tone was gentle, a switch from earlier. But I felt his gaze on my every move.

"I don't know."

"Really? Because I think you know more than you're letting on. This has really gotten you ruffled. And don't say it's because of seeing a dead body." His voice was quiet and comforting.

Noah was aware of a past part-time job of mine as a hairdresser and makeup artist for a funeral home. I worked drumming up something to pacify him for now until I called my dad.

"I think it's been a while. Beau turned into a recluse. Never left his apartment as far as I knew."

"I'll need his phone number, Andie Rose. Your dad's."

I glanced at him and quickly averted my gaze. "I'll

let him know."

"There's something more here you're not telling me. I can feel it. I think it's best if I talk with him directly."

I nodded and exhaled. "Fine. But not until he hears it from me first." Like I actually had a say in the matter. It was a murder, for crying out loud. But it didn't hurt to try.

He reached for my hand and helped me stand. Aspen stood as well, but he stayed against my leg.

"Fair enough. But just so you know, I'll be talking with him at some point *today*." He gave me a pointed look. "Understand?"

"Completely." What I understood even more was I had to get to my dad before Noah did.

"I'll need to talk with you again, too."

I looked at him and nodded. "I know."

Aspen and I turned to see Sister Alice and Quinn watching closely. We scampered toward them.

"What was that all about?" Sister Alice asked. "Why would he suddenly allow you within the perimeter of a crime scene? From here, it looked like he invited you in."

I blew through pursed lips, glanced at the daffodils and back to her. "I know who the victim is."

Her eyes shot open, and she touched the crucifix hanging on a chain around her neck. "Come again?"

"He used to be a friend of my dad's." I stole a glance at the body and frowned. "But I don't understand what this guy was doing here. A few years ago, he turned into a recluse. Wouldn't leave his home for nothing."

"Wait," she said, cocking her head to the side. "*Used* to be a friend of your dad's?"

I nodded.

"When did the friendship stop? When he stopped

leaving his house?"

I shook my head. "Earlier. Probably about a year; maybe more."

She sighed, closed her eyes, and ran a hand over her short, spiked white hair. "I'm sure it's not going in the direction I fear, that it was an amicable parting of ways, but *why* did their friendship end?"

I held her gaze. "Sister Alice, my dad is not a killer. You know him from living at the inn when you came to Spirit Lake." My dad would have been a teen when Sister Alice lived at the inn thirty-some-odd years ago, but still. She knew him.

She lifted a hand on my shoulder and rested it there. "If they had a falling out, Andie Rose, the police would have to explore that. When they do, what will they find?" She looked at Quinn before back to me, giving a discreet nod Quinn's way.

But Quinn was sharp, and it didn't get past her. "Don't worry. I'm used to keeping secrets from my brother. Don't all siblings keep secrets from each other?" She smiled.

Swayed by Quinn's confidentiality promise, Sister Alice said, "Detective Parker will insist on talking with your dad."

"I know. He's already asked for his number."

"Did you tell him about the falling out between the two of them?" Quinn asked.

I shook my head. "Not yet. And I hope you won't either. Just for now."

She made a zipping motion across her lips, twisted an invisible key, and pretended to toss it.

"Thank you," I said. "I know it's not fair to ask you to keep this from him, and I promise I'll let him know, but it's important for me to talk with my dad first. This might not look good for him, given Beau was a recluse. I can't imagine one would have too many enemies with that lifestyle." I heaved a sigh, pulled out my phone again, and stepped away to make the call.

The phone rang and rang until my dad's voice message began to play. Hearing his voice always made me happy. Not the same when I heard my mother's. Mom and I got on just fine, but she was the highest maintenance woman I'd ever known. She was far from the warm, comforting mother most of my friends had, but that part didn't bother me. It's not like I made it easy for her in my teenage years. The part which created the biggest problem in our relationship was, beneath the surface, I always felt a level of competition between us. If I did something, she wanted to do it better. If I did something with my dad, she gave him the silent treatment for a time. If I wore something people complimented me on, she went and bought the same thing. "We can be twinsies, Andie Rose," she'd said. "Won't it be fun?"

I rolled my eyes as I thought about it now. My dad was a saint for having dealt with it as well as he did.

I left a message asking him to call me back ASAP, telling him I really needed to talk with him.

I'd no sooner slipped my phone back in my pocket after leaving the message when it played the ring tone reserved for him, *My Daughter, My Darling*.

"Dad! Thanks for calling me back right away."

"What is it, Bug?"

"When's the last time you've talked with Beau Banks?" He made a sound from the back of his throat, making my stomach muscles tighten. "Think hard, Dad.

This is important."

"I just think the timing of the question is odd."

"Why?"

"Because I just saw him two days ago for the first time in five years."

I gasped. "Where?"

"His house. I tried to patch things over, but the ornery fart wouldn't have any part of it, so I left and let him know he'd never see me again. Why?"

"Oh my God," I whispered, looking down, my free hand over my forehead.

"Honey, what is this about?"

"I don't know how to tell you this over the phone, but—"

"Then don't. I was planning to surprise you, but the surprise has kind of been blown out of the water now."

"What do you mean?"

"I'm almost to Spirit Lake. Wanted to see my Bug."

My dad had been calling me Bug ever since I squished three of them to death in my hand from grasping them too tightly in an effort to keep them safe. I was four.

"Dad, go straight to the inn and up to my apartment. Do not talk to anyone except the staff. I'll be right there."

"Bug…"

"Dad, please," I pleaded. After he agreed, I hung up and turned toward Sister Alice and Quinn, who once again had Aspen's leash. "I need to go."

"Don't worry about me," Quinn said, handing me the leash. "I need to get back to the store, anyway. I'd love to meet your dad while he's here, though. I'm going to order his books for the store and would love to set up an author talk and signing as part of the bookshop's grand opening."

I frowned. "How did you know he's coming here?"

Sister Alice said, "Everyone knows now, dear. You had him on speakerphone."

I glanced around, only to find Noah standing feet away, a grim look on his face. My cheeks grew hot.

"Why didn't you tell me?" I asked Sister Alice under my breath.

"I figured you knew."

"I had the phone up to my ear," I said. "Would I have done that if I'd known?"

"Put the brakes on, Grasshopper. Everything will be fine." She looked at Noah, who now spoke with Quinn. Sister Alice whispered, "He's going to find out eventually, anyway."

"Later would have been better."

She pushed her glasses up, her finger smudging the lens as she did. As usual, she didn't even appear to notice. I, for one, had no idea how she could see through those things. They had to be more of a hindrance than a help. Which explained a lot, actually.

"Why, so he could accuse you of interfering with an investigation?"

Aspen's tail began swishing from side to side, sweeping the ground.

Noah startled me as he now stood beside me. He gave Aspen attention as he said, "It's never stopped her before."

Chapter 3

Noah faced me and said through a breath, "You sure have a knack for becoming involved in investigations, don't you? I'm sure you know now I have more questions than ever for your dad, right?"

Aspen turned away from him and plopped his butt on the ground, facing the opposite direction. Noah jerked his thumb toward Aspen. "What's up with him?"

"He knows when there's a traitor in the vicinity."

Noah's eyebrows rose, and he rolled his eyes. "Gimme a break."

"My dad didn't do anything wrong, Noah." I looked at him pointedly. "I assume it's okay to call you Noah since we're not in an investigatory situation right now." I cringed at the ugliness in my tone.

He frowned. "That's exactly what this is, Andie Rose. An investigation." He sighed. "Look, I'm not out to get anyone. My job is only to investigate and follow the evidence."

"Except that doesn't always give you the right answers either, does it?" I could have—and *should* have—stopped there, but no. Instead, I reminded him of the time last winter when I saved his life after I'd figured out who the killer was.

"Think of it this way. I'll be helping rule your dad out first and foremost."

"Yeah, right."

He thrust his arms out to the side. "I am not the villain here."

I nodded and exhaled. "I know. It's this case…It's really bothering me for obvious reasons. All the same, I'm sorry for taking it out on you, but it seems like you're holding all the cards right now. I'm only asking you not to make my dad out to be the villain, either. He'd never hurt anyone."

"Innocent until proven guilty. I know the law," he assured me. "And give me some credit. I have nothing to think your dad had anything to do with any of this. I'm only hoping he can answer some questions for me."

Aspen pivoted toward Noah again, apparently forgiving him. Quinn had left, and Sister Ida summoned Sister Alice. Given the look Sister Alice now gave me, it was killing her not to be part of the conversation with Noah.

"Just give me some time to talk with my dad before you do. Is that too much to ask? Please."

"It sounds like you've already talked to him. So consider your ask answered."

"More time, then. And without you listening in." He stayed silent, so I pleaded, "Come on. Consider it as paying me back for last winter." I fought the smile playing on my lips.

"How long, pray tell, are you going to hold that over me? And how many times will you ask me to pay you back?"

I shrugged. "Since I saved your life, maybe for a lifetime."

He tipped his head back and pressed one hand against the back of his neck. "Of course."

****

Aspen curled up in the front passenger seat and snoozed on the way back to the inn. One of his hind legs hung on the floor. Usually, he sat straight up, looking out the windshield, as if he were king of the world. I reached over and scratched behind his ear.

"Noah exhausts you too, huh, buddy?" In response, he lifted his head for a quick cursory glance, then settled his schnoz on his front paws.

Back at the inn, I scanned the parking lot for Dad's car. He hadn't said anything about my mother being with him, so I assumed she stayed to run their inn in Colorado, the second of the two inherited from my grandparents, my dad's folks.

Aspen dove over my lap and outside the minute I opened my door and trotted over to the daffodils circling a giant oak tree. "Aspen!" I called, attempting to sound stern. But when he looked at me through eyes that conveyed nothing but love, I caved. "That's okay, my friend. Just don't let Frank catch you." He trotted back to me, and I ruffled the fur on his neck.

Our master gardener could make anything grow. When I would have sworn something was dead and needed to be replaced, he'd tell me the only thing it needed was a little TLC. And he was right. Every. Time. So Aspen's so-called *help* wouldn't hurt.

I admired the vivid lime-green shoots of grass that poked through a scant, quickly disappearing layer of snow, and then scanned the small parking lot. Dad's Volvo wasn't in the lot, so Aspen and I went in and crossed the foyer to the reception desk. Jade was solo, so Lily must have left for the day. I looked at my watch. "Holy moly! Where has the time gone?"

"Flies when you're having fun," Jade said. She

snapped her fingers, calling Aspen to her, to which he was all too happy to oblige. "There's a hot guy who checked in about an hour ago. I'm happy to hang out here for the night."

I slapped my palm against my forehead. *Max!* I'd completely forgotten. If he'd only checked in an hour ago, he arrived much later than I'd expected, and it was a good thing I hadn't waited around for him.

The message behind Jade's comment a moment ago suddenly dawned on me. "You're married, Jade. Remember?"

"Doesn't mean I can't look at the menu."

I opened my mouth to reply, then thinking better of it, I shut it before offering a bemused smile. "You know what? I'm not even going there. The guy is Max Winters. He's here to check out Lakeview Pharmacy. He's interested in buying it."

"Want me to take him there? Show him where it's at?"

This time, I laughed and shook my head. "Do you have no shame? You just had a baby, Jade. Your hormones cannot be trusted right now. Obviously."

"Maybe we think about adding room service in the future." She looked at me and snickered. "Lighten up. I'm kidding. Besides, he asked for you."

My heart rate ticked up a notch. "Only because he knows me. Kind of."

She wiggled her eyebrows. "Wanna expand on that?"

Concealing a smile, I said, "No. But it's not what you think. I saw a box truck out in the parking lot. Is the piano here?"

She nodded toward the parlor. "Yep. They should be

31

just about done by now."

I turned toward the parlor and clapped my hands in excitement. Aspen's gaze jerked in my direction, clearly unimpressed at my sudden outburst. "Sorry, buddy. Let's go check out the piano."

My granddad and Honey had an old baby grand piano in storage, along with a load of other items my dad hadn't gone through yet. I remembered Honey's angelic music she made with the piano and asked my mother and dad if I could have it restored and transported to the inn. I was ecstatic when they agreed, and my dad said the parlor would be the perfect place to put it. The restoration process had taken a while, but it was well worth it to have such a cherished memory of Honey here. Now the only thing left was to contact a piano technician to come out and do a final tuning.

I'd determined to learn how to play one day and hoped to add lessons to my already full plate. When coaching clients claimed not to have enough time for what they wanted to do, I'd rebutted, telling them everyone has the same twenty-four hours in a day, and we fill those hours with what's most important to us. Maybe piano lessons would have to be bumped up on my important list.

The guys were packing up the equipment they used for transport while I stared at the beauty in front of me. In my mind's eye, I could see Honey sitting in front of those keys and playing, her fingers moving like magic. Except then the piano had been in the foyer and before they remodeled.

"Hi, Andie Rose."

I turned toward the entryway. "Max." I strode toward him and held out a hand. "Welcome to the inn."

His almost electric green eyes, unlike any I'd ever seen before, instantly drew me in. His hand was warm and soft in my own. No hard labor there, no sir.

"Nice place you have here."

"Thank you." I took in his striking features: thick black hair with the little curly-q that trailed onto his forehead, his angular face that showed little emotion and was mostly sober. But those eyes. Mercy me, were they gorgeous. Realizing I was still staring at him, probably looking like an idiot, I shook my head. "Can I get you a coffee? We have a coffee bar on the premises."

"I saw it when I gave myself a tour."

A smile played on my lips. "Anything, um...*odd* happen on your tour?"

He frowned. "Odd?"

"We have a ghost who lives here."

He lifted his chin and dropped it back down again. "Do you now?"

I laughed. "I've named her Lady Lucy." He only stared at me. "I was a skeptic at first too. Tried debunking everything. But I'll be the first to tell you, she's real."

Amusement tugged at the corners of his lips. "And how does one know if a ghost is female?"

"Intuition. Something females excel at."

He gave a quiet chuckle. "I see."

"So what about coffee? It's on the house." He merely smiled in answer. "Hey, Jade?" I said as we passed in front of the desk, "My dad's on his way. Can you tell him I'm in the coffee bar and to go there right away?" I turned toward the hallway before twirling back toward Jade. "One more thing. If Noah gets here first, tell him I'm not here. If he walks in at the same time as my dad, distract him—Noah, not my dad—so Noah won't realize it's him."

She tossed her thick sheet of black hair over her shoulder and wrinkled her forehead. "That's a little suspicious, isn't it? What's going on?"

"Nothing I want to get into right now."

She gave Max an appreciative glance. "Fine. But can I say your life makes the excitement of the ghost—"

"Lady Lucy."

"Whatever. She pales in comparison to your life." Aspen trotted toward Jade and lay by her feet.

I thought of my dad and a knot formed in my stomach. "Probably. Anyway, thanks, Jade."

The quick jaunt to the coffee bar was silent, me lost in my thoughts and Max being…well, Max being Max. Not that I knew him well, but all three times I'd seen him, he'd been consistently quiet and sober. One of those cliché strong, silent types. But I'd always found that attractive. And the times he did smile, his green eyes literally seemed to dance.

As he walked beside me, I noticed he wasn't much taller than me. Two inches at most.

Reaching the end of the hallway, we turned the corner into the coffee bar.

We bellied up to the counter, and Wendy the barista, who was steaming milk for someone's drink, turned toward us with a smile, her unnaturally white teeth almost luminous. Her tats and piercings rivaled those of any hardcore biker chick's tats and piercings any day. Except Wendy's collared dress confused what could be construed as the aforementioned biker chick image.

"Hey, Andie Rose. What'll it be?"

"Dark roast for me. Max?" I looked at him.

"The same."

Wendy laughed. "My easiest customers today. Go sit. I'll bring 'em right over."

Despite two coffee shops in town, Hallowed Grounds and Spirit Brew, the inn's coffee bar's unique ambience attracted Spirit Lake locals. It had pine walls and reclaimed pine floors with ebony stains and a darker finish adding a moody element. There were a handful of tables with charging stations for laptop users, comfy barrel chairs with side tables, and a few floor chairs strewn about. It was a mishmash of furniture that worked well together. People have claimed to hear the espresso machine when the room was empty, which drew a good many people. Despite having other, um, *spiritual* experiences, I was still waiting for that particular one.

After stopping off to greet a few inn guests, I swung by a couple of tables that held one person each, neither of whom I recognized. Either town locals I'd not yet met, or guests at The Raven Motel on the edge of town. It wasn't unusual for their guests to come to the inn for the coffee bar, and from there, to beg for a room. After stopping to welcome both people, I found out that was precisely the situation today. From all I'd heard about The Raven, it surprised me it was still in business.

I finally led the way toward a corner table at the same time Wendy brought our coffees to us. Max pulled the corner chair out for me, then sat across from me.

"Sounds like I was fortunate to get a room here."

I nodded. "It's booked from this time of year and into the first half of January of the following year. But life happens, so cancelations happen. We hold a waiting list for those occasions."

"And how did I get bumped to the top of the list?"

I grinned. "You know someone who knows

someone." Aspen turned the corner into the room and strolled toward me, firmly planting himself beside my chair and giving Max the what-for.

Max's green eyes glanced at Aspen. "I think your dog is questioning my place here."

I reached to ruffle my side-kick's fur. "He doesn't have a mean bone in his body."

"Speaking of knowing someone who knows someone, I was wondering if—"

Someone jerked the chair next to me from the table and my head swiveled to the culprit.

"Noah." Aspen, who'd just slid into a lying position a second before, sat up again. At Noah's presence, my heart rate soared farther north than was humanly safe, but I was unsure if it was being caught off guard with Max or fear Noah would be here when my dad arrived. I glanced at my watch. "What are you doing here?"

He stuck his hand out toward Max. "Hi. I'm Detective Noah Parker. You are?"

Yikes! Did I detect some kind of undertone there?

If Max had noticed anything in Noah's tone, he didn't let on. "I'm Max. An acquaintance of Andie Rose's."

"Noah, what are you doing here?" I jerked my hand up to tuck a strand of hair behind my ear, knocked my knuckle against my cup, coffee sloshing over the edge. I snatched a napkin to blot the table, my cheeks turning hot when I saw Noah staring at me, his chin quivering.

He reached for the napkin and finished wiping the coffee from the table for me.

"If I didn't know better, Andie Rose, I'd think my presence here makes you nervous. Hiding something?"

"Like what?"

A smile tugged at his lips, and he set the saturated napkin to the side of the table. "Thought I'd check to be sure you're doing okay. You were a little rattled earlier."

I twirled a strand of hair around my finger, the same strand I'd just a moment ago tucked behind my ear, and focused on Aspen. "I'm fine."

He glanced at Max and then back at me. "Has your dad arrived yet?"

I sucked in my cheeks and nodded slowly. "I get it. That's why you're really here, isn't it? To talk to my dad."

Max cleared his throat. "I should probably leave the two of you alone."

He pushed his chair back, and I placed a hand on his arm.

"You can stay, Max." I met Noah's eyes, working to hide the hurt in my own. "Noah was just leaving."

"Andie Rose—"

"As soon as I see my dad, I'll let him know." *Why did this bother me so much? So what if he was here to see my dad?*

He pursed his lips and narrowed his eyes. "So you say. But will you? This isn't just a fan wanting to meet your dad. I have a job to do and a killer to catch. I got his number and tried to call him. Imagine my surprise when he didn't answer or call me back."

I shrugged. "All I can do is tell you I'll ask him to call you. When I see him, which I haven't yet."

Noah exhaled, slowly nodded, and stood. I watched until he left the room.

"I'm sorry, Max. I'm sure this was a little awkward for you."

He pinched his thumb and forefinger together, his

dimples emerging with a small smile. "A little. Definitely some tension there." Instead of responding, I took a drink of coffee and focused on Aspen.

"I'd be lying if I said it hasn't piqued my curiosity, though," Max said.

I sighed and leaned back in my chair, the strand of hair still entwined around my finger. I disentangled it and circled both hands around my coffee cup.

"There was a murder in town today. An old friend of my dad's."

His gaze held mine as he appeared to process this information. Finally, he said, "So this stuff seems to have followed you from Birch Haven to Spirit Lake."

I mumbled, "You have no idea."

When I'd first met Max, little more than a year ago, I'd been staying with my cousin in Birch Haven, Minnesota, where I'd gotten in the middle of not one, but two, murders. Max had been there getting to know his sister, who my cousin worked with. And that's where I met Max.

"Is there something between you and this detective? Because I definitely sensed something."

"Depends what you mean by 'something.' " The sentence he'd started before Noah's interruption bounced into my head. *Speaking of someone who knows someone, I was wondering…*What was he about to say? My cheeks warmed, and I imagined their changing color. The hazards of being a fair-skinned redhead. "We have a history, but not like what you're probably thinking. I'm busy running an inn and don't have time for—" I waved a hand in dismissal, nearly knocking over my cup. Again. *Geez*! "Anyway, none of that matters. What were you going to say before Noah got here?"

He shook his head. "It's nothing." He pushed his chair back as he stood, scooping his cup as he did. "Do you have a to-go cup I could pour this into? I should probably get over to the pharmacy."

We strolled to the counter, and just as Wendy transferred Max's coffee to the paper cup and snapped on a lid, a familiar voice came from the doorway.

"Hi, Bug."

I spun around. "Dad!" Aspen trotted toward him and sniffed his shoes. I swooped in for a hug, standing on my tiptoes to match his six-foot-three frame. "I'm so glad you're here." I turned toward Max, who was already shaking hands with my dad. "This is a friend of mine."

"Nice to meet you. I'm Max."

"Chandler. How do you know my daughter?"

"Dad!" Now I was pretty sure the smattering of freckles across the bridge of my nose was even red.

Max smiled in amusement. "I get it. I have a daughter as well. Daisy."

"Doesn't matter how old they are," my dad said. "You always worry." He lifted a small section of his just-beginning-to-gray hair. "This is coming your way, eventually."

Max's dimples appeared again. "Mine is thirteen going on twenty, so the gray is quickly approaching."

My dad chuckled and turned toward me. "Well, hopefully she's easier on you than Andie was for her mother and me."

I playfully punched his arm and scowled. "I wasn't that bad."

"Your mom would say differently."

Dad laughed, and I waved my hand in dismissal. "Yeah, but that's just Mother being Mother."

"So what's this you had to tell me about Beau?"

I glanced at Max and then at my dad. "Let's go upstairs. Max was just leaving for the pharmacy, anyway."

After Max left, my dad said, "Why all the cloak and dagger stuff?"

"Hey, Andie Rose?" Jade said from the doorway. "Noah just pulled up in the parking lot again. He couldn't have even gotten to the end of the driveway before he turned around and came back. He might as well just rent a room here."

Aspen emitted a quiet whine. "Yeah, I know, Aspen," I muttered. "He's like a pop-up ad on a computer screen. He just keeps appearing."

Jade gave me a knowing smile. Seeing Noah every day would make her quite satisfied.

I grabbed my dad's arm and said, "*Now*, okay?" I tugged gently. "Please."

Chapter 4

"Exactly what happened between you and Beau when you saw him?" I snatched bottled seltzer water for both of us from the fridge and dropped beside him on the sofa. Aspen scratched furiously with both front paws at something imaginary on the rug. "Relax, Aspen." I reached over and gently stroked his head until he lay down and curled into a fluffy ball.

My dad took a drink and turned sideways and focused his eyes on me. "What is this all about?"

"Beau is dead, Dad."

His hand holding the bottle stopped halfway to his mouth, and he stared at me. "How did you find out?"

I studied him for a minute. "Did you know about it?"

"I told you, when I saw him—"

"You told him he'd never see you again. But—"

My phone rang. A quick glance at the screen said it was the front desk. "Hey, Jade, what's up?"

"Noah. He's on his way up to your apartment."

I tipped my head back and sighed. "Okay, thanks." To answer the door or stay deathly silent so he doesn't know we're in here—quite the dilemma.

Knuckles rapped on the door, followed by Noah's voice. "Andie Rose?" I stayed quiet and put my finger against my lips so Dad would, too. "I know you're in there. Open up."

Aspen raised his head, clearly unhappy someone

dared disturb him. My dad squinted his eyes at me, got up, and opened the door.

"You must be Detective Noah Parker," he said, shoving his hand to shake that of my unwelcomed guest.

Noah grasped it and nodded. "And you must be Chandler."

Both men turned toward me as I stayed seated on the couch, shrugged a shoulder and said, "What?"

"Exactly *my* question," my dad said. "What's going on, Bug?"

Noah caught my gaze. "Don't give me a death stare, Andie Rose. I have an investigation to conduct."

I bit the inside of my cheek and nodded. "I know."

"Mr. Kaczmarek—or should I call you Mr. Langston?" Noah asked.

"Chandler'll do. Is this about Beau?"

Noah nodded. "He's—"

"He's not just dead, Dad," I blurted. "Someone murdered him."

Noah gave me a side glance, and I frowned. Dad removed his glasses, ran a hand over his face, and let out a weary sigh.

"I was getting to it," I said to Noah.

"None too quick," Noah muttered. He said to my dad, "The victim's death was unusual."

I shivered. "To say the least." Taphephobia, fear of being buried alive, wasn't just any fear of mine, it was an irrational phobia. Add to that claustrophobia from which I suffered, and it didn't matter whether the coffin was above ground or beneath it. Or open or closed, for that matter. The possibility alone freaked me out. It saved my skin by avoiding tanning beds when they were all the rave. So there was that. When I suffered a nightmare about it, which wasn't uncommon for someone with such potent emotions about something, it could send me into a tailspin for days.

Noah exhaled and appeared to choose his next words carefully before looking at me. "Maybe it would be best if I spoke with him alone."

Since I knew he was unaware of my insane fear, he obviously wanted to say something he didn't want me to hear. Like accusing my dad of murder.

"Thanks, but I'll stay." As if I had any say in the matter if he decided otherwise.

Noah held my gaze, and I refused to budge, planting my weight ever deeper into the couch cushion.

My dad cleared his throat. "Apparently, there's something else going on here. Either of you care to fill me in?"

"When was the last time you saw the victim, Mr. Kaz—Chandler?"

"A few days ago."

"And where was this?"

"His apartment. Penthouse, really. I went there to set things right between us. But he wasn't having any of it."

"You had a falling out? Over what?"

"It's stupid and childish." My dad chuckled as he recalled the memory. "We used to be each other's best writing support network. He started getting really weird, and—"

"Weird as in how? What was he doing?" Noah took a break from the furious scribbling on his notepad to focus on my dad.

"He began comparing our writing, getting excessively critical of mine, and turned it into a competition. Honestly, I think his wife was behind it,

43

encouraging the rift, because she called several times after Beau had eventually stopped answering my calls. She didn't like anyone getting ahead of Beau. Professionally. That said, the last conversation we had was at his apartment. He was intoxicated. I told him I wasn't interested in the downward turn our friendship took, and he made some offhanded comment about how the only reason I'd made it big was because I had an agent and a big-time publisher. Then he said he was more successful because he did everything on his own. It was like we were on an elementary school playground." My dad sighed. "And there's truth to some of what he said. He *did* do everything on his own. And he did it well. But he made that choice when he started his own publishing company. Eventually, during his drunken rant—which was completely out of character for him, mind you—I suggested we pick this up at a later time when he could be more civil, because we weren't getting anywhere. And I left. He'd begun releasing his books at the same time as my releases. Figuring it wasn't a coincidence, but childish competition, I never went back to see him. Until a few days ago. I'd heard through the grapevine he'd shut himself in his penthouse a while back." He shrugged. "To be honest, it was a long while back, when there was media coverage about what happened to him. Speculation about why no one saw him out in public anymore. Some reporters even staked out his house for a while, waiting for him to come out. No one spotted him, only a woman going in occasionally and leaving again. When they approached her for answers, she shut them down instantly. Given all of that, I wanted to check in on him."

"And I gather it didn't go so well," Noah said. "He

didn't want to mend the friendship?"

Dad shook his head. "No." Heavy silence followed, and Noah studied him carefully.

"Were there any heated words exchanged?"

"Not on my part," Dad said.

My head bounced back and forth between the two as I waited to jump in at any time.

After volleying a few more questions and answers, Noah asked him, "What was his state when you left his apartment? His frame of mind."

My dad shrugged and shook his head. "Ornery. But that was just Beau. Gruff, rough around the edges, but a hell of a writer." He stared over Noah's shoulder a moment, then asked him, "What happened to Beau? How did he die?"

Noah said, his eyes not leaving my dad, "Cause of death is yet unknown until the M.E. completes the autopsy, but he was found in a closed coffin, on top of an empty grave."

My dad's eyebrows rocketed up, and he looked from me to Noah. "In a closed coffin you said? On top of an empty grave?"

Noah nodded. "Does that mean something to you?"

"Dad?" I jumped up and stood beside him, my hand on his arm. Aspen was wide awake now, standing protectively by my side. "What is it?"

"That's how they found the victim in my latest book."

"So it's public knowledge then," Noah said. "We'll have to look into that since it's so unusual."

I scratched my head in confusion, a finger getting caught in a tangle. I winced. "*Ouch.* I don't remember that one, and I've read every single book of yours.

Several times over."

My dad scrubbed the stubble on his chin and said quietly, "You haven't read it because it hasn't been published yet."

"Just so I understand," Noah looked at him sideways, "that means this is *not* public knowledge?"

My dad shook his head slowly. "No. Only a handful of us know about it. My publishing team."

Noah exhaled through pursed lips and combed his fingers through his silver hair. "Mr. Kaczmarek, you know how this looks."

I gasped. "Are you tagging my dad as a suspect? He didn't kill Beau Banks. Detective," I added, since Noah was apparently in major detective mode, referring to my dad by his surname. "There's no way he's guilty of *murder*."

A gust of wind howled outside, followed by a thud on my window. I gasped, my muscles going rigid. Aspen sidled up beside me and leaned against my leg.

"It was just a branch from the oak tree outside your window, kiddo. I'll get someone out here to trim that up before I leave, or you'll have a broken windowpane."

"I can do that, Dad. I guess my nerves are just a little frayed right now." I gave Noah a pointed look. "Because someone is looking at you for murder."

Noah frowned. "No, Andie Rose, that is not what I'm doing. My job is to collect evidence, not to judge whether or not someone is guilty. That's for a judge and/or jury to do."

"Well, he is not guilty of murder. And I intend to prove that."

Noah sighed and rubbed the back of his neck. "I know exactly what this means, and I need to caution you to please stay out of my investigation."

I held his gaze, not budging an inch, until he pivoted for the door. Before closing it after him, he turned toward my dad. "I'll need you to come to the station for a formal interview."

As angry as I was with him, his gentle tone toward my dad helped his case, if even just a little bit. I knew he had a murder to solve, but my dad? There's no way. But even *I* picked up on how bad it looked, and I was his daughter. My crime-solving team, Sister Alice, Aspen, and even Lady Lucy, who'd inconspicuously helped in the past, had work to do.

Chapter 5

I briefly entertained filling Quinn in on the plan but quickly dismissed the idea. That was a surefire way to get her brother on the warpath, and I couldn't have that. My dad's life and freedom were at stake.

First things first.

"Where are you staying?" I asked my dad as we trotted down the stairs from my apartment, Aspen hot on my heels. "Just because there are no available rooms here doesn't mean you can't stay with me. The couch isn't as comfortable as a bed, but it's not bad." I shrugged. "I'll even give you the bed and I'll take the couch."

"That'll work for tonight, but I'll figure something else out after that. On the way here, I got a call from my editor about some last-minute changes she wants made. The return window is…well, let's just say now. With that kind of deadline, I need to have some quiet, uninterrupted space to tie up the loose ends."

"Why can't you be one of those writers who works best with commotion around you? Besides, I'm hardly in the apartment during the daytime, so you'd have plenty of quiet."

He smiled and shook his head. "Why don't you understand my habits after knowing me as long as you have?"

"Touché. Doesn't mean I have to be happy about it, though." This was the first time he'd been here since they gave me this inn a year ago, and I wanted to spend as much time with him as I could. "Did your editor know you were coming here?"

He lifted his hands. "I don't know. Why? And what does that have to do with anything?"

I averted my gaze momentarily. "Maybe she has an issue with you taking a vacation."

Dad rolled his eyes and smirked. "Andie Rose, listen to yourself."

"No, thank you." I knew how crazy the idea sounded; I had no desire to hear it a second time.

"You've done well here, Bug. I'm proud of you. How's Tony working out as the lead chef?"

Since my folks were living in Costa Rica at the time of my granddad's death, they told me to choose which inn I wanted, the one in Colorado or the inn here in Spirit Lake. I was a Minnesota girl through and through, so it was a no-brainer to choose this one. They hired someone to run the inn for them in Colorado. Shortly after, they moved back to the States and took it over. I don't think Mother has been to Minnesota for years.

"He's better than the original one we had, Ivan."

"I figured that much." He tucked his hands in his front pants pockets. "I didn't know either of them very well, but I knew I liked Tony. Ivan, not so much."

"The sous chef, though—" I laughed. "As Honey used to say, *Uffda!*"

"I figured you'd have your hands full with that one when you told me you'd hired her. But you had to expect a seventeen-year-old to bring drama."

"She's not your average seventeen-year-old. She's a seventeen-year-old on steroids." I laughed again. "She keeps Tony on his toes. Always threatens to take over his job as lead chef."

Dad snickered. "You'll have your hands full so long as she's here. You learn as you go. You've got a lot of experience from the hotel industry, but owning your own business is a different ball game. And speaking of ballgame, how's your coaching biz going?"

Mere feet before we reached the kitchen entrance, I grasped his arm, we stopped, and I turned toward him. His casualness was disarming. "Dad, how can you be so calm about this whole thing? It's *murder*."

"I'm sad for Beau. Disbelief, even, that someone murdered him. But I have done nothing wrong. I have nothing to worry about. Besides, if I go to prison, I'd have plenty of writing time now, wouldn't I?"

I swatted his shoulder. "Not funny. Are you going to tell Mother?"

His eyes grew wide. "Not unless I have to. *That* would be something to worry about."

I giggled and let go of his arm. "Well, I'll make sure you don't have a reason to tell her."

He pulled me in for a side hug. Aspen squeezed between our legs before we entered the kitchen. Tony was resting against the stainless-steel center work island. The lingering smell of roasted chicken and basil tickled my nostrils.

Izzy snapped at Tony with a kitchen towel. "Out of my way. I'm trying to get outta here at a decent hour."

My dad laughed, and Tony spun around.

"What are you doing here, Tony?" I asked.

Izzy scowled. "Getting in my way. If he's gonna be here, at least he could help clean up."

Tony bent over, picked up a washcloth, and tossed it into the bin. "Done. Happy you little twerp?" He stepped toward my dad and hugged him, along with a couple of *manly* slaps on the back.

"Why are you here at this time of the evening?" I asked again.

"Heard your dad was in town. Thought I'd stop and say hi. See if he needs a place to stay since we're booked here."

I'd seen Tony's house once, and it was a king-sized bachelor pad. I'd teased him that clearly, I was paying him too much.

My Dad's eyebrows raised as he seemed to consider the offer. "That's not a bad idea. In fact, I'd appreciate it." He nodded toward me. "Andie Rose here seems to have drawn a little chaos to the place."

I slapped a hand against my chest and shot him a visual arrow. "Excuse me? I did nothing wrong." I looked at Tony. "But if he's staying with you, you'd better toe the line and not get him into any trouble, or you'll have to deal with my mother."

Tony made a move to shrink back and held up his hands in protection. "After what you've told me, I promise I'll bchave."

My dad looked at me. Amusement dimpled his cheeks, and I grinned.

"In my defense, you have to admit she's high maintenance."

"I've never disputed that. But she's still your mother."

I rolled my eyes. "Okay, okay. I know. I love her and I know she loves me. But it doesn't mean it was easy to live with her. Expecting perfection all the time."

Tony lifted his eyebrows and exhaled. "Well, now I just feel sorry for her expecting perfection and having you as a daughter."

My dad chuckled and draped an arm across my shoulders. "They clashed a time or two."

I elbowed him gently. "Don't think I didn't know you paid the price for sticking up for me." He gave me a blank look. "Come on, Dad. You can't tell me it was a coincidence you slept on the couch those nights."

He grinned. "Yeah, but the make-up—"

"Ew!" I stuck a finger in each of my ears. "Do not take that sentence any further."

Tony laughed and looked at my dad. "Ready to roll?"

He nodded once. "Ready. I'll follow you."

I watched through the window until the taillights from both cars were out of view. My mind, as if a crackling black and white film from an old projector, began replaying the crime scene, and when the crude headstone came into view, I shivered. If he was living the life of a shut in, who could he have upset so much they thought he deserved to die? His once devoted wife, now his ex? Or maybe he had a girlfriend, and she got fed up with him. But since he didn't leave his apartment, where would he have met her? Online? I cupped my chin with my hand as I thought about that. If he had met someone online, that would make sense. There were a million and one horror stories about people who meet online.

I jumped when Izzy spoke behind me.

"I'm outta here, Kaz." I'd become fond of Izzy's nickname for me. It was a whole lot better than nicknames I've heard teens call other adults.

"See ya mañana," Jade said, and to Izzy, "You, too, ya little brat. Stay out of trouble."

I sat on a lounge chair in the foyer, my back to the darkness outside, and leaned back as I called Sister Alice.

"Hi, trouble. What's up?"

"Oh, that I could tell you." I slouched down in the chair.

"Are you going to fill me in or make me ask?" She made a snorting sound. "Don't answer. I guess I just did. Ask. Is your dad there? I'm looking forward to seeing him. What, with him being a big celebrity author now and all, he probably doesn't have time for the little people like me."

I scoffed. "Right." My dad was the least judgmental and most humble person in the world. "He's staying at Tony's house. Maybe some of my dad's humility will rub off on him." I continued to fill her in until, from the corner of my eye, I saw Max come into the room. "Hey, I gotta go," I said to Sister Alice. "Stop by in the morning?"

"I work until noon. I'll swing by afterward."

I held a finger up to Max, who now stood beside my chair, looking out the window behind me. I indicated I would be with him in just a minute, and said into the phone, "That works."

"Tell Detective Parker to round me up if he needs help to prove your dad isn't the one he's looking for in this murder investigation."

I blew a raspberry. "I'm sure you would be the last person Noah would contact for help."

"You think? Who would be the first?"

I perched on the edge of my chair to stand. "Me. What a dumb question."

I hung up on her out-of-control laughter.

"Hi, Max." I nodded toward a book held loosely in his left hand and teased, "On your way to a book club somewhere?"

He gave a trace of a smile. "Thought I'd bring my reading down here and enjoy the parlor. It's an inviting room, and I assumed it would be empty at this time of the evening."

After I got my business degree, I used to manage a popular hotel in the city. There, nine o'clock in the evening was bustling with energy. People coming and going from clubbing, using the pool, and enjoying the nightlife. As a, what we call, *functioning* alcoholic, I hung onto my job by a loose thread. After a bonehead mistake while under the influence, I left. Not only did I feel shame my employer had discovered my addiction, but I decided it would be best to leave before he fired me.

Unlike in the city, people here were typically early to bed, early to rise so they could enjoy the countless benefits of nature. If they weren't early to bed, they usually holed up in the library, curled under a blanket in front of the fireplace with a good book and a cup of tea. The die-hard nightlife patrons hung out at Brewski's Pub in town until closing. Especially on Tuesday evenings for Pub Quiz Night. During the summer and fall months, there was usually a weekend concert or other entertainment at the pavilion in the town square behind Sweet Temptations Bakery. Usually, we could hear the music clear out here at the inn.

I gestured toward the parlor, one of the inn's most popular rooms. "Enjoy."

"Would you like to join me?"

My stomach did a little jig. Okay, maybe more than just a little one. "That would defeat your hope of a quiet room. Because as you might have guessed, I can talk. A lot."

He smiled, his green eyes almost glittering in the warm glow of the lamplight. "I wouldn't mind. In fact, I would enjoy it."

Faint piano music from the parlor reached us, and I raised my brows. I hadn't expected anyone to be playing the piano yet. I hadn't even had a chance to get it tuned. Surprisingly, it sounded beautiful. "It appears you wouldn't be alone in the parlor after all." I listened to the faint notes and gave a melancholy smile. I didn't want the person to stop playing, so I placed a hand lightly on Max's arm. "It sounds like 'Enchanted Moonlight' by Glen Brown."

He looked at me expectantly.

"It was a favorite of my granddad and Honey. My grandma," I explained when he looked confused. "Everyone called her Honey. This was their favorite song to dance to."

The music stopped, and I started across the room to the parlor, Aspen beside me and Max behind me. Through the doorway, I turned toward the piano and shivered at the chilly draft. The flame on the large candle decorating the table between two leather wingback chairs flickered. But the piano bench was empty.

I gave Max a quizzical look. Aspen, though, stared at the piano and cocked his head, as if trying to understand. *Did he see something?* Dogs have a keen sense of smell and can catch movement before a human can. And when it came to scent, Aspen was like a bloodhound.

"That's odd," Max said. "Is there another door to this room? Because no one left through this one." He jerked his thumb toward the arched doorway we'd just entered.

I smiled knowingly. "Lady Lucy." I reached for Aspen, who stayed rooted in place, unmoving. I'd heard animals can sense the paranormal, but I would have expected if that was the case, he'd be a bit more on guard. Instead, he appeared unconcerned, only curious, his gaze now traveling the room. A slight draft ruffled my hair as Aspen's focus crossed in front of us and toward the fireplace.

"You really think your," Max twirled a finger in the air, "ghost can play the piano?"

I shrugged. "Sure, why not? If it wasn't Lady Lucy, we're not only hearing something, but the *same* thing. That would be weirder than a ghost."

"Depends on your definition of weird," he muttered. "I don't think it gets weirder than a genuine belief in ghosts."

I grinned and wiggled my eyebrows. "Really? Because I believe, Max Winters, you just called me weird."

Aspen's gaze traveled to the piano again, and what felt like a breath brushed my cheek. The ivory and black keys depressed softly. I smiled as a warm feeling washed over me, like a hug from Honey.

Max's eyes grew, and then he laughed, jarring me from my moment.

"Okay, you got me," he said.

I tilted my head to the side. "What do you mean?"

"This is one of those pianos that plays on its own. Like in a hotel lobby. I've even seen one in a hospital lobby." He pointed toward Aspen, who strolled to the rug in front of the fireplace that had just turned on by itself.

He sprawled onto his belly, then rolled onto his side, completely at ease.

Max's eyes grew as his gaze, head unmoving, went from the fireplace to the piano to me.

I smiled, still feeling Honey's warmth. "Not to say you're wrong, but…Well, you're wrong. This piano used to be Honey's. It's been in storage for years and years. I had it refurbished and moved back in here just today."

He looked at me knowingly and nodded. "Well, that explains it. The company who did the work on it installed the mechanism that does that. Make it play on its own. Or maybe something broke in transport."

I exhaled in understanding. "You're doing what I did—trying everything you can to debunk the ghost. When I used to visit my grandad and Honey, I heard all the rumors and speculation, but I'd never seen any evidence of a ghost the whole time. So, naturally, I was skeptical. But ever since I took over the inn, there have been too many unexplainable incidents for it to be anything other than Lady Lucy. And how would you explain the fireplace just now?"

"The same thing? Or on a timer maybe." When I simply smiled, he asked, "Why would you be so calm if you have a ghost in your inn?" He narrowed his eyes as if waiting for the punchline.

I shrugged. "I wasn't at first. And I guess I don't have an answer for why I am now, except it's just not something that triggers fear in me anymore." Being locked in small spaces was quite a different story. And apparently death, since that's what started my panic disorder—a mistaken cancer diagnosis that rendered me mere months to live. "Besides, Lady Lucy isn't dangerous. Actually, the opposite. It's not like those horror flicks." He stared at me with a deadpan look. "Whether you believe or not doesn't change anything. And I wouldn't try to coax you into believing. You will when you're ready. Or not. But I believe in what I've personally seen and experienced." The piano was quiet again, and I extended my hand toward it. "Like that. And that it was Honey and Grandad's favorite song can't be a coincidence." A wave of nostalgia washed over me.

His focus switched between the piano and the fireplace, which was still on, and he whispered, "Do you think—well, do you think it could be *her*?"

"Honey?" I gave a sad smile and slowly shook my head. "I wish it was, but it's not."

"How can you know for sure?"

"The ghost was here long before Honey passed. Someday, I'm going to dig into a little research and find out who she was and how she died. The ghost, not Honey."

"I'm just saying, if you say there's one ghost in here, what's to say there couldn't be another? Like Honey."

"Because Honey would have crossed over to be with Grandad." I brushed a tear from my cheek with the back of my hand, and I felt the warmth of his hand on my back.

"I'm sorry," he said.

I sniffled and brushed the other cheek. "Don't be. These are happy tears. It's like Lady Lucy is telling me Honey is okay."

"Am I interrupting something?"

I startled at Noah's voice and turned to face him, running my palms over both cheeks. Max dropped his hand, and I stood.

"Noah. How did you get in?"

His gaze darted from Max to me. "The door was

unlocked. You should really be more careful."

I frowned. "It's an inn, Noah. And not quite nine thirty. I think we're safe."

"There's a killer out there, Andie Rose. Since your guests have key cards, there's no reason you can't lock up earlier, is there? At least until I catch this guy."

I met his eyes and wrapped my arms around me at a chill that passed through the room. "Unless you stop looking at my dad for this, you won't find the killer. I will find him before you do." Aspen roused from in front of the fireplace, stretched, and strolled toward me, planting himself on his haunches beside me.

Max cocked his head to the side. "Someone want to fill me in on what's going on?" He looked at me. "Why would your dad be a suspect?"

Noah's intrusion and the attitude accompanying him shattered the calming mood from the tune on the piano a moment ago.

"My dad knew the victim. They used to be friends until five years ago. And now suddenly Detective Parker has tagged my dad as a person of interest." Resentment bubbled up inside of me, drowning out Honey's hug, which only added to the resentment. I wrapped my arms tighter around my middle.

Noah took a deep breath, his tongue poking the inside of his cheek. "I'm only doing my job, Andie Rose, and you know that. If your dad didn't do it, then he has nothing to worry about."

Now I plunked my hands on my hips and scowled. "*If* he didn't do it? He *didn't* do it, Noah."

Max cleared his throat and lifted the book he still clutched in his hand. "Uh, listen. I think I'll go to my room to read and leave the two of you alone to figure this out. Whatever *this* even is." He waved his hand, his long fingers now wrapped loosely around the book. "Andie Rose, I'll see you tomorrow. Breakfast?"

I nodded. "I'll see you then."

Noah and I remained quiet until Max was long gone. I turned toward him and shook my head and said quietly, "I don't even know what to say, Noah."

His eyes became less intense, and he sighed. "You don't have to say anything. In fact, I'm asking you not to. Just trust me to do my job. Is that too much to ask?"

I lifted my shoulders and let them drop. "I don't know. It might be."

He pressed his lips together, nodded slowly, and stared at me for a moment too long. "I guess we have a problem, then." He blinked, looked at the floor, reached to scratch Aspen's head, and said quietly, "I guess I'll be going."

I watched as he turned to leave and crossed my arms in front of me, contradicting my weakening stance. "Noah?" I said as he reached the door. He turned towards me. "It's not personal. Toward you, I mean. But I have to do whatever it takes to prove my dad's innocence. That part is extremely personal."

He nodded, a small smile playing with a corner of his lips. "Well, I guess that makes us on the same side, after all. I'm just sorry you don't trust me enough to know that's what I'm doing." He reached the door, turned the knob, and faced me once more. "Not that it's any of my business, but is there something going on with you and Max?"

"You're right."

"About?"

"It's none of your business." When he lingered

there, I caved. "Max is the brother of a friend of mine from Birch Haven. He's a pharmacist and looking at buying Harvey's Pharmacy in town."

A ghost of a smile played on his lips before he turned and closed the door behind him.

Chapter 6

"Did Honey ever make her old piano into one of those self-playing ones?" I asked my dad on the phone after Noah left. Aspen trotted to the braided rug by the fireplace again and sprawled onto his side.

"Not that I know of. Why would she? She played it until she got sick. Then your granddad remodeled, and they moved the piano into storage."

"That's what I thought. Hey, Dad?"

"Yeah?"

"In your book—the upcoming one where the victim was buried alive in a coffin. Was the cause of death suffocation?" An involuntary shudder swept through me.

"No. Too ordinary. It's been done too many times."

I jerked the phone away as if it had burst into flames. Aspen lifted his head, appearing to weigh in on whether it was worth the energy to get up. Deciding not, he laid his head back down and repositioned himself onto his belly, nose on his crossed front paws.

"Andie?" My dad's voice, faint as it was, brought me back to reality. Taking a breath, I said, "I'm sorry, did you say ordinary? In whose world is being buried alive ordinary?"

"We're talking fiction, Bug. In the fictional world, it's been done to death. Pardon the pun."

"Gah! Should I be worried about Mother?" He chuckled. "So, how did the victim die in your book?" I pulled the phone from my ear again as a call came through, and I looked at the screen. "Hey, can I call you back in just a minute? Sister Alice is calling." And I was still trying to wrap my head around getting locked in a coffin as being too *ordinary*.

"Go. But call tomorrow instead of tonight. I'm beat and going to bed."

"Okay. Love you. Bye." Switching over, I said, "Hey there. What's up?"

"Everybody get settled in?"

"Yep. Guess what happened tonight?"

"I can only imagine. But when you say things like that, it scares me anyway."

I told her about the piano playing episode when Max and I were talking.

"While this is all entertaining," she said, "tell me about Max."

"Are you kidding me? There's a ghost playing a piano in my parlor and you want to hear about a mortal human being?"

"Right now, learning about Max is a higher priority. I need to know if I should intervene. Detective Parker is Catholic. Max could be—well, he could be a Baptist."

I laughed. "What about the fact *I'm* not a practicing Catholic? You still like me."

"But do I?" She chuckled.

"Did you call to harass me or what?"

"I called to see if you've received any further news about the murder."

"Why would I receive news?"

"Because that nice, young Catholic detective has a hard time staying away from you."

"Ha!" I crowed. "Subtle. And you're exaggerating.

He only comes by when he needs information."

"Well? You didn't answer me."

"He came by, yes. But after tonight, he may decide to stay far away from me."

"What'd you do?"

I swallowed a snicker. "You know, I'm insulted. Why do you always think *I* did something?"

"Hmm. Let's think about that one, shall we? Oh," she exclaimed, as if realizing something life altering. "I know. Because even though you assist others with their lives and relationships, you intentionally screw yours up."

"Rude," I scoffed. Except it was true. One hundred percent. I told her about the conversation with Noah.

"Well, that's unfortunate. The two of you need to realize you're in the same chapter, just on different pages. And speaking of books, Quinn Parker said she's ordered your father's books for her bookstore. She's going to ask him to be the special guest for her grand opening."

"Old news. She already told me. Dad will be thrilled, though. Especially with this being his hometown and all. What time are you coming by tomorrow? I'll see if she wants to come out too. If Noah hasn't disabled her car to keep her from seeing me," I muttered.

"Don't get all paranoid now. But in the event he did, I'll pick her up."

****

Sister Alice hung up from Andie Rose, grabbed the notebook and pen on the humble pine stand beside her bed and began jotting notes.

Andie Rose…goodness, there's so much to say there. She's more concerned with putting on other's oxygen

64

masks without attending to her own. But with her lack of relationship skills in the romance department, I worry she's going to end up an old spinster. She might as well be a nun if it weren't for her aversion to the church. I'm still holding out hope there, though. She laughed out loud at the image that popped into her head, taking a few minutes to enjoy the visual before writing it down. *Could you imagine Sister Ida if Andie Rose lived in the house? She'd pop an artery. At the very least, transfer to another parish. I don't mean to be nasty, but Sister Ida usually is. Nasty. No matter what I do, she's irritated. I'm surprised she hasn't put a pillow over my head yet when I'm sleeping. I should probably lock my door at night. Sisters are human too.*

She shook her head, tossed her notebook back onto the table, the pen on top of it, and said aloud, "Shame on me. I've no right to criticize Sister Ida for being different than me. Isn't that what I'm always telling Andie Rose? Don't judge others because they sin differently than you do?" She looked upward and whispered, "Sorry, Father. I'll get it right someday."

****

Aspen stayed tight against my side that night, forcing me to hug the edge of the bed. If I'd moved at all, I would have rolled right onto the floor. I wondered what made him so needy, Lady Lucy's obvious appearance or the disagreement with Noah. Though it was probably only because he sensed I was in need, therefore, making *me* the needy one.

I stretched each muscle slowly, working out the stiffness and kinks before finally setting my feet on the floor.

"Come on, boy. Let's get you outside to do your

business." He cocked his head and looked intently into my eyes. I grinned and ruffled the silky fur on his neck. "I swear you understand human language better than Izzy does. But if you start talking, we might have a problem."

When we stepped outside, the air was so fresh and exhilarating that despite the sunrise still a way off, I took him for a jog around the property, onto the wooded trail a bit, along the shoreline of Whisper Lake, and then back again. It was cool enough that my breath hung like frost in the air, but by the time we got back, beads of sweat formed on my forehead and the back of my neck.

When we reached the door, I leaned over and kissed the top of Aspen's head. "That'll keep you satisfied until we go on a longer run." When I looked into his eyes, it was evident he didn't think so. I laughed out loud. "Stop with the guilt trip."

He trotted to his water bowl, guzzled a good bit of it, and hopped up onto the couch and curled into a corner, leveling his gaze back on me.

I chuckled and shook my head. "You're out of control, Aspen."

While I showered and got ready for the day, I mulled over yesterday's murder: the details of the crime scene, Noah's determination to talk with my dad, my dad coming to visit for the first time in a year at the same time Beau—a recluse—was here *dead*! The squabble between Dad and Beau just days before he's murdered...My mind was like a hamster on a wheel, getting nowhere except defeated.

Finally, I headed to the kitchen. The warm smell of cinnamon and blueberries quickened my step. Tony was in the walk-in cooler, holding the door open with one foot while the rest of him was inside as he reached for something.

I helped myself to an enormous mug of steaming coffee until he finished and slammed the heavy door closed with his foot.

"Hey. Was my dad up when you left the house?"

"I didn't check up on him. Maybe that's why he wanted to stay at my house and not yours."

"Whatever you say." I popped a blueberry in my mouth from the bowl on the stainless-steel counter that ran down the center of the kitchen. "I was gonna call him, but I don't want to wake him up."

"I'd wait. Don't writers write until the wee hours of the morning?"

"With Dad, it depends on what he's doing, writing or revising." I popped another blueberry into my mouth before sipping my coffee. "Noah's twin sister is—"

"He has a twin?" He peered at me under the row of cabinets that hung above the island.

"Yep. Quinn. She's opening the bookstore in town. It's got the cutest name ever—Book Den & Pen."

"Is she hot?"

I shot a visual arrow at him, and he dramatically fell backward, clutching his chest. "Ouch."

"I'm already on her brother's blacklist. Don't make it worse. Besides, I like her."

He wiped his hands on the semi-white towel looped on the belt of his apron. "I asked a simple question, and you make it sound like I'm asking her to marry me."

I snickered. "Don't look all insulted, Valentino. I know how you Italians operate. Aren't you the one who told me you're a lover, not a fighter?"

"Everything I've told you and that's what you

remember?" He winked at me. "I'm not interested, anyway. I took a vow of celibacy."

I coughed, the coffee I'd just drunk spewing over the floor. His black eyebrows knit together, and he jerked his chin toward his chest.

"What's the matter with you?" He tossed me the towel he'd just used for his hands.

Catching the towel with one hand, I coughed into the crook of my elbow of the other arm. My eyes watered.

"Went down the wrong pipe." I coughed once more before squatting to wipe up the floor as Aspen looked longingly from the doorway at the wasted caffeine. "You've said some outrageous things in the past, but you've never outright lied to me."

He laid a hand against his chest. "*Moi*?"

"So when did this—this—celibacy thing start?" I stood, shoved out a hand, palm facing him. "Wait! Don't answer that. I'm your employer."

"Right? That's a pretty big offense." He snickered. "But I know you're curious, because let's face it, when aren't you?"

I shook my head and insisted, "No, really. I'm good." But I did kind of want to know.

"I'm waiting for the right woman. I'm tired of playing the field. I'm not getting any younger." I pressed my lips together. Tight. He pointed the knife toward me and said, "Go ahead, say whatever it is you're trying so hard not to."

"Just curious—"

"Which is always the case, but go on. Just say it."

"Well—I'm curious why? No one left in Spirit Lake for you to hit up? You've seen some pretty amazing women just since I've been here, and you always find something wrong with them. Or is it simply a phobia of commitment?"

He glanced at me while continuing to load the platters of breakfast goodies to transfer into the dining room. "You're a life coach. You know better than to listen to small town gossip or believe everything you hear." A smile tugged at the corners of his lips.

I nodded and smiled. "I do. But for a minute there, I thought Sister Alice got to you."

He laughed, tilting his head back. "Not for lack of trying over the years."

I pushed away from the counter. "I'm going to call my dad."

****

Two coaching sessions later—Tina Cartwright, a woman on a two-week stop as she investigates the *spiritual* aspect of the town, and Gemmalee Price, a guest at The Raven Motel—I attempted to call my dad again. Still no answer. Had Noah arrested him? He would have told me, wouldn't he? *Not if he didn't want you to jump his case.* I argued with myself whether to call Noah, deciding I needed to set aside our past confrontation, because my dad was more important here.

"Detective Parker," he answered.

"Hi. It's Andie Rose. Do you have my dad?"

"Why would I have your dad?" His tone was riddled with confusion, and I bit my lip, thinking of the right words to continue. As it turned out, I didn't need to. He sighed. "I haven't arrested your dad, Andie. I called him, though. Waiting for him to call back. Why did you think I arrested him? Do you know something I ought to?"

"Nope," I said too quickly. *I wouldn't tell you even if I did.* "I've just been trying to get in touch with him.

And no, he didn't."

"Didn't what?"

"Skip town. That's what you were wondering, wasn't it?"

"Actually, it hadn't even crossed my mind." Silence weighed on the line. Neither of us wanted to add a single word for fear it would snap. Finally, he said, "If you talk to him, let him know I called."

"Noah?" I asked before he could hang up. I felt a wee bit guilty about asking after I'd just been a turd, but not guilty enough to stop me. "Is there anything new in the investigation?"

"Nothing I can share."

A surge of hope rose in my chest. I wanted to get my dad off the hook right away. "So there is."

"All I can tell you is the autopsy has been completed."

"What—"

"I don't have any results yet, Andie Rose. And when I do, *if* I can tell you, I will."

"Hmm." I twisted my mouth. "Okay. Thank you."

Hanging up the phone, I glanced at my fitness watch. Twelve thirty and almost 10,000 steps. Not bad.

I'd come to understand it was the little things in sobriety that could become the catastrophic event and knew I should head to the noon twelve-step meeting, but my feet didn't follow my brain. Sister Alice usually went to the evening meeting since she started working in the library at Ravenwood and was scheduled until noon. I made a mental note to go to the evening meeting instead.

I finished filing a couple of things in my office before going out to mingle with the guests during lunch until Sister Alice and Quinn came by. I hadn't seen Max all morning. I stopped at the front desk to see if he'd left yet. I knew he was leaving today, and the checkout time was at noon.

"He left about three hours ago," Lily, Jade's sixty-something year old counterpart, said. Disappointment pinged in my chest. "He said he'd swing back around, though, before leaving town."

Jade smirked. "He said it was to let you know what happened with his final meeting with Harvey about the pharmacy. But we all know that's an excuse to come back and see you."

"Jade," Lily scolded. The two of them were as opposite as my mother was from my dad. "Mind your manners."

"Mind yours," Jade shot back. She liked nothing more than to goad Lily. And Tony and Izzy. I'd recently asked her if she saw the common denominator. She merely shrugged, snickered, and said, "Yeah, but you and Frank like me. And Aspen."

I couldn't argue. Aspen would be lost without Jade. He went to her whenever I wasn't around, and sometimes when I was. Frank was his third favorite.

My phone rang; I slipped it from my back pocket and glanced at it.

"Hey, Dad. Where have you been?" I wandered into the parlor so we could talk in private, and Aspen followed.

"Here. I was awake until four this morning. Finished the revisions my editor required. After that I wasn't tired, so I worked on a scene in my new book."

"*Message From the Grave*? I thought that one was set to be published soon."

"This is the sequel to *Message*. As yet untitled."

"Speaking of your books, in *Message From the Grave*—"

"Hey, Bug, I have to run. I'll call you back in a jiff. My editor is calling through. We're meeting up today."

"Fine." I sighed and hung up. Who knew trying to speak with my dad would be more difficult than when he was at his home in Colorado? And what was his editor doing here, anyway? Checking to be sure he finished the changes she wanted? Wouldn't email suffice?

Chapter 7

I was stitching together a few coveted minutes in the library with a cup of coffee and a good book when Sister Alice and Quinn came through the door, Quinn nearly hidden by a ball of long blue and cream-colored fur. Aspen perked up and sniffed the air.

"I hope it's okay I brought Lord Watson with me," Quinn said. "The guys are working on both the bookstore and my living quarters. The level of noise is insane."

I grinned. "Of course it's okay. By looking at Aspen's interest, it's *more* than okay."

Sister Alice smirked and pushed up her multi-colored eyewear with her pointer finger. "Neither you nor Aspen get as enthused to see me when I come here."

I hugged her and planted a kiss on each cheek. "Is that better?"

I'd thought about getting a cat for the inn after Aspen and I settled in. That has proven to be a slower process than I thought it would be. In one way, it felt like we'd been here forever. And yet, catastrophe seemed to rain down in one form or another, causing me to lose track of time.

Aspen lay back down, keeping one eye on Lord Watson, who was now planted on the floor, licking his paw and running it over his face as if Aspen didn't even exist.

"Aspen is either suspicious of Lord Watson or hurt

because the cat's not giving him a lick of attention," Sister Alice said.

"My guess is the latter." I bent to rub Aspen's head and stood again. "Give me a second to snag something for us to drink from my apartment. You both want a soda, bottled water, or coffee?"

"Coffee," they said in unison.

"It'll take a second to make, but two coffees coming up," I said.

Sister Alice said, "Why not just get it from the kitchen?"

I swiveled toward her. "Because my apartment is closer. And if I go into the kitchen, I might get delayed by Tony or Izzy. Two coffees coming right up." I pivoted toward the door and smacked into a cedarwood and vetiver-scented brick. Instinctively, I closed my eyes and gasped as two hands circled my biceps.

"Can you make that three?"

I looked up into Max's electric green eyes and flushed. "As soon as I catch my breath."

"I'll go with you and help carry them back here," Quinn said.

The thought of leaving Sister Alice alone with Max left me with some reservation. The poor guy was about to be submerged in questions. But that wasn't for me to worry about. Lord Watson had no intention of going anywhere, and Aspen remained still, watching the feline's every move. Maybe the two of them would distract Sister Alice from interrogating Max. *Nah, probably not.*

"He's cute," Quinn said as soon as we left the library. Her tone was more of an observation rather than with interest.

I shrugged and said nonchalantly, "I guess."

"You *guess*?"

I grinned. "Yeah, he is."

"Is there anything between the two of you?" she asked.

I cut a glance at her. "Why? Are you interested?"

One side of her mouth ticked upward. "I am not looking for anything. I'm still getting over some stuff I went through with my ex. But that doesn't mean I don't notice attractive men."

I turned my full attention to her. "Like what kind of stuff from your ex?"

She thought for a moment before she waved a dismissive hand. "Another time. I'd rather not get into it right now."

I smiled at her. "Fair enough. But let me tell you, in case you *are* interested in Max, your brother doesn't like him."

"They've already met? When? Sister Alice said he's visiting from Birch Haven."

"He is. And they have. Twice, briefly. But neither were positive experiences. For either of them, to be honest."

She chuckled. "I suppose not. Noah's probably jealous."

I pushed the handle down on the Keurig, the coffee pod making a whooshing sound as the metal point punctured the top of it. I inhaled the smoky, earthy aroma, closed my eyes, and emitted a dreamy sigh. "I love that smell." I glanced at her and smiled. "Sorry, got distracted. Back to your assessment. Why do you think Noah's jealous? And of what?"

She appeared to weigh what to say next, then waved

a hand, dismissing the conversation again. She was turning out to be a closed book regarding anything personal. It intrigued the coach in me.

"You know how men are," she said. "It's nothing."

But as we talked about the progress on Book Den & Pen, her statement loitered in my head. Sure, Tony, Jade, and Sister Alice teased me about Noah, but it was because of our banter. And because it was *them*. Noah was more often annoyed with me than anything else. And it wasn't about to get better with this murder investigation.

After refilling my own cup, we each carried two steaming mugs back to the library, where Sister Alice quietly studied Max, who looked everywhere except at Sister Alice. Aspen kept watch on a sleeping Lord Watson, who lay across the room from him.

"There you two lovely girls are," Sister Alice said. "Mr. Winters and I were having a delightful conversation."

I swallowed a smirk. "I'm sure you were." I handed a mug to Sister Alice, and Quinn handed one to Max. I watched for any interesting interaction between them but didn't catch a thing. Not that it was my business, anyway. Quinn and I plunked into chairs next to the window. I turned mine to easier face Max and Sister Alice. Quinn did the same.

"How's your coaching business?" Max asked.

I looked at Sister Alice.

"What? Word of mouth is the best form of advertisement," she said. "I've got you covered."

I chuckled and answered Max. "It's going really well. I've been offering a free session to guests during their stay here. That's ramped up business to where I might need to come up with a different promotional idea."

He frowned. "Doesn't the free session cut into your time and profits if it's part of the package for renting a room?"

"Yeah. But I'm willing to let go of both of those things for the sake of the inn's success." The minute the words were out of my mouth, I cringed. I sounded like a martyr tooting her own horn.

"I don't want to be intrusive or critical," he said, "but it sounds to me like the inn is doing well enough on its own. Attaining people who aren't from around here as free clients won't grow your business."

I caught my lower lip between my teeth. He stated the obvious, business basics I'd learned back in my college business courses.

"I know, I know. You're totally right." I sliced a hand through the air. "Business 101. Too often, knowing the material isn't the same as implementing it." I thought about my most recent clients—Tina Cartwright, Terry Finne, and Gemmalee Price, not from the inn at all. Two had scheduled another session, Terry and Gemmalee. Terry lives in Spirit Lake, Gemmalee not, but also not a guest at the inn. Tina isn't even from the country; she travels the world to places known as haunted, and then she blogs about them. From what she said, she makes a sizeable income from it. When I told her I wish I knew the story of Lady Lucy, she said to let her know if I decided to pursue answers, because she can put me in touch with the right people.

"Andie Rose?" Sister Alice snapped her fingers in the air. "Where'd you go?"

I shook my head to eradicate the thoughts. "Here."

"What's your coaching specialty? Your niche," Max asked.

Sister Alice suddenly coughed, but I knew it was only to cover a laugh. I tossed her a sidelong glance before answering Max. "I work mostly with mindset, addictions, and relationships."

Max looked at me sideways. "Do you coach family members of addicts?"

"I haven't yet, but I wouldn't rule it out either."

"And relationships? That seems like it would be a little complex."

I nodded, looked at Sister Alice, and narrowed my eyes. "Don't say it."

"Say what?" Quinn asked innocently. Her round denim blue glasses made her eyes appear larger than they were.

"That I'm a relationship coach who sucks at relationships."

"How does that work?" Max asked, running his hand slowly over his mouth and quivering chin.

"It's okay, you can laugh," I said. "I know how to coach people in their relationships; I just obviously don't do as I say." I shrugged. "Being single isn't a bad thing, though. It gives me the freedom to do as I please."

Quinn gave a wistful smile. "Yeah. Being married isn't all it's cracked up to be, anyway. At least I got out before we had any kids."

Max looked toward her and shifted in his chair.

I stood abruptly, rescuing him from the awkward conversation. But he *did* ask. I rubbed my forearms briskly. "Anyone else cold?" I pivoted toward the gas fireplace, but it turned on before I reached it. Lord Watson yowled, and his back arched. He stared at the fireplace before fixing his golden eyes on the ceiling. The commotion caught Aspen's attention. He sat up, looked at the ceiling and then toward the door, where Lord Watson's narrowed eyes were now laser focused, the fur on his back lifted. Aspen, growing as disinterested in Lord Watson's cat drama as Lord Watson had been in him earlier, let out a contented sigh as he slid back onto his stomach, resting his nose back onto his crossed front paws.

Sister Alice and I exchanged smiles. Quinn and Max remained motionless, except for their gazes traveling between the two furry kids in the room, Sister Alice, me, and the fireplace.

Finally, Max squinted his eyes and looked at me, his head turned toward the side.

I gave a small shrug and raised my eyebrows. "Yep. Lady Lucy."

"Lady who?" Quinn said, now standing.

"The resident ghost," Sister Alice said. "Andie Rose has taken to humanize it by assigning her a name."

Quinn removed her glasses, rubbed her eyes with her thumb and forefinger, replaced her glasses, and glanced at me and then Sister Alice. "Wait, what? There really is a ghost? Noah said it's just a tourist gimmick."

"No gimmick," Sister Alice and I both said.

Then Sister Alice jerked her thumb in my direction. "Andie Rose used to stay here when her grandparents owned the inn, and yet she was still a skeptic. Until last year."

"What happened last year?" Quinn asked.

I opened my mouth to talk, then closed it again, unsure where to even begin.

Sister Alice chuckled and said, "Cat got your

tongue?"

I looked at Aspen and then at Lord Watson, who had begun kneading the rug.

"Good one."

"Sister Ida would splash holy water on poor Lady Lucy in an attempt to loosen her from whatever has her trapped."

I tipped my chin toward my chest. "Loose her from *what*?"

"From staying stuck here in the in-between. But we must be careful with that kinda stuff."

"Well, so long as it didn't splash onto me. It would sizzle."

Sister Alice scoffed. "Stop talking such nonsense."

With a devilish grin, I said, "But it's so much fun."

"What's going on with the murder investigation?" Quinn asked. "My brother won't tell me a thing."

I snickered. "Probably because he's afraid you'll tell me."

"Well, he did say something to that effect," she admitted. "And that it's an—"

"Open investigation. And after he saw you at the scene with me, did he also tell you to stay *out* of his investigation?"

She opened her eyes wide. "Yep. And he was pretty determined about it."

"Did he share with you Sister Alice and I have helped him solve crimes in the past? Or that I saved his butt last winter?"

Max gave me a sidelong look. "If you've only been here a year, how many crimes could you have helped him solve? And why do I get the impression there's something more going on between the two of you than what you're letting on?"

That was more words than I'd ever heard Max say in one sentence.

"My brother has a strange way of showing an interest in someone," Quinn answered. "He could use your coaching magic, Andie Rose. But that might be a conflict of interest since you're the one—"

"There's nothing going on between us," I blurted, stopping Quinn from saying more. "We're just friends. And even that is probably overstating it." I downed the rest of my coffee, looked at Max, and then at Sister Alice, who watched with obvious amusement. "Want some popcorn?" I asked her wryly.

She smiled. "Maybe later. I should run."

I walked her to the door and said quietly, "See you at the meeting tonight?"

She nodded. "Of course. Nowhere else I'd rather be. No joke."

I swooped in for a hug.

"You have night meetings?" Max asked.

"You heard that?" With my voice, of course he did.

"Is it for coaching?" he asked.

I tilted my head from side to side then said, "Yeah, I guess you could say that." But what the heck? I had nothing to hide. "Twelve-step meetings."

He gave me a quizzical look before he glanced at his watch. "It's getting late. I have to run so I can be back to Birch Haven in time to pick up my daughter from her after-school program."

Quinn and I both said our goodbyes. After he left the room, she said, "Strange. Was that a quick exit, or what?"

"Men are so weird," I said, then chuckled. "Like I

said, being single isn't bad at all." I switched off the fireplace and said, "I should check in with the staff and see if anyone needs anything." I looked at Lord Watson, curled up in a giant fur ball in a chair by the window. Aspen lay at the foot of the chair. I smiled warmly. "I think the two of them are going to be friends. You're more than welcome to leave Lord Watson in here unless you have to go back to town." My eyes flew open. "Wait. Sister Alice was your ride and left without you. Give a holler when you're ready and I'll give you a ride back to town."

She shook her head. "Thanks, but no need. I drove my car."

I smirked. "You've heard about Sister Alice's driving, huh?"

She snickered. "Yeah. My brother was sure to tell me about her moped contraption. I imagine it's quite a sight to see and fun to drive, but it didn't sound appealing to ride on."

After popping into the kitchen briefly, we strolled to the front desk. Aspen had stayed with Lord Watson.

"Anything new?" I asked Jade and Lily.

"The person checking into Max's room canceled at the last minute," Lily said. "I'd no sooner hung up from them when a woman called to inquire about a room. Apparently, she had unexpected and devastating news, warranting a trip here."

I thought about the woman from The Raven Motel who wanted a room if there were any cancelations. I didn't ask her the reason for her trip. "Is her name Gemmalee?"

Lily shook her head and looked at the guest log. "Sara Banks."

Chapter 8

My eyes flew open. "Sara Banks?" I knew exactly what the unexpected and devastating news was. Had she and Beau reconciled?

"She said Terry Finne suggested she call here to see if, by some miracle, we had an opening. With two cancelations in as many days, that qualifies as," she made air quotes, "*some miracle.*"

Terry Finne, aside from being one of my clients, was the victim specialist at the police department. We worked through healthy ways of dealing with vicarious trauma. Despite his getting plenty of training in that area, having a coach was simply an extra layer of support. I worked with him on reframing thoughts and some neurolinguistic programming tools.

"Sara is the murder victim's ex-wife," I said. "Terry must have been the one to call and inform her about Beau's death." I shook my head sadly. "That would be a hard job. Giving someone news that would rip the ground out from under them, changing their lives forever."

"If the guy was her ex, his death might not be bad news for her. Maybe she's more bummed she'll no longer receive alimony."

"Jade!" Lily scolded.

I stared at Jade, my jaw agape. "Please tell me you're joking."

Jade lifted her hands. "What? I'm just saying what you all were probably thinking, but didn't have the guts to say."

Lily shook her head and blew through pursed lips. "Tasteless." She frowned. "But that the police would notify his ex must mean he doesn't have any other next of kin. Sad."

Jade's statement led me down a crooked path of new questions. Had Sara wanted him dead? Further, is she the one who killed him? If she did, how did she get his body to Spirit Lake? And why? Had she had help? What if there were two killers in town? And, again, why here? And why hadn't my dad called me back yet?

"Andie Rose." Jade snapped her fingers in front of my face, snagging my attention back to the room. Both Lily and Quinn were watching me intently.

I shook my head to clear the never-ending onslaught of questions. "What?"

"What are you thinking about?" Quinn asked. "Do you think my brother knows the victim's ex-wife is here?"

While I stared out the window, I said, "If Terry knows, your brother knows. Noah would have been the one to get Terry involved. And I'm sure Terry has to keep Noah apprised on any movement in the case on his end."

"But what about Terry suggesting Sara call here for a room?" Lily asked.

Jade spoke. "I can't imagine Parker would want anything or anyone associated with his case easily accessible to you."

I sucked in my cheeks. "Agreed. That part probably didn't know, because he never would have approved of it. He would try to keep anyone connected to the investigation in any way whatsoever as far away from me as possible."

Jade smirked. "Well, this is all terrible news, because this means Noah will be spending even more time here."

"Jade Hansen," Lily scolded again, shaking her head in disgust. "A man has been murdered. Have some respect."

"Lighten up, old lady," Jade said under her breath.

I shot her a look that warned her to knock it off and said, "Jade, maybe we need to enroll you in a sensitivity training course." I thought for a minute about the idea. "Hm. Actually, it's probably not a bad idea for all of us. I'll look into it."

"Great," Jade muttered. "She knows I was just kidding. Right Lily?" Jade gave her a hopeful look. I was sure the sole purpose was to get out of the aforementioned training.

Lily waved a hand in dismissal, then nodded toward Jade. "She's harmless."

"Did Sara give you a timeframe of when she'll be here?" I asked Lily. "And I *am* going to look into some sensitivity training for everyone who works here," I said with a cursory glance toward Jade.

Lily shook her head. "Nothing solid. Only that she will be here late afternoon, early evening." She glanced at the clock on the wall opposite her. "Which could be anytime now."

I nodded and said to Jade, "If Lily is gone before Sara gets here, can you let me know when she arrives? At the risk of annoying Noah—again—I'd love to talk to her."

"I'm going to go get Lord Watson and head back to town." Quinn crossed her fingers on both hands. "Here's hoping they've all but completed my living space so I can get out of my brother's hair. And if I'm on site, I can organize deliveries as they arrive, so I can be up and running sooner."

"Book deliveries?"

"Yeah. And everything else. Book Den & Pen is going to carry all kinds of stationery supplies. Pens, notebooks, journals, booklights, and any other merch readers will find useful and fun."

A smile spread across my face. "I cannot wait for you to open."

"Me too." She turned toward the stairs. "I'm going to the library to get Lord Watson."

I trotted beside her. "I'll go with you."

We hadn't made more than a few steps before Lord Watson and Aspen walked side by side toward us.

Quinn grinned. "Looks like Lord Watson made his first friend in Spirit Lake."

She scooped him up with one hand, surprisingly strong for her slight build, and went out the door. Aspen sat beside me and leaned against my leg. I reached down and rubbed his head.

"Let's take you out for a walk now, so we're back here to do some detecting work when Sara Banks arrives." I'd call Sister Alice at the same time, the multitasker that I am.

****

Sister Alice hung up the phone, intrigued by what Andie Rose told her about Sara. She didn't know what to think about it except grateful she'd never been involved in the complications of an earthly marriage. But if Andie

Rose didn't figure out her aversion to relationships sometime soon, she'd miss out on something she seemed to want but had never figured out how to get there. Sure, the girl said she wasn't interested in dating, but it's what she didn't say that caused Sister Alice to know Andie Rose longed for a healthy relationship. And Sister Alice laughed when she thought about Andie Rose having children, getting paid back for the sleepless nights she'd given her parents.

Chandler popped into her mind. Maybe she should pay him a visit. She'd only interacted with him a handful of times over the years, but she knew Honey adored him. And she'd been so proud of him in his career.

But first she wanted to speak with Father Vincent to check if he heard anything further about the murder. It was possible Detective Parker told him something he wouldn't tell herself or Andie Rose.

When Sister Alice entered the church, Father Vincent was in a side aisle of the nave, speaking with someone she didn't recognize, guessing it was an out-of-town visitor. Father Vincent's arms hung in front of him, hands clasped loosely. Sister Alice turned to leave.

"Sister," Father Vincent called, beckoning her with a finger. "Come meet Winston Dahl. He's Chandler Kaczmarek's agent and is staying with him at Mr. Valentino's house."

"Oh?" Why would Chandler's agent follow him here? Was Winston Beau's agent, too? "Did you know Beau Banks, Mr. Dahl?"

Winston shook his head, crossed his arms in front of him, and rocked back on his heels and back again. "Like a lot of us in the publishing industry, I knew *of* him, but I've never officially met the man. He's talked about in

87

the community. And I hate to speak ill of the dead, but it wasn't positive talk." His lips pressed together.

"Such as?" Sister Alice asked. Father Vincent gave her a guilt-inducing look. "Just what you know to be true," she specified. "Not gossip."

"As soon as Beau's book releases began coinciding with Chandler's, and Chandler began getting bad reviews on his books—which somehow, some IT guru traced back to Beau's server. Don't ask me how, because that's miles north of my paygrade. But when word about that got out—in fact, it spread faster than gossip in a small town—Beau began receiving a lot of hate mail. Death threats even. We think that's what caused him to go into hiding and become a hermit. Oddly, the only person he kept in contact with was his ex-wife."

"So they've reconciled?"

Winston shrugged. "Who knows?"

"I understand she just arrived at the Spirit Lake Inn. I imagine they'll release his body to her once they finish what they need to do with him."

Father Vincent slowly turned on a heel toward her, arms crossed in front of him, his thumb and forefinger of one hand stroking his chin.

"Sister Alice, are you getting involved in yet another investigation?"

She tilted her head to one side. "Well, *involved* sounds somewhat meddlesome in this context."

"Young Detective Parker will switch parishes if you keep getting in his way."

If he meant to be stern, he failed. Sister Alice couldn't miss the amusement bubbling in his chest as it shook ever so slightly. She looked at Winston. "Did Chandler get any hate mail over this, accusing him of…well, anything?"

Winston unfolded his arms and tucked his hands in his pockets. "On the contrary. He received mail, yes. Lots of it. But it was all supportive as far as I know. Some even went beyond supportive. Obsessed even, offering to quote," he made air quotes, "*take out* the competition. Some of those offers are quite disturbing."

She thought, *Some* of them?

Winston and Father Vincent gabbed about the writing business, Spirit Lake, the Minnesota football team, and…well, whatever else they discussed, Sister Alice didn't hear any of it. She was too absorbed in Winston's admission, and what it could all mean, about not only Beau, but Chandler as well. Who knew the writing community could be so…*deadly*?

Given what Winston said, Beau had enough enemies to keep the police spinning their wheels for months on end to narrow down a suspect pool. Which meant Chandler could be caught in the web of suspicion for equally as long. But how did Beau end up in Spirit Lake? Had they killed him here? If he never went anywhere, it didn't make sense. Had they killed him at his home and dumped him here? That seemed more likely, since the crime scene was so elaborately staged. But again, why in Spirit Lake?

She knew now, more than ever, she had to help Andie Rose find the killer. Because, once again, the girl has found herself in the middle of a precarious situation.

Chapter 9

When Aspen and I returned from our walk, we lingered in the parlor, which was right off the foyer. After the piano-playing incident the evening before when Max and I were in here, I felt close to Honey and grandad in the room. Had Max been right when he asked if it could be Honey's ghost? Because how would Lady Lucy know their favorite song? Unless she'd witnessed Granddad and Honey dancing to it. Was she somehow connected to Honey and Granddad? Had they known each other? I mentally jotted a note to look into Honey and Grandad's old friends.

Sister Alice called, breaking into my reverie.

"Hey."

"What's up, buttercup?" she asked and continued before I could utter a response. "Did you know your dad's agent is here in town? I met him talking with Father Vincent."

"That's peculiar. Why would he be talking with Father Vincent?"

"Probably to get information on Beau Banks' death."

"What do you mean, *probably*? Is that what he said?"

"I don't know. I didn't think of asking him *why* he was here. Even if I'd wanted to ask, there's a confidentiality thing. You know, the same thing we use

90

for not relaying information to Detective Parker about what we hear in our meetings. The thing that drives him absolutely nuts."

I frowned and caught my lower lip between my teeth. Frank's voice carried in from the front desk area, and Aspen trotted out of the parlor and into the foyer. "So, just curious...How could that question slip your mind to begin with? I need to give you some pointers on what questions to ask in a situation like this." I pressed my lips together to avoid snickering. Knowing from my coach training which questions to ask came in handy when investigating.

"Because finding out whether or not he knew Beau was top of my list. And if he did, how well?"

I listened, astonished, as Sister Alice relayed what she'd found out from Winston. "Well, that sure adds a twist, doesn't it?"

"Has Sara Banks arrived yet?"

I shook my head. One of those dumb moves people do when they're on the phone. "No. But I'm gonna try calling my dad again while I wait. I'm curious about his fan mail. My guess is there are answers in there somewhere."

"How about you tell the fine detective about all of this? It will help get on his good side."

"You're the one who found out all this information," I said. "You call him. He'd rather hear it from you."

"I'm trying to give you an opportunity to mend a fence, Grasshopper."

I poked the inside of my cheek with my tongue before I said, "We've been working together as sponsor-sponsee for a year now. I no longer qualify to be called Grasshopper. I've graduated from that."

"Ant. Better?"

"I give up." A call came through and I looked at the screen. "I have to grab this. It's my dad."

But as soon as I clicked over, he was talking to someone else and then said, "Crap, Bug. I'll call you right back," and hung up. *Are you kidding me*? I stared at the phone in disbelief.

Jade popped her head through the doorway. "Sara Banks is here. I have her waiting for you at the front desk."

I followed Jade to the foyer. Frank had left. I looked around for Aspen.

"Frank took Aspen out in the greenhouse with him," Jade said.

A woman as tall as me, with short black hair and a neon blue streak on one side, leaned her hip against the desk as she scrolled on her phone.

"Sara?"

She turned toward me, her fashionable jeans ripped up to *there*, revealed a lot of leg and dangerously close to more.

I extended my hand, struggling to keep my gaze on hers and away from the train wreck I feared would happen if she moved the wrong way. Or moved at all.

"Hi, Ms. Banks. I'm Andie Rose, owner of the inn. I'm pleased we were able to squeeze you in. I only wish it was under better circumstances."

She nodded, withdrew her hand, rested her phone face down on the counter, and rubbed her palms on her pants. "You knew Beau?"

"He used to be a friend of my dad's."

She laughed bitterly. "That had to be before he locked himself away. I'm surprised he had any friends left."

I touched the back of my fingers against my cheek, feeling the warmth. "They haven't talked for about five years now."

"So it *was* before," she said, knowingly. "People were so cruel to him about something so foolish, it forced him to live such a meager existence as a shut-in. Chandler Langston's sick followers," she nearly spat. "They didn't know the real story."

Here's my chance. "And what's that? The real story."

"Chandler Langston, that monster, set Beau up to fail. He's a miserable excuse for a human being. In fact, I think Langston is the one who killed Beau."

I shoved my hand toward her, palm out. "With all respect, and before you say anything more, I want you to know Chandler Langston is a good man. He's—"

The door swung open and in walked my dad. *Oh boy!* He didn't know what was about to hit him. Or I should say *who* was about to hit him.

"Hi, Bug." He strolled toward me and wrapped me in his arms, planting a kiss on top of my head.

"Dad, Sara Banks. Sara, meet my dad, Chandler Langston."

Her jaw dropped open. "I know Chandler Langston." Her eyes narrowed on me. "And you. Deceiving me like this. I guess the old cliché *The apple doesn't fall far from the tree* rings true."

"Sara—"

She pushed a hand toward me as if to keep me from moving toward her. "Zip it, lady. I cannot and *will* not stay in a place owned by the daughter of a killer." She glared at my dad. "And *you*. You should be ashamed of yourself."

"You know I didn't kill Beau, Sara," he said quietly.

"Do I?"

The venom in her voice and eyes scared me more than a murderer running around town. Unless she *was* the murderer. Which, after this outburst, made it appear she was more than capable of.

"Sara, other than a couple of days ago, I hadn't spoken to Beau for five years."

She stabbed a long, black polished fingernail at him. "Even if you didn't do the deed yourself, you are ultimately responsible. You and your sick tribe of followers. Like a pack of rabid dogs."

Aspen whimpered and covered his face with a paw. "Sissy," I whispered. He slid his paw down and stared at me. I resisted a smile.

"Sara," my dad began.

She spun on her heel, tripped over her suitcase, and caught herself on the edge of the desk. The unmistakable sound of ripping fabric made me cringe, and I was afraid to look. Not Aspen, though. He was no sissy after all. He jerked his head up and quickly put it back down, his paw back over his face with another barely audible whimper.

Sara gripped hold of the suitcase's handle, tugged the wheels free from the rug in front of the desk, and started for the door. "I will not stay here. I'd rather stay at the dump outside of town. The Crow's Nest."

"It's called The Raven Motel," I said. "I'm happy to call them to see if they have a vacancy before you drive all the way there." I knew they would. Rumor had it they were barely hanging on financially. But under the circumstances, I thought offering would be the courteous thing to do.

Ignoring me, she continued strutting toward the front door, revealing a large rip in her jeans at the back of her right leg. *Gah*! *That was close.*

"Sara?" I called as she turned the handle. "Where were you two nights ago?"

She came to an abrupt stop, paused, and in slow motion, turned toward me. "I don't have to answer to you." After a dramatic pause, she turned once more and slammed the door behind her, the pane of glass in the door rattling.

I turned toward my dad. "So what do you think? Can I count on her to hire me as a coach?"

He exhaled through pursed lips and muttered, "*Ei-ei-ei.* Poor Beau. I don't condone divorce, but this sure helps me understand it better."

I turned toward Jade. She'd been so quiet, I'd forgotten she was even in the room.

"You can close your mouth now, Jade."

"Holy crapola! Did you see those jeans?"

"I did. I wasn't sure which made me more nervous, her or the jeans."

Jade shook her head slowly, still looking toward the door. "I have to say, I'm impressed. That chick makes me look modest."

My dad glanced from me to Jade and back to me. "You girls have lost me."

My eyebrows shot up. "How?" He gave me a blank stare. "Are you blind, Dad? What man doesn't notice jeans like that?" Aspen even looked at him, head cocked.

"Me. I didn't exactly get the chance to see anything before she lit into me."

I tittered. "Fair enough." I slipped my phone from my pocket. "I'm calling Terry Finne to get a

95

professional's view of Sara. I want to know if you're in danger."

"Who's Terry Finne?" my dad asked.

"The victim specialist from the police department. He's the one who suggested she check if we had an available room."

"In case he doesn't know yet, you might also want to give him a heads up about how crazy she is," Jade said.

After leaving a voicemail for Terry, asking him to call me back as soon as he had a minute, I had an incoming call, an unknown number. I crooked a finger, indicating for my dad to follow me to the office while I answered, then patted my leg for Aspen to come along.

"The Spirit Lake Inn and Up Your Game Coaching. This is Andie Rose."

We continued to my office while I carried on the conversation. I sat behind my desk and my dad closed the door behind him and sat in a chair opposite my side.

When I hung up, I said, "That was one of my coaching clients. She needs to reschedule." I scribbled the changes in my planner, then looked at my dad. "Speaking of clients, I'm surprised Terry Finne referred Sara here."

"Why's that?"

I twisted my lips. "I guess I can't pin down a legitimate reason. It just feels weird. Maybe because he's never done it before, so why Sara?"

"How do you know he's never referred anyone here before? Have you asked him?"

I shook my head and glanced at my schedule. "You have a point."

"Tell me what you're thinking."

"It's probably nothing." I studied him for a moment.

"How can you be so calm when you're a suspect in a murder investigation? I know you said you didn't do it, so you have nothing to worry about, but still." I pointed my pencil at him. "And it's an investigation in which I'm going to prove your innocence, by the way. Detective Parker has no right to—"

"Do his job? Calm down, kiddo. I have nothing to hide." He slid down in his chair and clasped his hands in his lap. "Besides, even though someone found Beau in the same manner as the victim in my book, it's not like it's never been done before. Not every day, of course, but there's nothing new under the sun. Only the way we tell the story."

"Still, all things considered, you're so calm."

"The cause of death in my book is from a Golden Poison Dart Frog. As far as I'm aware of, no one has used that precise method before." He suddenly frowned. "What *does* disturb me, though, is the headstone, *Deserved to die*. That's in my book too."

Chapter 10

I exhaled, tilted my head back, and rubbed the back of my neck. "This is getting more and more confusing, not to mention disconcerting." I looked at my dad. "Any other details in your book that match up to this?"

"I don't know all the details of Beau's murder, but nothing more I'm aware of." He appeared to further ponder the question, then shook his head. "No."

"Dad, why would your agent come here? What's his relationship with Beau? He told Sister Alice he'd never personally met him."

"As far as I know, he doesn't have a relationship with him. Beau published himself. Winston just blamed him for the negative reviews and wasn't happy about Beau's business methods."

"Why? Were they unethical?"

"Not illegal. But unethical in the publishing industry, yes. And the way he ran business affected my sales."

I nodded slowly and caught my lower lip between my teeth for a moment. "How unhappy was Winston?"

"I don't know. You'd have to ask him." He heaved a sigh. "Wait a minute, Bug. I know where you're going with this. No, Winston wouldn't have killed Beau."

I shrugged and lifted my eyebrows. "How do you know?"

"He's not a killer."

"How well do you know him? Because everyone has a dark side, Dad."

"Only a year here, and you've gotten a third career as an investigator." He ran his hand over his mouth and chin, wiping away the grin. "It seems the inn and Up Your Game Coaching would keep you plenty busy. I see some hard times ahead for Detective Parker."

I narrowed my eyes. "Not helpful. And I do stay busy. Right now, it just happens to be trying to find a killer so you can enjoy your freedom."

He stood and motioned me toward him. Aspen rose to his feet and crossed to his water bowl. Dad wrapped an arm around my shoulder. "I'm not the one who's concerned about this, honey. So neither should you. The truth will come out."

"I think it's fair to say I'm rightfully concerned. And you know me enough to know not much shakes my world anymore, so when something does, there's a legit reason."

"That's fair." He gave me a consoling squeeze. "But how about we trust Detective Parker to do his job, huh?"

"Two heads are better than one. I helped before when he couldn't figure—"

He moved his arm around the back of my neck, pulled my head toward him, and gave me an affectionate noogie. "See, Bug. *This* is the kind of stuff that concerns me. You nosing around in dangerous situations."

Wrenching my way free, I said, "Trust me. And if you stayed here, in my apartment, I'd better be able to protect you."

Dad tipped his head back and laughed gently. "I don't need protecting, hon."

Jade coughed from the doorway, and I glanced at

her.

"What?" she said, suppressing a smirk.

"Coming down with a cold?"

She coughed again, this time into her elbow pit. "I must be."

I chuckled. "I'm sure you are."

"A call for you at the desk."

I followed Dad and Jade to the foyer and lifted the phone to my ear, but the person had already hung up. I looked at Jade with skepticism.

"There was someone there, I promise. Why would I lie?"

I rested a hand lightly on her arm and smiled at her. "Relax, Jade. I believe you."

After my dad left to go back to Tony's house, where Winston was meeting up with him to go over some business, I realized I never got an answer from him about what his agent was doing here in Spirit Lake. Since he had nothing to do with Beau and since most of his communication with my dad happened online via the internet, as far as I knew, anyway, there was no purpose for him to be here. Unless he's concerned my dad killed Beau?

I glanced at my watch and blew a long breath. "Come on, Aspen. We're late meeting up with the twelve-step gang.

I struggled to stay focused during the meeting, my thoughts like those balls inside a bingo machine.

"Andie Rose, you're up," Wes's voice cut through my thoughts.

"Huh?" I looked around the room, all eyes on me, and scrambled to put together a cohesive thought, unsure if it had anything to do with the evening's topic since I'd been zoned out. When several, "Thank you, Andie Rose," comments followed, I figured it couldn't have been too off base.

After everyone else left, Wes, Sister Alice, and I hung out in the church basement, my back to the wall. I wasn't afraid of ghosts, per se, but it freaked me out if my back faced the church basement's expanse of darkness that reached past the kitchenette where we held our meetings. I'd watched too many horror flicks in my earlier days, and too many evil things lurked in the darkness. Aspen gazed into the blackness, finally sprawling on the floor when he was apparently content nothing evil was present.

"You can relax. Except for us, no one's down here in the basement," Sister Alice said as she watched me get settled.

"Yeah? Well, it's not anything human hiding there that wigs me out."

Wes slapped my thigh with the back of his hand as he sat down beside me. Aspen glanced at him, looking none too pleased someone would dare touch his human.

"Can't blame you after everything you're going through," Wes said. "Again."

I turned to face him and lifted my eyebrows. "Don't start. You were the reason for the last nightmare in January."

"You gonna hold that against me for the rest of my life?"

I shrugged. "Depends how long your life is."

Sister Alice laughed. "The two of you need to play nice with one another."

"He started it," I said, knocking into Wes's shoulder with my own.

"Hey," he said, "I heard about the chick who bought the old bookstore. I also heard she's hot."

I scrunched my face. "Don't call her a chick. Some women find that demeaning."

"Excuse me," he said, initiating another shoulder knock. "The young lady. Is that better?"

"Much. But I wouldn't bother if I were you. It's Noah's twin sister."

"As in Detective Parker?"

Sister Alice's eyebrows lifted. "Do you know of another Noah in town, Wesley?"

"Nope. But I've learned to never assume." He grinned.

"Well," I said, "I think we can all be certain Noah wouldn't allow you to date his sister after last January."

He extended his arms, palms up. "Hey, this is the new and improved Wesley Wilson. Give a guy a chance to change."

"How about putting some time between your bonehead move and your self-professed change? That would convince me more."

He jerked his hand back and met my gaze. "You're on. I love a good challenge."

I reached and shook the outstretched hand he thrust toward me. "Deal."

"What's with the dude who's buying the pharmacy?" Wes asked. "Word is he might give Detective Parker some competition."

I scrunched my face. "Competition in what? A pharmacist has nothing to do with detective work, and vice versa."

They both stared at me, Sister Alice's jaw agape.

"Please tell me you're not so naïve, dear."

I scowled at Wes. "Where did you hear that, anyway?"

He shrugged and grinned. "It's a small town."

****

Sister Alice stood in the doorway and watched Andie Rose open her car door. Aspen jumped in and planted himself in the front seat as if he owned the car. She snickered as Andie Rose strapped him in, then herself, and watched until her taillights disappeared from sight. The girl was going to get herself into trouble if she insisted on solving crimes, making enemies of murderers. That said, who'd have thought the rising body count in Spirit Lake would threaten to outnumber the ghost sightings? Soon, the quaint little town wouldn't be so charming anymore. Instead of attracting tourists, they would run scared.

But right now, she couldn't worry about tourists. Andie Rose's sobriety and safety were more important. Since the girl moved here, this was the third murder investigation she'd got herself involved in. And solving the murders had become more important than attending the meetings. A normal person could get addicted to the adrenaline rush from high-stress situations because it triggers the fight-or-flight response. And while Sister Alice normally wouldn't be concerned with someone who had the tools and resources that Andie Rose did, with her solid knowledge of the brain's inner workings and all, people in recovery were susceptible to a setback before they even realized what happened. It had the potential to cause one's priorities to get out of whack, sending them hurtling down a slippery slope before they could adequately get their footing. Sister Alice would just need to make it a priority to help get this mystery solved as soon as possible so everyone could get back on level ground.

She locked the door behind her and set off across the lawn in back of the church toward the house. She needed to pray and devise a plan to get this settled quickly. And perhaps jot down a line or two of information to include in her writings.

****

I caught Jade as she was fixing to leave for the evening. Aspen trotted toward her, and she doted on him while she gave me the rundown on a newly arrived guest. Afterward, I patted my leg for Aspen to come with me to the parlor. I hoped I'd find some answers while there. The LED candlesticks on the window ledge, the fireplace mantel, and one on the top of the piano flickered, looking more real than most artificial candles I'd seen.

I settled onto the piano bench and ran my fingers lightly over the luxurious red velvet of the cushion. Aspen lay on his stomach in the middle of the room, nibbling on the treat Jade gave him clasped between his paws.

Then a realization hit me like a giant coffin dropped from a ten-story building. Not only was Winston in town, but as my dad's agent, he would be familiar with the manuscript. He would know exactly the cause of death and about the crude headstone. And if Beau's new releases competed with my dad's, causing a drop in sales, that would also mean a drop in income for Winston, wouldn't it? But just as quickly, I deflated. I had no idea how the publishing industry functioned. I had to ask my dad how the agent/author contract worked.

A list of the rest of the people who worked with my dad began to accumulate. I jogged to the foyer, snagged a piece of paper and a pen from Jade, and returned to the parlor. Aspen, so engrossed in his snack, paid little attention to me other than a brief glance. Note to self— don't give him this specific treat if I needed his assistance in an emotional crisis.

I got down to writing. Shirley Garcia, Dad's editor, would be on the list. For that matter, I bet anyone at the publishing house would have access to Dad's work if they wanted it. I jotted Shirley's name down beneath Winston's, followed by *Publisher*. I'd have to ask my dad how many people in the publishing house had access to his manuscripts, along with a list of names. It could easily be someone there who had it out for my dad for some weird reason. Weird only because no one ever hated my dad. Quiet, laid-back, amiable Dad.

I smiled as I thought of him. He'd been my savior countless times when my mother got mad at me for nothing at all. Well, okay, let's be honest, usually it was because I did something stupid. But Dad was still there for me, no judgement, no shame. Only the occasional disappointment he tried to hide.

"You spoil that girl rotten," I'd heard my mother tell him behind closed doors. But since I got my voice from my mother, a closed door didn't stop the sound.

The ringing of my phone popped my imaginary thought bubble. After hours and when no one was at the front desk, the calls rolled to my cell phone. Despite Jade still lingering at the desk, she'd apparently forwarded the calls to my phone all ready. I'd come to learn when she delayed leaving that it usually meant trouble on the home front or she was hoping her husband had her daughter in bed before she got home. I'd also come to learn not to ask about it.

"Up Your Game Coaching, this is Andie Rose."

"Hi, Andie Rose, this is Gemmalee Price. Some crazy lady in a snit just checked in here at The Raven Motel. She went into quite the rant at the front desk about canceling her room at your inn because of something to do with the murder in town."

"Great," I muttered. "I'm sorry you had to hear that. If you're concerned about coming here for your coaching session in the morning, I can guarantee you're safe. But if you want to cancel, I completely understand."

"Oh, no, I'm not concerned at all. My husband told me to call and check if you have an opening. This woman scares him more than the murderer." She laughed.

Unless Sara is *the murderer*. I jotted her name on top of the paper.

"I didn't put two and two together when we met for my first session, but you're Chandler Langston's daughter, right? You must be so proud of him."

"I am." I smiled warmly at the mention of my dad. "But how do you know that?" We'd discussed my dad briefly, but only as Chandler. Not that he was my father.

"Umm…well, I'm not exactly sure how to say this without causing you concern, but word has traveled through the town. You know, about the murder of your dad's nemesis?" She whispered the last sentence as if revealing a giant secret.

"Double great," I muttered.

"With the crazy lady gone, is her room still vacant?" she asked. "I would still pay for my coaching session, of course. I wouldn't expect that for free."

"The room she had booked for tonight is open, but someone else is checking in that room tomorrow."

"Oh, no worries then. Since we're only staying for

one more night after this, it would be more of a hassle than anything to switch for one night and then back here again. We'll just stay put. My husband will probably block the door with the suitcases." She giggled. "I don't want to sound insensitive to his feelings, but he's always been more afraid of things than I am."

In the first coaching session, she revealed her husband's irrational fear of other people and how it was turning him into a social embarrassment when they went out in public.

"Gemmalee, did your husband know my dad or the murder victim?"

"Oh, yeah! I told him if he ever switched gender preferences, Chandler Langston is the one I'd think caused it. He worships Chandler—your dad—and his books. And the conflict between Beau Banks and Chandler wasn't exactly private, so my husband wasn't sorry to see Beau gone." She gave a sharp inhale. "Oh, what a terrible thing to say. I'm so sorry. Stan isn't an evil man. In fact, he's really quite timid. Like I said, he's afraid of his own shadow."

After some parting pleasantries and confirming our scheduled session for ten the next morning, we hung up. I added *Stan Price* to my list of suspects.

I stayed in the parlor for a few moments longer until Jade called out her goodbye. After the door banged shut and the lock clicked into place behind her, I clapped my hands twice to turn out the lights. The LED candles glowed softly in the otherwise darkened room, casting flickering shadows against the walls and window the way this case cast shadows over my life of late.

I swung by the front desk to peer at the guest log for tomorrow, and trotted upstairs, my faithful canine right by my side.

****

The next morning brought gray, overcast skies. Thick, accumulating ominous clouds threatened to burst open. The weather forecast on the news predicted a fifty-three percent chance of a spring snowstorm, but that meant a forty-seven percent chance it wouldn't. I preferred to favor the odds on this one.

I groaned and rested my hand on Aspen's head. "We'd better get your walk in now, buddy. Because it looks like you might not get one later."

This was typical weather for March and April in Minnesota. It wasn't unusual to get snowstorms in springtime that could bury us under for an entire week. But knowing it was warmer, and the snow wouldn't stay long, it was cozy to snuggle in and watch it unfold. The heavy, wet snow would pile layer upon layer, watering the soil, which promised lush green grass and an abundance of wildflowers.

The inn's maintenance woman loved to shovel snow, but she was on vacation, leaving it to Frank, her backup. I appreciated all my staff, but if I was to be perfectly honest, Frank was one of my favorites. He was a seventy-nine-year-old Southern gentleman with smoky-quartz colored skin, white hair, and tobacco-stained teeth, who'd called me Miss Andie from the first day I came here to stay with my grandparents. I think he'd secretly been Honey's favorite too, and Granddad might've been a wee bit jealous. Being on the brink of eighty didn't slow Frank down a bit. And he wouldn't even think about letting me pick up a shovel if he was here.

Thinking of Frank gave me the energy to get out of

bed. Since sobriety seven years ago, I'd always loved mornings. But when the weather was like today, staying in bed tucked beneath the covers with Aspen for a little longer held more appeal.

I slipped into my running clothes, closed the door after us, and led the way down the back stairwell. The backyard held the lake, the boathouse, the hot tub, the bonfire ring, the horseshoe pits, and pretty much everything else, so it was usually the busiest area except in the early morning.

Two lakes, Big Spirit and Little Spirit, formed a triangle of sorts between the inn and Spirit Lake proper. The trail around both lakes was one of mine and Aspen's favorite running spots. The town plowed the trail in the winter months and it offered enormous trees, benches, and hidden seating areas for the times one needed to get away from it all.

We jogged to Little Spirit Lake and followed the lakeshore trail halfway around where it merged with the trail that followed the shoreline around Big Spirit Lake. Aspen continued in that direction while I slowed to survey the sky and get a bead on when the precipitation would start. Which was now. Just like that, sleet spit on my face in tiny pellets, but I knew it would only get worse.

Aspen was already a few yards up. I cupped my hands around my mouth and said, "Aspen! Come 'ere boy." He stopped and turned to look at me, but he didn't budge. "Come on. Now's not the time to be stubborn. We're gonna get soaked."

After another moment of hesitation, probably making sure I really meant business—he was so spoiled and my not giving in wasn't something he was used to—

he strolled back toward me, head hanging low.

I laughed. "Seriously?" When he reached me, I stooped to kiss the top of his head. "Stop pouting." I started at a good speed back for the inn, Aspen matching my stride.

When we entered the foyer, I grinned at voices inside the parlor. Dad. The second voice was somewhat familiar, but I couldn't place it. I stomped my shoes on the rug, brushed my mittened hands over Aspen's fur to dry him off, and brushed off my jacket before greeting him. When I turned the corner, Dad and Winston sat in the chairs beside the fireplace. Aspen made a wide circle around Winston until he reached my dad, who ruffled the fur on Aspen's neck.

"Hey, Bug."

"Are you talking to me or Aspen?" I plopped down on a chair and turned it to face him.

He glanced at my hair and sniggered. "Got caught in the rain, huh?"

I smoothed my hands over my red hair, trying to tame the wet frizz. "It's sleeting. I hope the roads don't ice up." I rubbed my hands together, cupped them and blew into them. "What brings you by so early? Tony wake you up?"

"No. I didn't even hear him leave. I popped into the kitchen as soon as I got here to make sure he was there."

"Then why—"

"I wanted to have coffee with my daughter. Is that okay? Should have called first, I suppose."

I glanced at him warily, heart heavy. "Are you leaving?" I had hardly any time with him, and I couldn't imagine Noah didn't insist he stay put.

"Whenever I get the green light. With Sara Banks

on the warpath, hopefully they'll clear me to leave before I wind up the next one dead." He chuckled.

I scowled. "That's not funny, Dad. We don't know she didn't kill Beau. And you should probably keep a low profile. Move your stuff over here."

"I spend most of my time locked up in a room on my computer. I can't keep a much lower profile than that. And I'm safer at Tony's house than here in the middle of things."

He had a point. I stood. "Regardless, I'm glad you're here. Give me a half hour to shower and change." I started for the door; Aspen lay by my dad's feet, on the opposite side from Winston. "I guess he's staying with you."

Chapter 11

I trotted back downstairs after a glorious hot shower with a eucalyptus shower steamer. My dad and Winston were in the kitchen with Tony, and Aspen lay on the rug just outside the kitchen doorway. His head was up, carefully studying Tony's every move, probably hoping the superb chef would toss him some of the goods. Heck, with the smell of bacon permeating the air, I hoped Tony would toss *me* some of the goods.

I strolled to the oven and opened the door, inhaled deeply, and grinned. Tony preferred to bake bacon because it got it crispier, more evenly done, and took less attention. I liked it because it didn't splatter grease onto everything within the vicinity and beyond.

"Oh, my God, Tony, that's heaven." I closed the oven door and glanced at my dad and Winston. My eyebrows shot up. "No coffee yet? What gives?" I grabbed three giant sized mugs.

"How about we drink from coffee cups instead of soup bowls?" my dad said.

Tony laughed. "Andie Rose loves her coffee."

"She's never been one for moderation."

I grinned at my dad before I said to him and Winston, "We can hit up the coffee bar if you want something other than black coffee."

Winston shook his head and scratched at the stubble on his chin. The diamond stud in his ear glinted off the stainless-steel countertop. "Real men don't drink that fancy crap. Black coffee with whiskey is the only way to go."

Tony and I locked eyes as he struggled to hide a smirk. Finally, he turned toward the grill.

"No whiskey. Sorry." I shook my head.

My dad spoke. "Andie Rose doesn't drink anymore, Winston. I couldn't be prouder of her."

Winston grimaced. "I couldn't be sorrier for her."

I totally understood his statement. Too well. I used to feel sorry for people in restaurants who didn't have a drink in front of them. Wasn't that the point of going out?

"Thanks, Dad." I filled the mugs, handed one to him and another to Winston before leading the way back to the parlor. Aspen followed by my side.

"Dad, the old bookstore on Spirit Lane is reopening."

"I heard. Music to an author's ears. The young lady who bought it—"

"Quinn Parker."

"She asked if I would be the guest of honor for the grand opening. Since it will coincide with the release of my new book, the timing couldn't be more perfect."

Winston made a low sound in his throat and said in a surly tone, "And you won't have competition this time. Or random bad reviews." Seemed to me he hadn't talked with Father Vincent long enough. But then, who was I to talk? It opened wide the door to ask a burning question, though.

"Winston, if Dad's sales dip, does that affect your income as well?"

He sipped his coffee. "It affects the publisher more. If an author doesn't earn back his or her advance, the publisher loses money."

I digested the info and looked at my dad. "Your editor obviously knows your books inside and out prior to publication, but does everyone else at the house have access to your manuscript, too?"

My dad gave me his *I know where you're going with this* look. "Don't go down that rabbit hole, Bug. Beau's murder has nothing to do with me or my manuscript."

I held my tongue—the gift of sobriety that kept on giving, unless it didn't, which still happened more than I'd like—and instead drank my coffee. But then, surprise, I couldn't hold it any longer. "We need to convince the police of that. If Detective Parker finds *more* connections to your book, I can't imagine he won't want to talk with your editor." I looked at Winston. "And you."

Winston scoffed. "Good luck with that. I'm leaving today before Beau's bitter ex-wife gets to me like she did Chandler. Besides, I had nothing to do with the man's death." He nabbed a pack of Marlboros from his shirt pocket and tapped one out, balancing it loosely between two fingers.

"You'll have to step outside if you want to smoke, Winston."

He stuck the tip of the cigarette between his lips. "I won't light up. It's my security blanket, is all. The thought of Sara Banks—"

My phone rang, interrupting him. But it didn't take a genius to know what he was about to say. I looked at the screen. "Speak of the devil. It's Detective Parker." I put the phone up to my ear. "Hi, Noah."

"Good morning." His tone was pure business. "Are you going to be around for a while?"

"Yeah, I'll be here, but I won't be available the entire time. I have a client coming at ten."

"Is Chandler there?"

I met my dad's gaze. "Why?"

"So I can tell you both at the same time. And maybe if he's there, you won't beat on me so badly."

I snickered. "You poor, poor man. Yeah, him and Winston, his agent, are here having a cup of coffee with me before we all get busy for the day."

"I'll be there shortly. And Andie Rose," he said then fell silent.

This sounded serious. I sat on the edge of my chair and caught my lower lip between my teeth. "What is it?"

He drew a breath and exhaled. "Just ask both of them to hold tight. I'll be there as soon as I can. I just have one other thing to do. Shouldn't be more than a half hour."

"Well, I, for one, can hardly wait," I said.

"Your level of enthusiasm tells me just how much."

I relayed the message to Dad and Winston.

"Well, I have to stay for this," Winston said. "I want to know what kind of evidence they have. But if surly Sara pops in before then, I'm making a beeline for the back door."

I listened as they chatted about the publishing industry, Dad's new book release, whether they thought Beau's book will be released on schedule despite his death. I drank in every word as I tried to piece together anything that might fit with the murder and permanently release my dad from any suspicion.

A half hour turned into an hour, which then turned into two. Guests came down for breakfast and wandered in and out of the parlor. I kept an eye on the baby grand in the corner, wondering if Lady Lucy would entertain us this morning.

Finally, Dad glanced at his watch. "It's getting kind of late, Bug. I had hoped to tie up some loose ends on my manuscript."

"Yeah, I gotta hit the road," Winston said.

"Dad, when's the last time you've talked with your editor?"

"Shirley? We talk frequently on the phone. Why?"

"Curious. Winston?"

He shrugged. "Within the last couple of days. I suggested she meet us here for a gathering of the creative minds in the beautiful woods of the North Country. We could say our *fond* farewells to Beau Banks."

My eyes grew wide. "A little bitter, aren't you? You might want to tamp it down a little, given the circumstances."

"Eh, I'm not worried."

I glanced at my dad. Given someone was murdered, and he used to be a friend of my dad's, Winson's comments seemed not only cruel, but inconsiderate.

"Why would you invite Shirley here? I'm sure she has a lot more authors than my dad."

Winston snickered. "Shirley's my ex-sister-in-law. I like her better than my brother she was married to."

"Oh. What did she say when you suggested she meet you guys here?"

"She was going to try but couldn't make any promises. She's long overdue for a vacation, but the timing isn't great."

I frowned. "Well, I wouldn't exactly call these vacation-worthy circumstances, anyway."

Winston stood and asked, "Which way to the

restrooms?"

I gave him directions and when he was outside of hearing range, I said, "Dad, what is wrong with that man? He's got to be the most insensitive person I've ever met."

My dad gave a small smile and nodded. "He's not an awful man. Just better in small doses is all. And he's good at what he does."

I raised my eyebrows. "Which is what, annoy people?"

He glanced at his watch again, folded his arms loosely in front of him, and began bouncing his leg up and down with the ball of his foot.

"I'll call Detective Parker and see how long it's going to be," I offered.

I hadn't even touched my phone yet, and it rang.

"Hi Noah. I mean Detective." I shook my head. "Whatever. What should I call you?"

"You can call me anything you want so long as it's nice."

"That's a big ask." A smile played on my lips. "I was just going to call you. My dad needs to go, and Winston is leaving for home. What's taking so long?"

"It's going to be a while. Chandler's not going back home yet, is he?"

I drew in a breath and kept my gaze on my dad. "No. He's going back to Tony's house to work."

"Okay, that's good. Could you do me a favor and ask Winston to stay put until I've talked to him?"

I clutched my phone in a death grip. "What's going on?" Aspen roused to a sitting position and looked at me. The beep of an incoming call sounded, but whoever it was would have to wait.

"There's been another death, Andie Rose."

I gasped and bounced up from my chair. My dad stood in front of me, concern etched in his face. Aspen rose and lifted his nose toward me.

"Who this time?"

"Sara Banks, the ex-wife of victim number one."

I swallowed hard. "What happened?"

"I'll explain whatever I can when I get there. It's just going to be a bit."

I glanced at my watch. Nine forty-five. My client would be here in fifteen minutes. I pulled the phone from my ear to see who had tried calling a moment ago, hoping it was her to cancel or reschedule. But it was Sister Alice.

"Are you there?"

"Yeah, yeah," I answered absently.

"I gotta run. I'll be there when I can. And Andie?"

I shook my head, clearing my mind. "Yeah?"

"Do not come to the church and interfere. Am I clear?"

I inhaled sharply. "The church?"

"Good Lord," he muttered, apparently aware of his error.

"The same place as Beau? That means it was definitely murder."

"Andie Rose…" He huffed an exasperated breath. "I didn't say that."

"Unless it was suicide. But I can't imagine an *ex*-spouse would be so distraught. Murder is the only thing it can be." I looked at my watch again, willing Gemmalee to cancel her appointment.

"You said you have a coaching client at ten. Focus on that and stay away from my crime scene."

The line went dead. *Crime scene*. Yep. It was murder. I recalled the confrontation between Sara and my dad when it suddenly felt like I'd swallowed a rock that hit the bottom of my stomach. This wouldn't help my dad's case at all.

Chapter 12

Sister Alice draped her simple silver crucifix around her neck as she prepared for work. Unlike her coif and veil, which she only wore to church or when she represented the church, the crucifix was a staple she never went without.

She'd just slipped her glasses on—yellow frames today to add a little sunshine on a cold, dreary day—and stepped through the door when Father Vincent's voice drifted her way. But it was the second voice that piqued her interest. Detective Parker.

She glanced at her watch; she had time to go 'round and say hi. And, of course, to see what was up. She couldn't imagine the good detective popped in at this time of day for a mere early morning chat with Father. Her curiosity had been a problem a time or two, but she'd managed to keep it in check. Mostly.

As she turned the corner, a police car parked by the church's cemetery instantly snagged her attention. Its red and blue strobing lights pushed relentlessly against the dark sky. Interesting, to say the least. Had there been a new development in Beau Banks' death? Only one way to find out.

She strolled up to the two men, deep in conversation.

"Detective Parker. How are you this fine, fine morning?"

He sighed. "Sister. Why did I have a feeling you'd

show up here?"

"Why wouldn't I? It's practically my backyard."

Father Vincent cupped his hand around his mouth, but she caught a slight hitch in his chest. He knew her all too well.

"Good morning, Alice," Father Vincent said.

"Morning, Father. What's going on this morning, Detective? I didn't hear any sirens."

Noah crossed his arms. "I had hoped to avoid unnecessary onlookers. Catch my drift?"

"Something new with the Banks case?"

His lips formed a flat line, and he ran his hand over his head. "You could say that."

"It appears we have another victim," Father Vincent said. "The first victim's ex-wife is dead."

"She's what?" Sister Alice said, eyes wide, as she made the sign of the cross, her hand knocking her glasses askew. "What happened?"

"I don't have any answers yet," Noah was quick to explain. "And, Sister, if I could please ask you not to call Andie Rose." He narrowed his eyes. "I understand that's probably a lot of pressure to put on you, but I'll call and tell her myself. I was supposed to be at the inn by now anyway, to speak with all three of them."

"All three of them?"

"Andie Rose, her father, and his agent."

Father Vincent said, "I met the agent yesterday. Winston."

"What did he want?" Noah asked. Father Vincent hesitated. "If it's not confidential, of course."

"I thought he was here to ask me about the church, but I think he was more interested in information about the first victim."

Noah groaned. "If he was here yesterday—well, did he say when he got to town, Father?"

"A couple of days ago, I believe."

"He's staying with Chandler at Tony Valentino's house," Sister Alice said.

She began side-stepping slowly, trying to see around the police car.

"Please stay away from my crime scene, Sister."

She dropped her jaw. "Me? I wouldn't dream of interfering."

This time, Father Vincent didn't bother hiding his amusement. She raised her shoulders and let them drop. "What? I wouldn't."

"Um-hm," Noah said through closed lips.

"I promise I'll stay on this side of the police car. Deal?"

"About all I can ask, since this side isn't cordoned off." He looked at Father Vincent. "Thank you, Father. If I have anything else, I'll be back."

Father Vincent nodded. "Happy to help."

"One of many," Noah murmured, and left.

Sister Alice leaned in toward Father Vincent. "Did you already do a blessing over the body, Father?"

"Of course." He straightened his biretta, then his stole.

"Did you notice anything…shall we say, *unusual*?"

He frowned. "It's a murder victim, Alice. Everything about it is unusual."

She wrestled for her next words. Finally, she leaned toward him and in a loud whisper asked, "But anything that especially stood out? You know, like a murder weapon?"

He tipped his chin toward his chest and said, "Alice,

I will not scratch your curiosity further involving you in Detective Parker's investigation."

"I understand, Father."

"Do you?"

But she didn't hear him, as focused on the crime scene as she was. She crept to the side of the police car she'd agreed upon as a boundary, hoping to see anything at all, without breaking her promise to Detective Parker. A few stray snowflakes floated in front of her, one of them landing on the lens of her glasses. She wiped it with her hand, accomplishing only to smear the entire lens. She slipped them off and tucked them in her pocket.

Police stood guard as the medical examiner squatted beside the body, one arm resting on a knee as he spoke with Detective Parker. Sister Alice leaned in, hoping to hear something, but Noah was too smart for that. He glimpsed her from the corner of his eye, turned his back, and spoke in hushed tones while he punched a number into his phone and walked away from the medical examiner.

"Alice," Father Vincent said, startling her. "Aren't you supposed to be on your way to work?"

"Yes, Father. I'll be on my way now." She smiled sheepishly and turned to leave, but not before she glimpsed a knife protruding from the woman's back and a makeshift headstone that read, *Backstabber*. Well, now, she thought and absent-mindedly retrieved her glasses, only to tuck them away again. She reached for her phone and turned toward her moped to leave for Ravenwood school.

****

I quickly called Sister Alice, who answered on the first ring.

"I tried to call you," she said. "I wanted to give you and your dad a heads up on the latest news. But I fear it won't look good for him given the altercation last night you mentioned."

"I know. Noah beat you to it. Telling me, I mean. But you can give me details. Noah wouldn't, not that it's a surprise. What do you know to help better prepare for my dad's defense? Him and Winston are here right now."

"Father Vincent stumbled upon the scene this morning. A woman was lying where Beau's body was, but without the coffin. A knife was in her back. Like Beau's crime scene, there was a makeshift headstone, but this time it read *Backstabber*."

"Poetic, in a sick way, since the killer stabbed her in the back," I said and shivered at the image in my head.

Sister Alice relayed the rest of what she knew, as well as Noah's typical admonishment to stay out of his investigation.

"I'll bet he practices that speech in his sleep."

Sister Alice chuckled. "He wouldn't have to if you didn't overstep."

I rolled my eyes. "And yet it was you he gave the warning to." She remained quiet. "Okay, fine. He gave me the same one."

"Of course he did, Ant."

"Between your and my dad's nicknames for me, I'd be surprised if Noah doesn't call me *pest*."

"He's smarter than to say what he thinks."

"Pshaw," I muttered.

"The first thing we need to do is establish a firm alibi for your dad for last night."

"He was at Tony's."

"Can Tony corroborate that?"

"Probably not. It's not like they sleep in the same room."

"Winston?"

"I didn't ask." I drew a sharp inhale. "But since my dad sometimes pulls all-nighters when he's in the zone, he may have done that last night."

"That won't necessarily work in his favor unless Tony or Winston were up with him."

I groaned. "Grrr. If he was up all night working, Winston or Tony wouldn't have been with him. He'd have been alone."

"Don't a lot of authors work better in a busy environment? The images romanticizing the author's writing life by working in cafés and coffee shops have to come from somewhere."

"My dad has never worked that way."

She blew a long breath. "Pity. Okay then, first things first. Talk to your dad." The door opened and in walked Gemmalee. I smiled at her, the greeting betraying my disappointment.

"My ten o'clock client just walked in," I whispered into the phone. "It'll have to wait until after I finish."

I hung up and greeted my client properly before leading the way to my office. Once we settled in, Aspen lying beside my chair, I asked her how it had gone with practicing the tools I'd given her in our last session only a couple of days ago.

She pushed her hair behind her shoulder. "I'm a work in progress. And while I'm looking forward to practicing this long term, I appreciate you getting me in again so quickly before we head for home. My husband's going to drive me crazy if I don't do somethin', Andie Rose. I'd sure like to travel again, but it's no fun alone."

"How did the reframing exercise do that we went over?" I asked again. Reframing is a technique that improves one's mindset by changing negative experiences into positive thoughts. After a time, it retrains the brain and creates new neural pathways. In Gemmalee's case, I had hoped to help her overcome mama drama, which bled over into her marriage with Stan.

"I've tried teaching him how to do it, but he just gets irritated with me."

"Seeing a life coach is about changing *your* thoughts and behaviors, not someone else's. You said you had drama with your folks as you grew up. If Stan has issues, that's an entirely separate matter *he* will have to work on. You can't do it for him."

"Yeah, I know. I'm just desperate, you know?"

"Did you work on reframing *your* negative thoughts?"

She nodded. "Not as much as I'd have liked to. I got distracted by the crazy lady." She shook her head and frowned. "Like legit crazy, Andie Rose. She was going off like nobody's business about your dad and how she'd probably be the next one dead, like a premonition or something." She gasped. "Oh! And speaking of nuts, the guy from The Raven Motel said the woman is Beau Banks' ex-wife and that she's dead now too." She sliced a finger across her throat. "Did you hear anything about that?" She hung on the end of her chair as if waiting for the winning Powerball numbers.

I knew it wasn't professional to get into this with a client, but the need to defend my dad took priority. I needed info. "Did she say why she thought she might be next?"

"She's convinced your dad had something to do with Beau's death. She said since she was his business manager and his business coach, that your dad would try to get her out of his way like he did Beau. My husband is so upset about this. He doesn't consider Chandler Langston a mere mortal."

I slumped back in my chair, tipped my head back, and exhaled. "Great." Aspen looked at me, then rolled over so he was lying on his side. Across my feet, as if keeping me grounded.

"Chandler Langston is successful based on his own merit," she said. "You don't have to worry about him. No one—and I mean *no* one—will believe he killed anyone."

It sounded like she was trying to console me, so to keep what little professionalism I'd managed to maintain from completely flipping on its head, I regained my composure and flipped the conversation instead.

"The truth always comes out. I'm one hundred percent convinced of that. Yes, my dad will be fine." Now to convince myself of that for real.

After I wrapped things up with Gemmalee, which included giving her some resources to work on at home and a lead on a new life coach in her area, I wished her well and walked her to the door. Dying to know the truth, I called my dad to get an answer to whether or not he knew Sara Banks was Beau's business manager. My call rolled into voicemail, but I hung up without leaving one.

I wished I could be as calm as my dad was in all of this. Though I think he was more concerned than he let on. How could he not be? Maybe it was divine intervention that made him not answer my call. Maybe I could find out some more to ease any additional stress he had to be under.

I told Lily I'd be back in a while and turned toward the kitchen to let Tony know I'd be back before Izzy arrived but stopped when the front door opened. Two women came in; one I knew, the other not.

"Hey, Quinn," I said and laughed at Lord Watson's leash clipped to a rhinestone studded collar. Aspen cocked his head to the side as if trying to figure out the situation. Neither of us could take our eyes off the enormous feline. Lord Watson appeared less than impressed with his predicament.

"A cat on a leash?" I finally said.

Quinn sighed. "Yeah. As you can tell, he's not thrilled with the idea. He's just gotten way too big for me to comfortably hold."

"Is it possible for a cat to feel embarrassment? 'Cause I think he does."

Lord Watson meowed his displeasure. Aspen laid down, appearing to bow to the grumpy cat. Aspen's snout rested between his feet, his rump in the air, tail wagging.

"Well, now that you're here," I said, chuckling, "why don't you put Lord Watson out of his misery and take the leash off? He can wander with Aspen."

The woman behind Quinn, still holding the door open while Quinn bent to unclip Lord Watson's leash, cleared her throat, startling Quinn.

Quinn stood, and Lord Watson, relieved at his freedom, rubbed against my leg, back arched, and crossed the room to Aspen.

The second woman came in and closed the door behind her. I smiled and extended a warm welcome.

"My apologies for the delayed greeting. I was taken

in by the entertainment ahead of you. Welcome to the Spirit Lake Inn."

"Thank you."

I stepped aside so Lily could get the guest checked in.

"Do you have time for a cuppa joe?" Quinn asked me.

"With you? Of course." I began leading the way to the coffee bar but stopped short when the woman who came in with Quinn asked for Chandler Langston and Winston Dahl. I spun around, retraced my steps to the front desk, and extended my hand to the woman. "I'm Andie Rose Kaczmarek, owner of the inn and Chandler's daughter."

Her hand gripped mine and held it for a moment. "Wonderful to meet you. I'm Shirley Garcia, Chandler's editor." My heart skipped a beat. "Winston invited me here to collaborate together in an inspirational setting and told me if I could make it, to come here to the Spirit Lake Inn." She looked around with obvious appreciation. "And I can see why. You have a gorgeous place here. Is it true what they say?"

I offered her a bemused smile. "It depends on what you've heard and who said it."

She wiggled her eyebrows. "That it's haunted."

"Well, then, yes, it's true. Are you a believer or a skeptic? Or on the fence? I've discovered more in that camp than any other."

She tilted her head from one side to the other. "Undecided, I guess you could say." She gave an appreciative glance around the room. "Why hasn't Chandler written a book about this place? That would land me squarely in the believer's camp." She looked at me and fanned her face with her hand. "I adore your father. He's my favorite client. Your mother is one lucky woman."

I didn't have an aversion to physical touch, but that Shirley still had hold of my hand was awkward, to say the least. But it gave me plenty of time to notice the thick foundation under too-red rouge, drawn in eyebrows, and thick mascara and smoky eyeshadow. I favored blackest black mascara, and used it liberally, but Shirley's use of the product made me look naked.

After she uttered another flattering comment about my dad, I slipped my hand from hers, and discreetly as possible, I wiped my palm on my jeans. Her over-the-top adoration of my dad creeped me out a little. As my dad's self-appointed coach, I made a mental note to talk to him about it. Men were sometimes so clueless how a woman feels about them. And if he spent much time with her, whether it be online, over the phone, or in person, he had to know what he was dealing with.

Quinn, leaning against the desk and to the side of Shirley, caught my eye and grimaced. I think she, too, recognized Shirley's potentially problematic affection for my dad.

Shirley laughed. "I'm so sorry. I didn't mean to hold on to your hand. Nothing like embarrassing myself with Chandler's daughter." She repositioned her handbag on her crooked elbow and said, "So, are they here?"

"No, I'm sorry, they're not. Can I give them a message? Tell them where they can find you?"

She waved her hand in dismissal. "No, thank you. I'll call one of them directly and meet up wherever they are."

"I think Winston was planning on leaving today."

She grinned. "Sad. I would hate to have time alone with Chandler."

Eww! I couldn't hold my tongue over that one. As if they knew what was coming, Quinn's eyebrows shot up and Lily cleared her throat. Aspen, who had been intently watching Lord Watson prowl the room, looked up at me.

"Shirley, I don't intend any ill will when I say this, but Chandler is my dad. He's still very much married to my mother. I don't see that changing."

"Oh, dear," she said, condescension clouding her face, her smokey gray eyelids heavy. She rested her hand on my arm. "It's all in light fun, honey. And I'm only one of thousands who finds your dad attractive. There's something irresistible about a quiet, mysterious author." She shook a finger at me. "Trust me when I tell you those people, the ones Chandler *doesn't* know, are who you should watch out for. The ones hiding behind social media. Trolls in sheep's clothing. Fans can be dangerous, dangerous people."

Her uncomfortable statement hung in the air between us, as heavy as the clouds outside earlier, until I glanced at Quinn. "Ready for the coffee bar?"

"More than ready," she murmured with one more look at Shirley.

After a few steps, I turned toward Shirley again.

"Shirley?" She looked at me as she held her phone to her ear, most likely waiting for my dad to answer. "When did you get into town?"

"Only this morning."

I nodded as she began leaving a message for my dad with a sickening, sultry tone. Lord Watson padded into the parlor. When he didn't come back out, I peeked in to see he'd curled into a ball on the rug in front of the fireplace. Just in case he woke, I asked Lily and Jade to be sure he didn't get outside. Aspen, however, had enough of Lord Watson and trotted beside me.

Once down the hallway, Quinn jerked her thumb over her shoulder and asked, "What do you make of all that?"

"For starters, I have got to talk with my dad about her gross affection for him." I shuddered. "Eww. And her warning about dangerous fans. Has she looked in the mirror? She's about as much of a fangirl as one could be." I made a sound in my throat. "Again, gross."

"Do you believe she just got here this morning?"

Turning into the coffee bar, I glanced at Quinn. "Not for a minute. And she just made it onto my suspect list, along with Winston."

Chapter 13

After Cindy, the coffee bar barista on shift for the day, made our drinks, Quinn and I sat on two enchanting, mismatched chairs. Aspen lay facing the doorway.

"I don't think Lord Watson is interested in you, buddy." I rubbed the side of his neck.

The coffee bar was one of my favorite rooms and one my Granddad added onto the inn shortly after Honey died. Not only was I a coffee addict—a coffee snob, really—but the ambiance here was unmatched. Granddad clearly hadn't designed it himself, because he didn't have a creative side. That was Honey's gift. I'd never asked him, and now wished I had, whether Honey planned it before she died or if he had someone else do it. I had been too self-involved to be interested in anything else back then. A sliver of sadness threatened to wedge its way under my skin of what I'd all missed out on in my hell-raising days. But I kicked it outta the park with relief I was no longer that person.

People have claimed to hear the espresso machine when no one was in here, drawing non-inn guests here as well. While I searched for a valid explanation, I came up empty except for the obvious answer—the resident ghost, Lady Lucy.

"Hey, Andie Rose," Cindy called over her shoulder as she wiped down the steaming wands. "Can I have Saturday and Sunday off? Terry's taking me antiquing out of town. Martha said she could fill in for me."

I frowned and shook my head. "Wait, what? Terry who? Terry Finne?"

She gave me a sidelong look. "Yeah. Why?"

"Umm—no reason." I shrugged. "I only recently met Terry. Surprised me is all. The two of you are dating?" *Duh, Andie Rose.* If they're going away for a weekend together, they're dating.

"Not really."

I chewed the inside of my cheek for a moment. There was so much I wanted to ask, but as her boss, it was none of my business. Cindy, along with the rest of the coffee bar employees was part time, and I didn't work closely with them like I did with Tony, Izzy, Jade, Lily, Frank. Even Marcie, the maintenance woman; although Marcie was a hard one to crack.

I turned my focus back to Quinn, who leaned back, taking in the exchange. She brushed a strand of long brown hair from her face, and with her knuckle, nudged her large round frames up further onto the bridge of her nose.

I lowered my voice and said to Quinn, "Terry is the one who suggested Beau Banks' wife, Sara, stay here. I wonder how well Terry knew her."

"Does it matter?" Quinn lifted her cup to her lips.

Lord Watson ambled in, searched the room, then settled alongside Aspen, who was now sprawled in the sunshine that had miraculously broken through the earlier cloud cover. The snow was off the radar, apparently. The rays streamed through the window, highlighting floating dust motes and creating prisms on the floor.

I smiled. "I stand corrected, Aspen. Lord Watson

apparently is interested in you." I shifted my thoughts back to Quinn's question. "No, probably not. Maybe it's that right now I don't trust anyone who has a connection to this case. Someone killed Beau and then Sara, and he's trying to frame my dad."

She sipped again and set her cup down on the table, her petite hands hugging the mug. "Maybe I should hire you as a P.I. to dig into my ex."

"What is it you want to find that your brother probably already hasn't unearthed?"

"I don't know." She sliced a hand through the air. "It's not even important anymore. Except I still feel incredibly stupid. And it's why Noah treats me like such a helpless child."

I leaned in toward her, loosely circling my hands around my mug. "Are you up for telling me about it?"

"There's not a whole lot to tell except he was already married when he married me."

I sat back and grimaced. "That's saying a lot in only a few words. I take it you didn't get married in a church?"

"That's the weird thing. He wanted to, and I didn't. You'd think it would have been the opposite, right? And he has two kids with his legal-slash-legitimate wife." She shook her head as if trying to clear away unwelcome memories.

"Yuk. Stories like this are why I shy away from relationships." I thought about Max. How well did I really know him? Not well at all, actually. Only that he used to be married and has custody of his daughter. "How long had you been married before you found out?"

"Only about three months. But we dated for a year and a half before that, and he hadn't revealed a thing. I mean, he traveled a lot, but he was a sales rep for a huge corporation." She rolled her eyes. "That's what he told me, anyway. And I was gullible enough to believe him." She met my gaze. "To make matters worse, he'd been charged with the attempted murder of his first wife—the one *before* the one he was married to when I married him. The court later dismissed that charge for lack of evidence, but Noah's not convinced he's innocent. I know they say love can be blind, but it totally blindsided me." She sighed. "I thought Noah was going to kill him. He scared me so badly that I was searching for the best attorneys in case Noah ended up needing one."

I nodded, my train of thought taking a detour to the murders, opening new possibilities. Did either Beau or Sara have a bitter ex prior to their marriage to each other? Or had either of them recently broken off a relationship with someone, leaving them *murderously* angry? Beau was a shut-in, but had he met someone online? And it wasn't too far out there to think Sara might have poked a murder hornet's nest.

"Andie Rose?"

Quinn's voice jolted my attention back to the room.

"I can see why Noah would be angry. And he has every reason to worry. You're his sister."

"Well, all I know is since then, he's been extra protective of me."

"But you can understand, right?"

She raised her eyebrows. "Sure. But showing up at a restaurant I'm at, or other places I go? No matter where I go with anyone male, there he is. Boom. He's in overdrive protective mode."

I chuckled. "Poor Max has no chance since your brother already doesn't like him."

Now it was Quinn who chuckled. "I told my brother

how cute Max is and he got pretty uptight about it. I just did it to antagonize him." She grinned. "Besides, Noah's dislike of Max has nothing to do with me and everything to do with you."

I touched my hand to my chest and frowned. "What have *I* done?"

She shook her head slowly. "And you're a relationship coach?"

"Speaking of that, Max and coaching, I mean, what did you make about his abrupt departure yesterday?"

She drew her eyebrows together. "Yeah, that was a little weird. I know I'm an introvert, and if I could live inside books with the characters and never have to deal with real people, I totally would. But Max makes me look gregarious." She shrugged. "Maybe it was as simple as that. Nothing more." She sat back in her chair and looked out the window, then back at me. "That would be awesome, wouldn't it?"

"What would? You as gregarious?"

"Living with the characters inside a good book."

"Not if you lived inside my dad's books. You'd be doomed living inside the minds of certifiable insane killers. Sometimes it scares me how he comes up with these characters." Mention of my dad brought the seriousness of the situation back to the forefront of my thoughts. "Geez, for a minute there, I was able to think about something else. Thank you for that."

"Anything to help. By the way, your dad's books are phenomenal." She pushed her chair back, earning Lord Watson's attention. "I should go so you can get back to getting on my brother's nerves."

I quickly placed my hand on her arm. "You can stay. I enjoy your company." I nodded toward the canine-feline friendship as I picked up my phone. "Aspen and Lord Watson are too cute together. Just give me a second to try calling Dad again. I'm hoping to talk with him before Shirley does." I snapped a photo of the blossoming furry friendship before dialing my dad's number. It rolled into voicemail; I groaned and left him a message to call me before he returned any other calls. When I hung up, I said, "Anyway, back to Max. Maybe it was the ghost who freaked him out. But it wasn't his first exposure to it, so I wouldn't think that's it."

"The conversation about marriage and relationships we were having would more likely scare off a man than talk about ghosts. Even if the ghost *was* present."

I snickered. "Good point. Usually it scares me off, too. After hearing the story about your ex-husband—wait, can we even call him your ex-husband?" I twisted my lips, then shook my head. "Your ex, whatever it is he was, doesn't help ease my fear of relationships any." I gazed at the coffee bar, where Cindy was taking the drink orders for a couple of guests. Pondering her relationship with Terry Finne, I blinked and sat up straight when none other than Terry turned the corner into the coffee bar. Aspen sat up, appearing to consider the change in my body language.

I whispered to Quinn. "Terry Finne just walked in. He's talking to Cindy."

Quinn turned toward the bar at the same time Terry looked our way; we all waved in acknowledgement before he focused on Cindy.

"He's probably finding out if she got the weekend off so he can make their plans. If it's a weekend thing that includes hotel reservations, he'll need as much notice as possible."

I thought about that for a moment and shook my head. "It's just so strange."

"What is?"

"I didn't even know Terry Finne existed until this case."

"How long has he been at the police department?"

"I don't know. I'd think it's been a while if he and Cindy are—well, whatever they are. But if he's new, I'm curious what brought him here."

Quinn shrugged. "I'm new to Spirit Lake, and I'm not a killer. Besides, people move for work reasons all the time."

"Yeah, but...I don't know. You're probably right. Anyway, working at a police department and with victims would require a thorough background check."

I looked at him again as he said goodbye to Cindy and strolled our way, straightening his tie with one hand, the other tucked in his pants pocket.

"Andie Rose, thank you for giving Cindy the weekend off on such short notice."

I smiled at him. "She found her own replacement, so it's no trouble at all. Terry, I was wondering about something." He sat and waited for me to go on. "How well did you know Sara Banks?"

"I went to high school with their daughter, Fawn. We dated for a short while." He made a face. "It didn't end on good terms, I'm afraid. That woman can hold a grudge like no other."

"Their daughter or Sara?"

"Sara."

"Do you know why Beau, a shut in, would have been here in Spirit Lake?"

"He and I remained close after I broke things off

with Fawn. Being somewhat new in town, I invited him to come see me. It took some coaxing before he eventually agreed, but then he backed out again. That was a month or so ago. So how he ultimately ended up here is a mystery, because he didn't tell me he'd changed his mind since then."

I looked at him, trying to read any telltale signs of anything, well, *telling*, but there was nothing. "What about Sara?"

"Oh man. Where to even begin." He leaned back and clasped his hands behind his head. "She hated me. But that doesn't make me special. I think she hated everyone except Fawn. And sometimes Beau."

"Did she have a lot of enemies?"

"That's putting it mildly. But to her credit, she was a fantastic mother to Fawn. Fawn was her entire world."

"So where is Fawn now? Does she know about her folks?"

He exhaled through pursed lips, stretched his arms, and re-clasped his hands behind his head. "That's another story. Fawn hooked up with one of those communities." He made air quotes around the word community. "You know the ones. They take you away from your family and take all your money for the common good of the community." He made air quotes again.

"So, have you told her about her parents? I assume as the victim witness person, you'd have to notify her, correct?"

"I'm working on it, yeah. No one has any contact info for her, though. The community she hooked up with moved to another state and I'm running into dead ends at every shot. I guess Beau and Sara made multiple attempts at contacting her, but they didn't get anywhere. She cut them off completely. Which turned Sara into an even bigger monster."

Curiosity prickled my thoughts. "Was Fawn angry with them about something?"

Terry lifted his hands in an *I don't know* fashion, before he stood. "Couldn't tell ya. But I need to get going and try more avenues to contact Fawn. See if I can find one that's *not* a dead end."

"Thanks, Terry."

He stopped back at the coffee bar, said something to Cindy, who looked our way, then he left.

I stared at the doorway after he'd gone and said to Quinn, "Exactly how close could Terry have been with Beau if he only dated Fawn a short time, as he claimed?"

"Well? If the town they're from was small, he could have known Beau and Sara for a long time, not only while he and Fawn dated."

"I find it strange that Terry has lived here for such a short time and knew not only both murder victims, but he was in a relationship with their daughter. A relationship that didn't end amicably, by the sounds of it." I tucked my lower lip between my teeth as I stared at the doorway Terry just exited. "I'll have to find out more about that."

Quinn gave an amused smile. "I'm beginning to see why you and my brother butt heads."

I splayed a hand across my chest. "I don't get in his way. Usually. But when I have something at stake in the matter, I can't merely sit back and not do anything about it."

"You don't trust Noah to solve it?"

I glanced at Aspen and Lord Watson, still lounging

despite the sun all but disappearing again. The branches blowing in the breeze cast shadows across the room.

"It has nothing to do with trust. It has to do with a need to protect my loved ones."

"Maybe you should tell him that."

I looked back at her. "Maybe."

She stood. "Hey, I really need to get going. I've been trying to stay out of the way of the guys working at my place, but I'm eager to see the progress since I was there last evening. They think they'll have my living quarters done this week. It looks so perfectly perfect. Simple with lots of bookshelves."

I laughed. "The books in the store aren't enough. You need more shelves?"

"Can one ever have too many books? Plus, I want my own stash. I don't want to dip into the inventory and sell used goods."

"Read eBooks."

She shook her head. "Nah. There's nothing like holding a physical book in my hand. Even the smell." She closed her eyes and smiled as she inhaled.

"I'm in your camp on that one."

"I'm thinking about eventually adding a used book section to the store too, though. A leave one, take one kind of thing. What do you think?"

"It's genius. But it'll take away from your sales. Besides, there's the town library for that."

She nodded. "Good point. I just don't want anyone to have an obstacle to getting their hands on a good book, ya know?"

"You could always ask the town to put up one of those little free libraries, just not in front of your bookstore. Get your brother on it, so he stays out of my way." We both laughed, and I glanced at my watch. "I'll walk out with you. I've been itching to go see what's happening at the crime scene. Sister Alice gave me a lot of deets, but I want to see what I can from my own perspective. And I've given Noah enough time and space so he can't say I'm interfering with his crime scene."

"I'm impressed you've stayed away as long as you have."

"It hasn't been easy. Trust me."

"My brother should be happy. Are you going to tell him about your conversation with Terry and about Fawn?"

"Timing is everything."

Aspen and Lord Watson trailed behind us. After checking in—and out—with my staff, Quinn clipped Lord Watson's leash to his harness, and we each got into our cars. Aspen assumed his usual spot in the front passenger seat and settled in.

I looked at him and laughed. "If I didn't know better, Aspen, I'd think you are feeling superior to Lord Watson because you didn't need a leash."

After leaning over to plant a kiss on his schnoz, I snagged my phone and punched in the number for my dad. First things first. His freedom was at stake, and my patience had run dry. If he didn't answer, I would go to Tony's house. I just hoped he was there and not off with Shirley somewhere. Fully expecting his voicemail, his answer jolted me from the too-recent recall of the conversation with Shirley.

"Hi, Bug. I just picked up my phone to call you."

"Did you get my voicemails?"

"Just now. I turn my phone off when I'm writing. But it sounds like it's important."

"Extremely. Have you talked with Shirley yet?"

"Shirley?" His tone was riddled with confusion. "I have a missed call from her but haven't called her back yet. Why are you asking?"

"Because she's in town, Dad." I proceeded to relay the full conversation I'd had with her. "And I'm not the only one who picked up on the gross vibe. You should not be anywhere alone with that woman. *Nowhere*."

My dad chuckled. "You have nothing to worry about, Andie Rose. I'm a big boy and I don't walk my way into trouble."

"Yeah, but men can be so clueless sometimes. That's why there are so many office romances."

"Take a breath, kid. I'm not just any man, I'm your dad. You know me better than that. And that was a rather sexist thing to come out of your mouth. Women aren't guilty of that, too?"

"Yeah, well…" I knew he was one hundred percent right, but still.

"I have all I can do to take care of my relationship with your mom. As you know, relationships are hard work."

"Your message beneath that seemingly simple statement is loud and clear. But that's not why I'm single, Dad. I'm not afraid of hard work."

"Not of hard work, no. You've always been a hard worker. But when it comes to relationships…well, the bottom line is you're just afraid. Your mom and me—"

"Don't worry, Dad. It has absolutely nothing to do with you and Mother and the example you set. Anyway, I'm not even sure how we got to that topic. I just wanted to be sure you were aware of Shirley's affection." I grimaced. *Gross*.

He laughed softly. "Received. Anything else?"

"One thing. Do you have an alibi for last night?"

"Other than Winston snoring loud enough downstairs, I heard him upstairs on the opposite side of the house? I think Tony was here, but I can't be sure. Did you ask him?"

"Dad, I'm not going to ask Tony if he was home last night. I'm his boss. I strive to keep a professional relationship with my staff." *Yeah, right.*

"How's it working for ya?" He chuckled.

I blew through my lips. "Sometimes better than others. Some of them, Tony included, are like family, you know? Frank, Izzy, Jade, Lily…"

"I do."

Tony and I had especially gotten chummy in my short time here, and I guess some could misconstrue it as something inappropriate. But he was more of a brother figure. Still, if I didn't have to ask him if he was home last night when my dad was here to ask him, all the better. I hadn't exactly been professional in Gemmalee's coaching session, either. *Sheesh*! Maybe I needed to take a class in professionalism. I planted my face into my empty palm.

"Andie Rose?"

"Yeah, sorry." I proceeded to tell him the details I'd learned from Sister Alice about Sara's murder. "We need to find you a solid alibi for last night."

My dad blew through his lips. I imagined him taking his glasses off and chewing on one of the temple tips.

"I'm afraid I don't have one."

"Winston or Tony didn't get up for anything, a glass of water or to pee, *anything*, so they can vouch for your being there?"

"Honey, I don't know." He sighed. "They wouldn't have come into my room for either of those things. And when I'm in the zone, an earthquake could level the town, and I wouldn't know it."

"You know how weird and uncommon that is, right? I can't imagine any author who wouldn't want to wring your neck out of envy for having that superpower."

"I didn't say it's always that way. Only when I'm dialed in to my work. Which is where I was last night." The phone beeped, and he said, "Shirley is calling. I'd better let you go."

"Remember what I said about her, Dad."

"How could I forget, Bug? And remember what I said, too."

"I'm going to the crime scene to see what I can find. Over and out."

I hung up and curled my lip at the thought of Shirley talking with my dad. It wouldn't have bothered me so much had she not been so blatant and crude about it. But her comments about crazed fans stayed in the back of my mind. Could Beau and Sara's deaths have something to do with one of Beau's deranged fans who'd gotten upset with him? The idea of a peeved past flame from one of them came to mind again. But what about the killer knowing about my dad's manuscript? Maybe that was to throw suspicion on my dad, using him as an easy fall-guy but had nothing to do with the writing industry at all. I heaved a sigh. *Boy, oh boy.*

When Aspen and I got to town, I parked along the curb in the front instead of alongside the church in the parking lot so Noah wouldn't see my car. Anything not to give him a head start on preparing a speech for me. This way I could walk around to the back and go unnoticed as long as possible. I wished Sister Alice was here with me and looked forward to the summer when she wasn't expected to be at the school library every morning. Even when she worked at the hospital, her schedule was more flexible than it was now.

The sky seemed conflicted as to what it wanted to do. At least the clouds weren't spitting anymore, but by looking at the bank of gray incoming, I wouldn't rule it out in the next hour or so. One of those frequent bipolar Minnesota days.

As it happened, Noah wasn't at the scene. In fact, there were only a two people left, one of them an older man with his arms crossed in front of him, who I knew from past escapades as Chief Romero. He stroked his mustache with his thumb and forefinger. The second was a younger man in his police uniform, feet planted apart, hands resting on his duty belt.

"I expected you'd be here a lot earlier than this. Had my speech all ready."

I jumped at Noah's voice inches behind me and scowled. "Not funny," I said. "Where did you come from?"

Aspen sniffed the cuffs of Noah's pants before he sat beside my feet.

"You're not the only one hoping to go unnoticed."

"Can you tell me anything about Sara's murder?"

"Nope. The crime scene isn't even cold yet. I can't imagine that stopped your cohort from telling you what she shouldn't have, though."

I knew not to fall into that trap and ignored the comment all together. Addressing it, whether in the affirmative or denial, would land both Sister Alice and me in trouble.

"Anything new on Beau's case? Another murder contaminated his murder scene anyway, right?" I zeroed in on the crime scene. "This is all so bizarre."

Noah said, "I was just on the phone with the coroner's office about Beau's case."

My heart leaped, hoping he was going to give me some morsel of information, no matter how small. I felt like Aspen waiting for a crumb. "And?"

"She gave me the preliminary cause of death."

When he didn't say anything more, my jaw dropped open, and I placed my hands on my hips. "You cannot just leave me hanging like that."

"It's the most unusual thing. I'm still trying to process it. Just when I thought I'd seen it all."

I raised my eyebrows and made a rolling motion with my hand, encouraging him to continue.

He squinted his eyes and said, "Death by the toxin of a Golden Dart Frog."

Chapter 14

I choked on my saliva, coughing and sputtering. Aspen nudged my leg with his nose, then licked my hand.

"Are you okay?" Noah asked, concern etched on his face.

I leaned over, held up a hand, palm facing him, the other hand on my knee. My dad said the reason he wasn't overly concerned was because that very thing was the cause of death of the victim in his book and was such a rarity. And here it was. It jumped off the page of his yet-unpublished book, to an actual murder. And to someone he knew. Someone was going through a lot of trouble to set him up.

When I finally stopped hacking, I stood and said, "I'm sorry, I thought you said a Golden Poison Dart Frog."

"I did."

I looked through him and into the distance, my brain scrambling to make sense of it. Aspen trotted toward the police car and marked one tire. I sucked in my lips to keep from smiling my satisfaction.

"Tell me."

I shook my head a bit and averted my gaze from his. "Tell you what?"

"Andie Rose, I've come to know you well enough to know when you're hiding something."

"We haven't known each other that long, so—"

"The length of time means nothing. I know you more than you think I do. And I'm a detective. Reading people is what I do. And let me tell you, you're terrible at hiding things. Don't take up poker. Or deception."

"Rude," I mumbled and glanced at my phone, my watch, behind me. Anything to buy time to figure out my next move.

"You might as well tell me. You know I'll find out, anyway."

I hesitated another moment longer, and Noah sighed and said, "If you're keeping something from me that's critical to this investigation…Well, trust me when I say you don't want to do that. With murder, a double murder in this case, I'll swim the depths to solve it regardless of who gets in my way."

A flash of something in his eyes, sadness mixed with dogged determination, captured my attention, but I turned my focus on Aspen, who was making his way toward me from the edge of the property.

Noah cleared his throat. "Andie Rose, if it's about Chandler, you know I will do literally everything in my power to prove his innocence. You need to trust me."

I shifted my weight from one foot to the other, hands on my hips, and said quietly, "The victim's cause of death in my dad's upcoming book was from the poison of the Golden Dart Frog."

Noah blew through pursed lips and ran a hand over his face and down his chin. "Okay. Let me think about this for a minute."

"Noah, not only is my dad incapable of murder, but he's not stupid either. He wouldn't set himself up like this."

"No, but *someone* is." He chewed the inside of his cheek and briefly glanced back at the crime scene where Chief Romero and the officer were wrapping up their conversation.

The young officer waved at Noah and trotted off to his car. Chief Romero strolled toward us and briefed Noah on a couple of items, but nothing of any significance to the investigation. He nodded toward me.

"Ms. Kaczmarek, I don't think I need to tell you this is a police investigation and not open to assistance from amateur detectives. Am I clear?"

I looked down briefly before I met his eyes. Warmth crept into my cheeks at the sternness there. "Clear, sir. Understood."

Another awkward moment of holding my gaze, the heat from my cheeks reached up to my scalp. Chief Romero patted Noah between his shoulder blades and said, "Stay focused, Parker."

We watched until he turned the corner. Noah turned back to me and said, "To be honest, this revelation helps Chandler's case instead of hurting it."

I sucked in a breath. "It does?"

He narrowed his eyes and tucked his lower lip between his teeth, the wheels in his head churning.

"Yep. First of all, you're one hundred percent right when—has Chandler traveled outside of the country anytime recently?"

"No. Not since they moved back here from Costa Rica."

He sighed and tipped his head back and rubbed his neck. "Oh, man. That's right."

I asked tentatively, "Why do I think this just went from getting better to worse again?"

"Because it might have," he said with some reluctance. "The M.E. said she did some quick research on the frog before calling me. Golden Poison Dart Frogs live in the jungles of Colombia in an area people can't easily get to because it's loaded with drug cartels and illegal gold miners."

"I don't understand. What does that have to do with my dad's past in Costa Rica? It's not like Colombia and Costa Rica are neighbors. Heck, it's not even the same continent."

"It's probably nothing. I just need to find out if these frogs live in Costa Rica, too. If they do…well, you can see how that won't be good for Chandler."

"You don't know if these toxic little critters are in Costa Rica?"

He frowned. "It's not exactly like I've had one of these deaths ever before. Your dad would probably know a lot more than me since he's the one who would have done the research on them."

Tina Cartwright came to mind, and I thrust a finger in the air. "A recent guest, and one who sought out the free coaching session, Tina Cartwright, travels the world checking out places people claim are haunted."

"And?"

"Maybe one of her locations was Colombia."

"You said she travels to *haunted* places." I lifted my eyebrows and cocked my head to the side. "Andie Rose, I don't know that Colombia is haunted. By ghosts, anyway."

"Well, if you won't check it out, I will."

He shook his head slowly. "I will. You won't. Got it?" He jotted Tina's name on his notepad.

"You have to admit, the timing is a little sketchy."

"I said I'd check into it."

"Did the M.E. say anything else?"

"Only that the frog releases the toxin when it's agitated or threatened. And some indigenous groups use it to tip blow darts as self-defense measures. Or any other reason they have, I suppose."

"But that doesn't explain how it got here. Someone can't just get in a car and drive from Columbia. And with airport security measures as tight as they are, it's not like a person can just dip a blow dart in poison and carry it onto a plane." I snatched my phone and began furiously pushing keys.

"Who are you texting, your partner in crime?" He shoved his hand out in front of him. "Don't."

The gruffness of his tone caught my attention for all of a second. "I'm not texting her or anyone."

"Then what are you doing? This is an odd time to surf the internet."

I glanced at him briefly and then went back to my phone. "Not when I'm looking up information on dart frogs."

He tipped his head back and groaned. "Oh, good Lord. Don't tell me you're trusting a search engine for such sensitive information."

I frowned. "Of course I am. The internet is a treasure trove of free information." I scanned an article that popped up. "Says here most poison dart frogs are poisonous but not deadly. And according to this site, it's their native diet that makes them poisonous. They eat little bugs which feed on toxic plants. So when they're in captivity, they're not poisonous."

"Let's remember this information is from a website of which you know nothing about as far as accuracy, huh? Just because it's on the internet doesn't make it true."

"Thanks for the AI lesson." I glanced at Aspen, who darted toward a squirrel, the little varmint scrambling up a tree just before Aspen reached it.

"No need to be defensive," Noah said.

I dipped my chin toward my chest and looked up at him. "I'm not. But this at least gives us something to go on, right?"

"But it's not helpful if it's not true."

"Pshaw. And you call yourself a detective." I watched Aspen, planted at the base of the tree as the squirrel chittered furiously, taunting him from a low-hanging branch. "Now, back to the wealth of information I was generously handing to you before you rudely interrupted me. A question, really. If they're not dangerous in captivity, then someone had to get the poison while physically there."

I held his gaze as we processed everything. Or at least I was processing. He might have been wondering how I'd gotten this far in life, feeling sorry for my dad and Mother.

"So, that makes me wonder about something," I said. "Would it be possible to bottle the poison somehow and transport it that way?"

He held up a hand toward me. "A lot hinges on that answer, so do me a favor and let me find an accurate answer to that question."

"Whoever you ask will probably have gotten it from the internet just like me."

"But a professional source thoroughly vets the information for accuracy."

I held up a finger. "Did the medical examiner tell

you the symptoms of getting poisoned by one of these things?" I kept talking without waiting for an answer, reading from my phone. "Muscle contractions, respiratory and muscle paralysis, convulsions, and it goes on from there. Which means Beau died a pretty horrific death. Oh!" I stabbed my finger into the air again. "It says a victim can die within three minutes if the poison gets into an open wound. Given he was in a coffin," I paused and shuddered, "I hope that was the case with Beau. Can you imagine being in a coffin and paralyzed so you can't move, just lay there tortured as you know you're dying?" I shuddered again, fearing I might just puke.

Noah stared at me, unblinking. "Are you done? Because I have valid answers to get instead of information from an unreliable source."

"Before I go, can I get something in writing proving you said I was right about something? I'm happy to record it on my phone if you don't have any blank space left on your notepad."

He pressed his lips together, but his eyes shone with amusement. "Doubtful. Putting it in writing or a recording."

I folded my palm around my phone and turned to leave. "Never hurts to ask. Keep me posted?"

He scoffed. "Right."

"It wasn't a no, so I'm holding out hope." Aspen trotted to my side and followed me.

"Hey, Andie Rose."

I pivoted to face him again.

"How well do you know Max Winters?"

His tone collided with his casual stance. *Was he jealous?* I swallowed a lump in my throat.

"Why do you want to know?"

"I don't want him around my sister if he's not trustworthy."

My curiosity crashed, shattering my psyche to shards. Not sure what I was hoping for, but it obviously wasn't that. I let out a soft puff of air through my lips.

"How about you let Quinn make that call instead of you doing it for her?"

"Asking you about the man isn't doing anything *for* her. It's investigating. It's what I do."

"Except this isn't one of your cases. It's your sister's business," I said as gently as I could. "I'd suggest not interfering, Noah. She told me what happened to her, and it's pretty awful, but you have to trust she's learned from it and is all the wiser. Trust *her*. She's a smart lady." I made a face. "Now her brother, well…" I rolled my eyes, chuckled, and turned again toward my car.

"One more thing," he said. "What makes this Max guy so attractive to you two?"

Oh heck no. I wasn't making that mistake again. "Ask Quinn," I called over my shoulder with a wave.

"I'm asking you."

I turned the corner as if I hadn't heard a thing. Except the unsettled sensation in my stomach let me know I'd heard it all right. Loud and clear.

The minute we got into the car, Aspen perched on the front seat while I wrapped the seat belt around him. Sister Alice teased me mercilessly about using a seatbelt on a dog. That in her day, dogs and kids alike rode in the back of pickup trucks with no restraints. My reply was less than appropriate to say to a sister, but you can probably guess what it was. Or close to it, anyway. I also reminded her Aspen wasn't a *dog*, and if she didn't believe me, to just ask him. But she only asked me if I'd gone back to the bottle because of suggesting such an absurd thing.

I buckled my own belt and punched in the number for my dad, switching it to Bluetooth. It shocked me senseless when he answered on the first ring. "Dad?"

"Hi, Bug."

"Oh, it's Andie Rose," Shirley's voice rang from the background. "Tell her Shirley says hi."

I rolled my eyes. "I heard. You're not at Tony's, are you?"

"Nope. At Hallowed Grounds Coffee Shop."

Hallowed Grounds was one of the two unique coffee shops in Spirit Lake, the other being Spirit Brew. The locals delighted that two independently owned coffee shops ruled the town and no big corporations had come and driven them out of business.

"Well, that's good at least." He chuckled. "We need to chat about something I just found out."

"What is it?" His voice took on a tone of concern, unlike most of the time up to this point.

"Not on the phone. I'm in town. I'd come to the coffee shop, but it's not something I want to say in front of Shirley. Can you meet me back at the inn?" But then something occurred to me. "Wait! I'll come to you if you two are up for company." Maybe I *did* want Shirley to hear, so I could witness her reaction. The killer, knowing the details of my dad's book, involved her completely. I realized he'd said something. "I'm sorry, what?"

"I'll wait for you here."

Chapter 15

When I walked into Hallowed Grounds, I searched the crowded room and spotted my dad waving his hand at me.

Shirley was first to stand and swooped in for a hug. "You get your height from your dad. And your looks."

I scowled and squirmed away from her before I hugged my dad.

"What do you want to drink, and I'll go get it," he said.

"Lavender-vanilla latte with oat milk, please. And can you get some whipped cream for Aspen?" At the mention of it, Aspen sat, his tail furiously sweeping the floor, his gaze on mine. Dad looked at me, eyebrows raised. "He knows human speak."

Dad strolled toward the counter, leaving Aspen and me alone with Shirley. My canine pal, though, was much more enthused about it, knowing what was upcoming. Whipped cream was like doggy crack to him.

"Chandler said you had something important to talk with him about. Sounds so mysterious." She wiggled her eyebrows. "What's it about?"

I gave her a thin smile. "I'll wait for my dad to get back to the table."

She sighed and reached for my hand. "I think we might have gotten off on the wrong foot. I'm an acquired taste," she said.

One I hadn't acquired yet, for sure.

"Maybe we can start over. Please," she said when I left silence hover between us.

And this is where I can get hung up from healthy relationships. I could teach people how to have them, but I seemed to lack the skill in the *doing* part. My dad used to say, *Those who can, do; those who can't, teach.* There was a reason I teach.

"Sure," I finally said and glanced at my dad, still at the counter.

"So what is it you wanted to tell your dad?"

"I'm going to wait until he gets back to the table," I said again. Her suggestion for us to start over hadn't changed my mind about telling her ahead of my dad.

We sat in silence until he put my latte in front of me, along with Aspen's paper cup piled high with whipped cream. He settled back down in his chair, stretching his legs out in front of him. Aspen licked his lips and pawed at the cup before I'd even set it in front of him. He grasped it between his paws.

Dad said, "Shirley heard about Beau's death and came to see how we were doing."

"We?"

"Winston and me."

"Winston stayed in town then?" I didn't see any evidence of a third person having been at the table. I glanced around the coffee shop. "And I thought Winston said he'd invited you here," I said to Shirley.

Dad said, "Detective Parker caught up with Winston before he left. Noah gave him the go-ahead to leave with the condition he didn't leave the country."

"Why was Winston in such a hurry to leave town?" I asked. "And why was he trying to avoid talking with

Noah?"

Shirley took a drink of her coffee, leaving a bright red outline on the ridge of the cup. "He said he didn't want to get caught up in drama."

My eyebrows arched toward my hairline. "Drama? Someone—excuse me, *two* people were murdered. That's not exactly everyday drama."

"What I meant was—"

"Sorry," I said. "Winston's view of what drama means just seemed tasteless. And hurrying away at a time like this makes him look guilty, is all."

Shirley shook her head slowly. "Oh, honey, I know Winston, and he has nothing to feel guilty about. He had nothing to do with the deaths of Beau or Sara."

"Dad, remember when I asked you about the similarities to your book and Beau's cause of death?"

"Yeah?" He lifted his cup and took a sip.

"And you said you weren't worried because the cause of death to the victim in your book was so unusual?"

"Oh, it was absolutely brilliant!" Shirley exclaimed. "Deliciously unusual."

Dad, his eyes not leaving mine, hesitated before saying slowly, "Yeah?"

I took a deep breath and looked at Shirley. "I just found out Beau's cause of death was poison from a Golden Dart Frog."

Shirley gasped, and her hand flew up to cover her mouth. "Oh my, God!"

I briefly glanced at my dad's genuinely shocked expression, then I turned my attention back to Shirley. The lack of concern in her eyes betrayed her reaction. I was good at reading people during a coaching session, but to be fair, this wasn't a session, and I didn't know Shirley. Not to mention our rocky start could taint my interpretation.

"If you'll excuse me," Shirley finally said, "I need to go and speak with Detective Parker. I have some news I think he should know about."

"What news?" I asked.

She looked at me a moment as if weighing whether to tell me before she said, "The less you know, the better, Andie Rose."

"Do you want me to call him to see where he is? So you know where to find him."

She shook her head as she stood and adjusted the strap of her handbag on her shoulder. "It's a teensie-tiny town. I'll find him easy enough."

She air-kissed my dad's cheek before she slipped out the door. I almost gagged.

"What do you think that was all about?" He didn't reply, only seemed to process what I'd told him. "Dad, do you know what she needed to talk to Noah about?"

He shook his head. Aspen's attention was heavy on me. I reached down to pet him. "No more, Aspen. You'll get an upset stomach." He slid onto his belly, his nose lying on his crossed front paws, his eyes still focused on me should I change my mind from sympathy for his situation. "Dad, do you think whatever Shirley wanted to tell Noah had something to do with Winston?"

He shook his head again and said solemnly, "I don't know. What I *do* know is I'm now a wee bit concerned." He held his pointer finger and thumb a breath apart from one another.

"Someone is setting you up."

"But who? My book isn't published yet. The ARCs

haven't even gone out."

"ARCs?"

"The advanced reader copies. The publisher sends them out to get early reviews." He exhaled and leaned back as he clasped his hands behind his head. "Unless they have, and she didn't tell me. I didn't think of asking."

"Maybe that's what Shirley had to talk with Noah about. Do you think she suspects someone?"

"I don't know."

His tone startled me. I can't remember the last time he snapped at me. Even when he had every right to. But his life hadn't been on the line before, either.

"I'm sorry. I don't mean to add pressure to an already stressful situation. I'm only trying to find out who's doing this to you."

"You have nothing to be sorry for. It would seem like the most likely scenario. This isn't the time I'd planned on having with my daughter. Hate to say it, but I'm looking forward to getting out of here and back home."

"To Mother? You *are* desperate to leave."

"Andie Rose, she's your mother. And she's my wife."

Message received. My cheeks burned with shame from a tasteless joke. But those few words revealed just how worried my dad had become.

"I know. I'm sorry, Dad. Again." I rolled my eyes. The snarky comment was ugly, and I regretted it.

The ring of my phone sliced through the accumulating tension like a bolt of lightning through thick clouds.

"Hi, Sister Alice." I looked at my watch. "Are you

done with work?"

"I've been done. I saw your car by Hallowed Grounds. Want company?"

"Always, if it's you."

She laughed. "Oh-oh. Something's wrong. I'll be right there."

Not even five seconds later, she whizzed up to our table and pulled out a chair.

"Where were you when you called?" I asked. "Outside the door?"

"Pretty much." She looked at my dad. "Nice to see you, Chandler."

Startled, my dad stood and enveloped her in an easy hug. "Sorry, Sister. I guess my mind is somewhere else right now."

Aspen nudged her with his nose. "Aww, even the pup missed me." She leaned to rub his head and plunked into the chair.

"Don't let Aspen's baby browns fool you. He's hoping for another pup cup."

She looked at me with a quirked eyebrow. I filled her in on the latest, choosing my words carefully so I didn't add to my dad's stress. But no matter how I phrased it, there wasn't a gentler way than telling it exactly like it was. Sometimes there was no way to soften the prickly truth.

Finally, I stopped talking, sighed. "What do you want to drink? I'll go get it."

"Nothing."

My dad rose to his feet, drained the last of his drink, and tossed the empty cup in the garbage. "If you ladies will excuse me, I have something I need to do."

I raised my eyebrows. "That sounds cryptic. Want

help?"

He shook his head and planted a kiss on top of my head. "I'm good."

"That's weird," I said after he left.

"That he wanted to do something alone?" Sister Alice asked.

I told Sister Alice about Shirley's recent strange departure. "I wonder if both he and Shirley have someone in mind. Like Winston. Shirley said she didn't believe Winston would ever do anything to Beau or Sara, but I wish you could have been here. It was odd." I plucked up a napkin and reached over to wipe one of the many smudges from her glasses.

She jerked back. "Boundaries, dear."

Sister Alice had eyewear frames in every bright color and pattern imaginable. A highlight of my day had become witness to her choice of frames for the day, but her lenses were usually so smudged I don't think she could see a hippopotamus two feet in front of her. It drove me crazy, and she knew it.

"You do that on purpose. I know you do."

She smiled. "It doesn't bother *me*."

"How do you afford all those, anyway? Don't sisters have to take a vow of poverty?"

She dipped her chin and looked at me as she wiped her lenses with the napkin I provided for her. "You've been doing some reading, I see."

"Trying to understand you." I smiled at the ever-present mischief glittering in her eyes.

"There are a lot of dimensions to being a religious sister. It's not a one-size-fits-all kind of thing. But I have good news for you."

I leaned back and sighed. "Oh, boy. Could I use that

right now."

"I know how much you miss me, so you'll be happy to know you'll see more of me than you have this past week."

I raised an eyebrow. "Why? You get fired from the school library already?"

"It was only temporary to begin with. It just wasn't clear *how* temporary."

"Oh, I get it. You couldn't see well enough to file the books appropriately, could you?" She only stared at me, unblinking, and I rolled my hand for her to continue. "Go on. The suspense is killing me."

"They got a full-time applicant who's more than qualified for the position. Of course, they offered it to me first. Except other duties demand my attention."

"Are you going back to the hospital? And where does that leave Sister Eunice since she took your place there?"

"My replacement at the school won't start until next school year. After that I'll still substitute at the library, but the community needs someone to provide care for the housebound, the ill, and the spiritually bankrupt. Sister Ida balked at me filling the position. Said I'm not couth enough." Her tongue rolled dramatically over the word *couth*. "But Father Vincent insisted I was the perfect candidate."

"And you want to do it to irk Sister Ida, am I right?"

"Don't be so cynical," she scoffed. "I enjoy working with the community I've been a part of for so long."

But I knew the teensiest part of Sister Alice was gloating about getting the position despite Sister Ida's objections. *Especially* because of that. Sister Alice was, how should I put it, rough-hewn? Unrefined? But she loved people and always gave everyone, no matter what they were accused of, the benefit of the doubt. Thank God, because I needed that benefit of the doubt more times than I cared to admit.

"Why does this employment change mean I'll see more of you? Will your time be more flexible again?"

"Yes. But that's not why. You're one of the spiritually bankrupt I'm charged with tending to." She snickered.

And there it was. I laughed, reached toward her, and ran my pointer finger over one of her lenses. "Let's go find some evidence to prove my dad's innocence."

Chapter 16

As we were leaving, Gemmalee pulled the door open to come in the shop, but stepped back onto the sidewalk when she saw us. We skirted off to the side of the door while Aspen scoped out the traffic on the sidewalk, greeting a little schnauzer walking its humans.

"Hi, Andie Rose."

She looked at Sister Alice and smiled.

"This is Sister Alice from St. Michael's," I said. "Sister," I gestured toward her, "meet Gemmalee Price. She and her husband, Stan, have a room at The Raven Motel." I scanned the immediate area. "Stan didn't come with you?"

She waved a hand through the air. "He's in Handy Hardware. I'd rather have coffee than stroll through the tool section. Cleaning supplies and tools aren't really my thing. And gloves? Don't even get me started with how many he has already." She waggled her head.

Sister Alice shook Gemmalee's hand. "You have a beautiful name. Welcome to Spirit Lake. How long are you staying for?"

The two of them chatted a bit, but I didn't hear a word of it. Her husband's shopping list snagged a hundred percent of my attention.

With a quick apologetic glance at Sister Alice for interrupting her in mid-sentence, I said, "Gemmalee, why did your husband need cleaning supplies and gloves? I can't imagine he'd have a burning need to clean the motel room before you leave. Couldn't he wait and get those things when you get back home?"

She shrugged. "Does one ever know why a man does what he does?"

Sister Alice laughed. "Amen to that."

"Agreed." As if insulted, Aspen tossed me a look I wasn't aware he was capable of and went back to willing another canine to happen by.

"The guy at the front desk from the motel told him about some massive sale going on at Handy's, and my husband will do anything for a sale. Even if he doesn't need it." She rolled her eyes. "I'll have to go back to the corporate IT world if he keeps it up. He's worse than a woman at Macy's." She shuddered. "I'd have to kill him before I'd get forced back into the cutthroat IT industry." She gasped and her hand flew to her mouth. "Oh, my God! That was the wrong thing to say right now. Me and my big mouth." She shook her head, the worried look still plastered in place. "That gives me an idea, though, to get him back to traveling with me. Wherever I want to go, I'll just tell him there's a hardware store there. But first, make darn sure there *isn't* one."

"You don't think he'd catch on to that gimmick?" Sister Alice winked at her.

Gemmalee toyed with her coat zipper, grinned, and said, "Eventually, probably."

She said her goodbyes and slipped inside the coffee shop.

After the door closed behind her, Sister Alice snickered. "I like that lady."

"Yeah, I do too. But something about Stan doesn't sit well with me."

"Because he's buying things on sale?"

"Cleaning supplies and gloves after there've just been two murders?" I stopped walking and stared absently down the sidewalk in front of me before I set my focus in the direction of Handy Hardware. "Maybe Aspen and I'll hang out here and wait for him to meet back up with Gemmalee."

Sister Alice screwed up her lips. "Loitering and/or stalking isn't a good idea, Ant. Neither of those falls in line with what the Program teaches us about doing the next right thing."

I waved a hand through the air. "I know. And you're right. I think I'm trying so hard to clear my dad that I'm looking for something that's not there." I let out a breath of frustration. "I don't even know where to turn from here, Sister Alice. It seems the more answers I get, the more it throws my dad into suspicion. I wish I knew what Shirley had to tell Noah. She knew something significant."

"Well, from what you've told me, we know it's nothing that will cast suspicion on Chandler, but the opposite. Her admiration for him has its upsides."

I frowned. "It's still gross."

"Your father is a handsome, successful man, Andie Rose. Why is that gross? Most of all, you need to trust him. And realize that in this case, whatever she had that was so important to tell Noah, it will help clear your dad."

I nodded. Something was still niggling at me about Stan Price. Since I didn't have the means to do a background search on him, the only way I could get one was by telling Noah. Desperate means call for desperate measures, as the old cliché goes. And I could always hope if I told him something, maybe he'd give me information on what Shirley revealed to him. Or information he might have on Shirley or Winston. Both of them had early access to my dad's manuscript, and they both knew of the murder victims. And what about Terry Finne? He knew both parties. And then there was Fawn. What kind of community was she in? Was it a dangerous one that would kill for finances? It wouldn't mean Fawn killed her own parents, but someone else in the community could have to get the money. I groaned. That opened up a bottomless box of suspects. And if Terry couldn't find Fawn, he sure wouldn't be able to find an entire commune. The biggest obstacle I couldn't get over, however, was how they'd know about the contents of my dad's as-yet-unpublished manuscript.

There were so many questions I wanted answers to. I hadn't told Noah about my conversation with Terry yet, but I couldn't imagine he hadn't mentioned something to Noah about Fawn or that Noah had found out Fawn was the next of kin. Terry and Noah worked in the same building. Wouldn't Noah know Terry was looking for Fawn for victim notification purposes, if nothing else? Maybe we were looking at two killers. I doubted it, but at this point, I was willing to entertain every possibility.

"Kid!" Sister Alice's voice snapped me back to the moment, and I looked at her. "Where were you just now? You forgot to take me with you. And your pup got so bored waiting he fell asleep."

I shook my head. "Sorry." After filling her in on everything romping through my head, I said, "I think the next step is to call Noah. So many answers to my questions lie with him."

She pressed her lips into a thin line before the

corners of her mouth curved in amusement. "And he's going to tell you? No matter how much the man likes you, he's not about to reveal his hand. No chance."

"This isn't poker. Which he told me not to take up, by the way. Apparently I'm an open book."

She shook her head. "I'm not touchin' that one."

"I'm helping him catch a killer or two. The least he could do is throw me a morsel of information now and again."

She emitted a slight huff. "I don't think he wants your help except for *you* to give *him* helpful information. It's a one-way street thing."

"I'm hoping if I give him some info, he'll return the favor. You know, paving a new lane on that one-way street."

"Again, I tell you, don't get your hopes up."

"Yeah, yeah."

"I'm glad you hit up the meeting last night. It's imperative you stay connected during times like these."

I looked at her and frowned. "That reminds me. We added the evening meetings to accommodate your new job, and—"

"Hold up there. Before you go any further with that, the group didn't add the evening meetings just for me. Several members appreciate the added time because it works better with their jobs, too."

"True."

"It wouldn't hurt to have two meetings a day so you could attend both. Double the pleasure, double the fun."

"I was only asking out of curiosity."

"You know what they say about curiosity. And you don't have nine lives like a cat supposedly does."

I smirked. "Come on. Let's go see if Noah's at the

police department."

We crossed the street and hiked our way to the end of the block to Town Hall, which also housed the police department. Noah pulled into the parking lot as we arrived.

He slammed his car door closed and punched the lock button on the fob.

"If it isn't the dynamic duo. Here with questions I cannot and will not give you answers to? Because you know I can't give you ladies information on an open investigation." His tone was flat, and he casually glanced at his watch.

"Are we boring you? Sorry-not-sorry." I wasn't surprised though since he issued the same monologue numerous times.

He shook his head slowly. "Not bored, just busy catching a killer and trying to prove your dad isn't that person."

Ouch. My face grew hot. "What would you say if I told you I'm here to give you information?"

"I'd say you've got to be kidding. Unless you want information in exchange for what you have for me. And you can probably guess what my answer is to that."

"You don't even want to hear what I know?"

He nodded. "Oh, I do, and I think you'll tell me. Because withholding information is a crime, remember?"

"Only if you ask me a question and I don't tell you an honest answer. It's kind of a gray line there, you know? Easy to wiggle out of."

He frowned, plunked his hands on his hips, and fought a smile. "Actually, it's pretty black and white." He nodded toward the station. "Come on into my office and let's talk."

I nudged Sister Alice with my elbow and discreetly mouthed, "Watch this."

Noah snagged a stray chair from the hallway, dragged it into his office, and cleared files from another. He motioned for us to sit and took his place behind his desk. He leaned forward and clasped his hands in front of him. Aspen perched beside my chair.

"Talk," he said, his focus glued to me.

"You first?" I squirmed and cringed at the timidity of my tone.

"Hard no." He wasn't wavering on this one iota.

I swallowed. Apparently, I was going to have to give info and then hope he gave anything at all. "Did you know Beau and Sara have a child?"

He cocked his head to the side and didn't so much as blink. "A child?"

Huh. So he didn't know. Exactly what has he been doing to clear my dad?

"Yes. Her name is Fawn, and—"

"Okay." He exhaled and sat back in his chair, a pencil tucked between his forefinger and middle finger. He alternated tapping both ends of the pencil on his desk but lost the rhythm. The pencil fell to the floor. Aspen stood and sniffed at it before Noah reached to pick it up. "Don't eat lead, Aspen." He brusquely rubbed Aspen's neck, sat up and forward again.

My mouth opened to speak, but nothing came out. There were absolutely no words. Finally, I found them. "Don't eat lead? Is that like a police department slogan or something?"

Sister Alice shrugged. "If it is, at least it's a healthy one."

Noah, ignoring the peanut gallery comments, said, "Of course we know about Fawn. But she's an adult, not a child."

"Have you located her yet?"

He shook his head. "Nope. Terry Finne's working on it. Sometimes those communes, cults, whatever you want to call them, are impossible to find if they don't want to be found. All we know is they've gone to another state."

Sister Alice shifted in her chair. "There's always a trail, Noah. Just depends on how hard one looks."

Noah cleared his throat. "Excuse me, Sister, but are you implying I'm not doing my job?"

"Not at all. That in no way referenced *your* detecting abilities."

"Then—"

"She meant Terry. Did you know Terry used to date Fawn in high school, that he remained close with Beau, and he didn't like Sara?" I felt bad for ratting out Terry, but if it helped prove my dad's innocence. Well, it was my dad. There's nothing I wouldn't do for him. To be fair, for Mother either.

"So what we're curious about," Sister Alice said, "is you admitted Terry is the one looking for Fawn. Can you be sure he's doing whatever it takes to find her? *Anything* it takes."

Noah cleared his throat. "The dating information is new to me." He jotted something down on a scrap of paper.

I leaned forward, but he flipped the paper over before I could read what it said.

"I'll talk with Terry, nosey."

I flinched. "Harsh."

Sister Alice sniggered.

Maybe I was a bit quick to feel bad for ratting on Terry. He obviously didn't want Noah to know his personal connection to Fawn. I wondered why that was? It seemed a significant piece of information to withhold. Might as well tell Noah the rest.

"Terry invited Beau to come to Spirit Lake. Beau finally agreed but then backed out and said he wasn't coming."

Noah lifted his shoulders and let them drop again. "Clearly, he changed his mind."

"But did he?" Sister Alice asked.

Noah ran his hand over his face. "Beau coming here on his own would be the only thing that makes sense in this entire case. I can't think of another reason he ended up here in Spirit Lake, of all places. Can you? It's not like someone would have killed him in his home and think to do a body dump, in a coffin, on *top* of a grave, at a cemetery in Spirit Lake, Minnesota. Even though it follows Chandler's book. It's not like Chandler lives in Spirit Lake." He frowned, looked absently beyond me, and said slowly, to no one in particular, "Unless they wanted to draw Chandler Langston here."

I drew in a sharp breath. "Say what?"

He brought his gaze back to mine, his thoughts still elsewhere. "Just thinking out loud."

Everything in my body came to an abrupt stop. I thought about Shirley's gross infatuation with my dad, about her comment on dangerous fans, about Stan Price's zealous interest in my dad and his books.

"What are you thinking?"

I jerked my attention back to him. "Noah, do you think my dad's in danger?"

Instead of answering the question, he said, "Andie Rose, does your dad make his location public? What I mean is, does he post his home address anywhere in his books, social media sites, website—anything like that?"

I shook my head. "Uh-uh. He's really careful about what information he puts out there into the universe. He even tries to avoid photos taken in easily identifiable locales in case someone recognizes something. During interviews, when they ask where he lives—which is stupid, by the way, but people have asked it—the only thing he'll say is he grew up in Spirit Lake."

Noah released a long exhale and ran a hand over his face, which was suddenly too serious. I got a sinking feeling in the pit of my stomach.

"What are you thinking, Noah?"

He stood, his chair spinning out from behind him and hitting the wall. "Stay put. I'll be right back."

I turned my chair so Aspen was between my feet. He sat up, and I buried my hands in his silky mahogany fur, then planted my cheek against the top of his head.

Sister Alice rested her hand on my back. "You okay?"

"What do you suppose Noah is doing? It sounds like he's worried about my dad's safety. Did you catch that?" I sat up and gripped my phone. "I need to call him."

"Whoa," she said, her hand now on my arm. "Hold the phone. Literally. Don't do anything that's going to cause your dad to go into hibernation, following Beau's habits. We don't want to frighten Chandler based on a *feeling* you have. Let's get a little more information first so we know more about what's going on."

Noah came back into the room and closed the door behind him before once again settling behind his desk.

"Noah, do I need to call my dad to warn him?"

"I'd tell you no, I'll call him, but that would be fruitless. You'll call him, anyway."

"And you—"

He held up a hand. "Before you throw your phone at me, I didn't say I'd blame you. I'd probably do the same thing. I've arranged for an officer to stay close to Chandler round the clock until we solve this case. Or until someone proves my theory wrong."

I sat up straight and cupped my hands around my knees. "That's it. He needs to stay at the inn."

"If there's cause for concern, it won't matter where he's staying. And for your safety—"

"This is about *his* safety, Noah. I need to be sure *he's* safe."

"And how do you propose to do that if you're not safe? And you have innocent people here at the inn you need to think about." His mouth set in a hard, stubborn line.

"Fine." I thought about Shirley's mention of dangerous fans again. "What have you found out about Tina Cartwright?"

"I can't find anyone by that name. I'm still looking into it."

I exhaled through pursed lips. "That's not concerning at all."

"Who's Tina Cartwright?" Sister Alice asked. "By the look on your face, she's a potential suspect?"

Instead of answering her, I told Noah, "Check into Stan Price."

"Who?"

"My dad's editor, Shirley Garcia, told me about the dangers of deranged fans. I heard Stan is a super fan of

177

my dad and his books. And Shirley—well, she has a, shall we say, an interest—in my dad."

"Why wouldn't she? His success brings her success, doesn't it?"

"Not that kind of interest. More personal." I shrugged. "And honestly? I have no idea how the publishing industry works. I've never really asked him for many details."

"Wow," he said, a bit taken aback. "I'm going to have to ask him how he does that."

"Publishing? You'd be better off asking Shirley."

"No, I meant how he keeps you out of his professional business."

Sister Alice chuckled and pushed her glasses further on her nose with her pointer finger.

I offered a bemused smile. "Hysterical."

"Excuse me," Sister Alice said, raising her hand. "But I must ask—shouldn't we be more worried about Beau's distraught superfans hurting Chandler? Chandler's own fans wouldn't want to hurt him. And if it was a fan of Beau's, why would he or she have killed him? There are arguments against both scenarios. And you never answered my question about Tina Cartwright. Who is she?"

I looked from her to Noah. "Tina was a recent guest at the inn and travels the country ghost hunting."

"Well, that sure clears things up. Not."

"I'll fill you in, but first," I looked at Noah, "what if one of Dad's fans killed Beau? If he's deranged enough to kill, who's to say he wouldn't go after Dad?"

Sister Alice's eyebrows shot up. "Oh, of course! Like that one book by the famous author about the woman who captures a novelist and keeps him hostage, eventually feeding him to pigs."

Noah tamped his hand in the air. "Okay, first of all, this isn't fiction."

"Might as well be," Sister Alice said. "It can't be coincidence that the murder is following a fictional book."

I shuddered. Aspen sat and rested his nose on my knee, and I laid my hand on his head.

Noah exhaled a long breath and rubbed the back of his neck. "You're not helping here, Sister."

"By the way," I said, "what important news did Shirley have for you?"

He frowned. "I have no idea what you're talking about."

Grr. "Come on, Noah. Can't you just tell me that much?"

He shook his head. "I can't tell you *anything* about that."

I folded my arms across my chest and tapped my foot. "You won't give me even a crumb of information?"

"It's not that I won't, but I can't, because I haven't talked with her yet." He looked at his watch. "And time's a tickin', daylight burnin'." He pushed his chair back and stood. "Now if you ladies, and dog," he nodded toward Aspen, "will excuse me, I have work to do."

I opened my mouth to speak, closed it again, then opened it once more.

Sister Alice said, "You look like Quinn's cat when he's focused on a bird, his lower jaw going up and down like that."

I shot her a look. "I'm trying to figure out how I want to approach this."

"Head on," she suggested.

Noah nodded his agreement, sighed, and sat back down in his chair. "This is the one and only time I'm happy you got involved, Sister."

"When you told me Beau's cause of death, I told my dad. Shirley was standing there. Something about it upset her, and—"

"Understandable," Sister Alice said. "Given the accumulating information."

"But she suddenly had to leave to find you, Noah. Said she had something important to tell you. And the less I knew, the better."

Noah's eyes widened. "I haven't seen her. Do you have her number?"

I shook my head. "But my dad would. I offered to give her your number, and she declined. Said she'd just come to the police department and if you weren't here, Spirit Lake is a small town, so she would find you."

Noah picked up the phone receiver and punched in a number. "Sherry, it's Parker. Did anyone come to the front desk asking for me while I was out?" He frowned. "No one?" Another frown and he hung up the phone. "She didn't come here."

"She knows the details of my dad's book, Noah. You have to find her before she gets to my dad. I'm just glad she didn't do anything to him yet." I snatched my phone and punched in my dad's number, surprised when he answered. Twice in a row. Wow! I put him on speakerphone. "Dad, is Shirley there?"

"Not anymore. She left."

"From the coffee shop, I know. But you haven't seen her since then?"

"No. She called, though. Said as soon as she gave Detective Parker some information he might find useful, she was going back to the office to put out a fire."

"She didn't talk with me, Chandler," Noah said.

"Maybe she left a message with the receptionist," my dad offered.

"I checked with her. No one has been in for me."

"Did she call and leave a message that way? I mean I know she didn't want the phone number from Andie Rose, but it's not hard to get the number for the police department."

"I'll check again," Noah said.

"There's a police car that just pulled up in front of Tony's house. The officer's walking to the door. Did he do something to warrant a police visit?"

"You have a cop in the room on my end listening in on this conversation. Do you think I'd tell you if I thought Tony did something criminal?" I planted my face in my hand for a second. "It's not for Tony, Dad. He's there for you."

"What—"

"For protection," I blurted.

He exhaled. "You gave me a heart attack, Bug. I thought something happened. But that begs the question, why—"

"Chandler, are you going to be there for a while?" Noah asked. "I want to talk to you and then I'll tell you what's going on."

I stood, Sister Alice and Aspen following. "I'm going too."

"Of course you are," Noah mumbled under his breath.

"We'll be right there, Dad. And don't go out anywhere without your detail."

I hung up, and Noah covered his mouth with his

hand, attempting to conceal a snicker.

"What's so funny?"

"His detail?" he finally asked.

"Isn't that what it's called when an officer follows someone for safety reasons?"

He pressed his lips together, making them all but disappear as he fought back a laugh. "In the movies."

My cheeks flushed; I imagined they probably matched my hair.

I turned, nearly tripping over Aspen. "I'll see you there."

"Take a breath, dear," Sister Alice murmured.

"Come on, boy," I said to Aspen.

When Sister Alice stepped through the door behind Aspen and me, I said, "So that wasn't embarrassing at all."

"By the time he gets in his car, he won't remember it."

"Yeah, right," I scoffed. And then I wondered why I even cared. It's not like I was interested in anything other than helping solve this crime. I opened the back car door for Aspen, who balked at the suggestion I dared expect him to sit in the back.

"Aspen can claim his front seat spot. I can't go with. I have a home visit to do. And it's not at Tony's house. Stop off at the pharmacy on your way, though. Maybe some fiber will loosen you up a bit, dear."

Chapter 17

I got to Tony's a breath before Noah pulled up behind me. The sun had been a magician today, disappearing and reappearing again. Now it was beginning its descent just beyond the tree line, a glowing ball of yellow orange. It almost looked like the treetops were on fire.

As I took in the sizeable dove-gray with black trim house, I realized how unavailable I'd been to my staff for far too long. Not physically gone so much, but when I was there, I wasn't *really* there, because my mind was saturated with other things. I couldn't even remember the last time I'd done some yoga. I missed my staff and normal, everyday living. Except if it didn't happen soon, I'd forget what normal even was.

I desperately wished there was a vacancy so my dad could stay at the inn. If he was on site, it would make things so much easier. Except, now I knew it wouldn't be an option, even if there was an available room. I heaved a sigh and grumbled, "Doggone you, Noah."

Maybe I could persuade them with the fact if Dad was at the inn, Lady Lucy could then help as well. Except there were two problems with that argument: one, Noah didn't believe in ghosts and thinks I'm plum crazy; two, Noah hasn't made it a secret he doesn't want my help, anyway.

So far, Lady Lucy's assistance has helped with two

murders. While Grandad and Honey had agreed to leave the ghost alone in peace, careful not to disturb it, I made a mental note to look into the inn's past when we wrapped up this thing with my dad. Hopefully, with everyone alive and unharmed. But I wanted to do what I could to help Lady Lucy cross over. There had been speculation and rumors over the years, but as far as I knew, no one had dug deep for factual information. Surprising, since it was so well-known throughout the country. Why wouldn't a ghost-hunter stay here and see what he or she could find? Given there weren't any historical murders here, and the ghost had never been menacing, maybe it held no appeal. Then again, maybe someone had been here and had discovered nothing. And that brought Tina Cartwright to mind again. Or whatever the heck her name is. Why *was* she here in Spirit Lake? I desperately hoped Noah would find something out soon. In the meantime, I'd keep my antennae up for any sign of her.

My thoughts traveled back to Lady Lucy. Now that I'd gotten used to her presence—her existence at all, really—I didn't want her to leave, but I didn't want her to stay in limbo either. Of course, maybe that was only in the movies, too. I felt my cheeks flush again as I thought about the *detail* comment.

I glanced at Noah, who had finally exited his car, and I strode up to the front door ahead of him. Noah stopped at the patrol vehicle, said something to the officer inside, then caught up with me.

"I was beginning to wonder if you were taking a nap in your car before coming into the house."

"Business call. And don't bother asking me what it was about."

I shrugged. "I wasn't."

"Yeah, right. Your innocent tone doesn't work with me."

I smirked and reached up to knock on the door when Dad pulled it open.

He stepped to the side, allowing us to pass by him. I motioned for Aspen to follow me inside. With interest in the unknown, Aspen began checking things out, leading with his nose like a hound.

"Don't pee," my dad said.

I frowned. "Excuse me?"

"I was talking to Aspen."

"Obviously. You wouldn't be telling me or Noah not to pee. But you insult Aspen when you say things like that."

Dad rolled his eyes. "Always drama with girls."

"Again, rude."

He ruffled my hair like he did when I was a kid, and I jerked away with a grin.

"Tony's house has probably never had so much excitement as it has since I've been here," my dad said.

Noah smirked. "Somehow I doubt that."

"Now, now. Play nice."

I scanned the part of the house I could see. Aspen continued his investigation, nosing into every corner and crevice. I expected Tony's house to look more like a bachelor pad, so it shocked me to see it so orderly and clean. It even smelled clean. I knew it wasn't my dad who cleaned it. He wasn't dirty, but he was messy. Clutter didn't faze him, and it always drove my mother crazy. Me too, to be fair. But he claimed to know where everything was in each stack on his desk and on the floor around his desk, warning Mother to not interfere and move things around.

The three of us settled around the kitchen table.

"What's this all about? Why do I need protection?"

"I don't know that you do," Noah said. "But at this time, I don't know that you don't, either. So we're playing it safe." He slipped a side-eye toward me, then focused back on my dad. "I'd hate for anything to happen to you. Because Andie Rose scares me. To death."

Dad laughed but sobered quickly as Noah explained the new information and plausible theory. He chewed the inside of his cheek, took his glasses off, then chewed on the temple tip. He'd done that as far back as I could remember. It was as much a part of him as Sister Alice's smudged lenses were for her.

"Dad, Shirley never went to see Noah like she said she was going to do when she left. She beat the trail fast. Why, I don't know, but it wasn't for her given reason. That's suspicious, don't you think?"

He frowned and shook his head. "No, not suspicious at all. She probably just didn't have enough time before she got called back to the office to put out the fire."

"A fire that's more important than relaying information in a murder?"

"We don't know what the information was, Andie."

"But—"

He put up his hand, stopping me right there. "Listen, Bug, I know you don't like her, and I understand that." He tilted his head and frowned. "Actually, I don't. You usually like everyone." He shook his head slightly. "Anyway, it's obvious she has gotten on the wrong side of you for some reason."

"Not only for *some* reason. We both know exactly what that reason is."

"Care to fill me in?" Noah asked, looking from me to my dad.

"She made some extremely inappropriate comments about how cute my dad is and how lucky she was Winston left so she could have time alone with my dad."

Dad chuckled. "I think you've embellished that a bit."

"I didn't. In fact, I probably underplayed it."

Aspen, apparently accepting there was nothing of interest in the house, trotted to the door, plopped his butt down and stared at the doorknob. I opened the door and let him outside to explore, knowing he wouldn't go far from his needy human.

Noah said, "So Shirley thinks your dad is attractive. He's a successful author she admires. What's wrong with that?"

My jaw dropped, and I frowned. "He's married."

Noah lifted his shoulders and dropped them again. "And? You've never thought a man was attractive, even though he had a ring on it?"

"I would never act on it," I argued and grimaced. "And it's my *dad*."

Noah reached over and placed a hand on my shoulder. "Relax. I was only teasing." He sat back in his chair.

I gave him a small smile. "Sorry. I might be just a tad worried. But with good reason."

"I know," Noah said gently. "But we'll figure this out. I promise you."

My shoulder tingled from his brief touch. Aspen scratched on the door, so I crossed the room to let him back inside, inadvertently brushing against Noah as I did. Initial embarrassment turned into gratification. *Don't mind if I do, thank you very much.* It's not like it meant anything, anyway.

I scratched Aspen's head and opened cupboards until I found a bowl, filled it with fresh water, and set it on the floor. Aspen lapped at it like I hadn't given him water in the last week. The bowl skidded along the floor as he drank. "Were you running from hungry bears, Aspen?" I sat back down and looked at Noah. "What about Winston? He left in a hurry, too."

"He's on my radar. I've made a call to the police department in that jurisdiction, and they've agreed to keep an eye on him for the time being."

"Dad, do you know Stan Price?"

He appeared to ponder the name, then shook his head. "No, it doesn't ring a bell. Why?"

"He's a super fan of yours. Shirley mentioned fans can be dangerous."

"It's not like I'm a million-dollar household name."

Noah spoke up. "You have a very devoted, loyal following, Chandler. I've read some of the social media posts. One in particular I would classify as dangerously obsessed. What can you tell me about Simone Holloway?"

"I think I may have gotten a disturbing letter or two from her, to say the least. One offering to, quote, *take care of* my competition. But I dismissed it as nothing more than crazy words, not a genuine threat." He leaned forward, crossed arms resting on the table. "Maybe I was wrong. I've also gotten mail from prisoners who read my books. One guy said he was on death row and offered to kill the ongoing overall antagonist in one of my series." He shrugged. "That's why I don't give those a second thought. They're obviously not firing on all cylinders."

He tapped his temple with his finger. "Lights are on, no one's home."

I frowned. "Geez, Dad."

"What?"

"That's not a politically correct thing to say."

"When have you known me to be politically correct? I was just explaining why I didn't think much of it or turn them over to the police."

"How could a woman have gotten Beau's body to the cemetery, though? Unless she lured him there and drugged him. Not that women are weak," I added quickly, "but a dead body is dead weight. Pun intended."

Noah looked at my dad. "Chandler, do you still have those letters?"

He nodded. "I keep all fan mail in boxes in my home office."

I screwed up my face. "Even the creepy ones?"

"Sure. It's proving useful now, isn't it?"

"Do you think your wife could take a photo of them and send them to you so I can have a copy? And of any other odd fan mail. Looks like someone wanted to lure *you* to Spirit Lake so they could have access to you. I'm sure of it."

My dad frowned. "Except I was on my way here to see the kid," he nodded at me, "before I even heard about Beau."

"But this person might not have known that."

Dad nodded. "Okay. I'll call my wife right now. But I have to warn you it might take a while. The letters aren't in any certain order, just thrown into a box all together." He picked up his phone while Noah excused himself to go speak with the officer again, and I wandered around the house, justifying it by wanting to

189

be sure Aspen hadn't gotten into everything. But anyone who knew me would see right through that. I was simply nosey. Or curious. Yeah, curious. That sounded nicer. Not that nice had ever been a favorite word of mine. Women have been degraded forever from the expectation of being *nice*.

Every room was as clean and orderly as the kitchen. No way could this be Tony's doing. He had to either have a cleaner come in or else a secret girlfriend. But there wasn't anything feminine to suggest that. The possibilities intrigued me.

When Noah came back into the house, I flipped the light switch, illuminating the quickly darkening kitchen. "Let there be light." My dad hung up from my mother, deep in thought.

"Chandler, just a few more questions before I go. Is there any way someone could trace your home address?"

His eyebrows pinched together, the temple tip of his glasses back between his teeth. "Anything's possible, I guess. I don't announce it anywhere, but nowadays, with technology the way it is, anyone can find anyone."

My eyes grew wide. "Noah, do you think my mother could be in danger?"

Dad focused on Noah. "She said she's been getting hang up calls, and she thought someone might have been following her a little while ago."

Noah picked up his phone. "Okay. That concerns me on a couple of different levels. You live in Colorado, which means there might be more than one person involved."

"Or the person who killed Beau and Sara is gone," I said.

Concern etched my dad's face. "And in Colorado.

Could you reach out to that jurisdiction, Detective Parker, and arrange for someone to watch the house until I get back? I'll call the airport and get on the next flight out."

He snatched his phone; Noah and I watched him as he made reservations. When he hung up, he stood and started down a hallway. "I'm on a flight that leaves in three hours. I'll grab my things."

I sprang to my feet and called after him, "Dad, it takes at least two hours to get to the airport on a *good* day."

"I'll drive him to the airport," Noah said.

"I want to do it," I insisted.

"I have a police vehicle and can get him there faster."

I blew through pursed lips. "Okay. Then Aspen and me will ride along."

He gave me a pointed look. "Go back to the inn, Andie. The fewer of us there are will make it quicker and easier in the long run."

"Yeah, yeah. Even though I understand, it doesn't mean I like it." I stared at him, neither of us wavering. "I'll go back to the inn."

Getting my dad to the airport on time was the number one priority, so he was home and so he could protect my mother. Everyone would be safe. And it wasn't such a disappointment I could be at the inn I've neglected for the past couple of days.

Dad came back within five minutes, clutching a backpack and his computer bag in one hand. He slid a key off his keyring and tossed it to me. "Do me a favor? Hang onto this. I'll fly back out here soon and get my car. I can't imagine Tony will mind it staying here for now." He hugged me tight with his free arm and planted a kiss on my head. "Love you, Bug."

I swallowed a lump in my throat. "I love you, too, Dad."

He locked the door, handed me Tony's house key, and followed behind Noah, who turned and asked him, "Do you know a Terry Finne?"

The question rocked me on my heels. Did Noah have an unspoken concern about Terry?

"Only that he used to date Beau's daughter. He and Beau stayed in contact, I think."

I pinched my eyebrows together as I trotted close on their heels to the car. "Does anyone else find it strange Beau and Terry would stay friends so long when Terry dated Fawn for such a short period of time?"

"It wasn't a brief time at all. They were together for quite a few years," my dad said. "Engaged at one point, but she joined a commune of some sort, and that was the end of the engagement."

Noah and I locked eyes.

"I'm sure Terry wasn't too happy about that," I said.

Noah grumbled, "This changes things a bit. It might be nothing, but I need to make a quick phone call on the way to the airport."

"To who?" But he didn't hear me. They were already in the car, doors closed.

Noah rolled his window down. "Do me a favor and stay out of things while I'm gone."

When Aspen and I got back to the inn, I stopped at the front desk; Aspen immediately trotted toward Jade. I asked her if we had any further visitors that weren't guests. *Like Simone Holloway or Tina Cartwright.*

"Nope. Not a physical one."

I raised my eyebrows. "What does that mean?"

"It means the piano you moved in here seems to have a mind of its own. I went in there to see who was playing and—"

"Enchanted Moonlight by Glen Brown?"

Her eyes widened. "How did you know?"

I nodded and smiled, my eyes misting. "It was Grandad and Honey's favorite song to dance to." Warmth spread from my head to my toes.

"But how did you know that's the song that was playing on the piano?"

"It happened when Max and I were talking the other night."

Her eyes widened. "Do you think it could be the ghost of one of them?"

I shook my head and said quietly, "I hope not. That would mean they're stuck in between here and there." I pointed up. "When this whole fiasco with the murders is done, I want to help the ghost who's here get to *there*."

Jade raised her eyebrows and tugged the neckline up of her shirt. "You've only recently believed in the ghost and now you want to be a vessel to help them cross over? Don't you need like training or something to do that?"

"I'll try to find someone who knows about that stuff."

Jade gave me a sidelong look. "Have you gone back to drinking?"

I made a face like I'd burped something up. "Ugh. Not a chance."

"But I don't get it. Why would you want to take the spirit out of Spirit Lake? That's what people come here for."

"The inn can't be the only place people suspect the

ghost inhabits. Granddad and Honey said people believed there to be one at Town Hall too."

Jade tugged her shirt up again and said, "Well, I think we have another one here besides the one you call Lady Lucy. And the second one's not as nice. Maybe check into that one and send it packing instead."

I drew a quick breath. "What happened?"

"In one episode, the stapler fell," she made air quotes around the word *fell*, "on my toes, and it wasn't even close to the edge of the desk. And Tony said just yesterday a knife slipped," she made air quotes again, "from the counter and stuck into the rug, just missing his foot."

Izzy came toward us. "I was listening from the kitchen doorway. This ghost has an anger problem toward feet or what?"

Jade scowled. "If it was your foot, you wouldn't make light of it."

"Jade, why didn't you say something before?" She shrugged. "And why didn't Tony say something?"

"He didn't want to add more to your plate with what you're already going through."

I blew a long breath and ran my hand through my hair. "I'll be in the kitchen scrounging for something to eat."

"Leave Aspen with me," Jade said.

I looked at Aspen, comfortably lying on the floor beside Jade.

"Traitor," I mumbled through a smile. "He only loves you because of the treats you give him. You know that, right?"

"Whatever works," she said.

"Nah, he loves you." I turned toward the kitchen and

said over my shoulder, "I was just showing a little unhealthy jealousy."

Tony was chopping vegetables at the kitchen's center island.

"Hey, Tony," I said, leaning over and resting my forearms on the counter. "What are you doing here?"

"Izzy has to leave early for a family deal."

In answer, Izzy breezed by us, tossing her apron in the laundry. "See ya, Kaz. Thanks, Tony."

My eyebrows shot up, and I said to Tony, "Did she just tell you thank you?"

He smiled. "Yeah, she can be okay."

Perplexed, I said, "But—but it sounded genuine."

"Ha! I take it when I can get it. Anyway, figured so long as I was here, I'd get a jump start on meal prep for tomorrow."

"Got it. Hey, do you have a cleaner who comes to your house or are you keeping a secret from us?" I grinned and snagged a slice of red pepper and popped it into my mouth.

"What kind of secret?"

Tony was extremely attractive and what the single women in town called the *Italian Stallion*. The problem was, those single women, and some who weren't single, knew he was an *available* Italian Stallion. Six months ago, he'd decided to turn things around. "I'm not getting any younger," he'd said, adding, "I wanna find that special someone to grow old with." I told him he'd have to look in a different town if he hadn't already found that someone, because there wasn't anyone left for him to go out with in Spirit Lake. He'd told me not to believe everything I heard, that just because someone says something doesn't mean it's true, and I should know that.

It felt like he'd slapped my hand. The sad part was, I knew exactly what he meant.

"What kind of secret?" he asked again.

"Do you have a special someone? I just left your house from seeing my dad, who left to go back home, by the way, but no bachelor has such a clean house." I slid his house key across the counter toward him.

He stopped chopping and tucked the key in his apron pocket while I snagged another slice of red pepper.

"He called and told me he was on his way to the airport. It sounded like it was a sudden decision. What happened?"

"He didn't tell you why he left?"

He shook his head, keeping his gaze on me.

"And you didn't ask? What is it with the lack of communication with guys?"

"We're not all as nosey as you."

"Yeah, but you're curious now. Just another term for nosey, you know."

"I'm concerned. There's a difference."

I grabbed a coffee cup and filled it, taking a sip before spilling the details of my dad's departure. I plunked onto a stool but then stood so quickly coffee splashed over the side of the mug. "If someone knew he was staying at your house and they don't know he left, you could be in danger."

"Don't get ahead of yourself. I can protect myself just fine." He pointed the knife toward me for emphasis and went back to chopping.

"Seriously, Tony, I think we should ask Noah if he can increase security by your house."

"No."

One word, so forceful, surprised me. "Why?"

He scooped the chopped peppers into a bowl. "I don't want someone watching my every move."

I frowned. "If you have nothing to hide, what's the problem?"

He pushed the bowl aside and looked at me while he gathered onions and placed them beside the cutting block.

"Would you like someone tailing you around, knowing your every move, however harmless it was?"

I dropped my weight back onto the stool again and rested a foot on the lower rung. "I'd hate it. I just worry, Tony."

"I can take care of myself, Andie Rose. I promise. Don't waste your energy worrying about me."

"Easy to say. You're like a brother to me."

He grinned. "Aww, shucks."

I lifted my other foot and placed it on the rung, too. "Hey, I hear you had a knife fight with a ghost the other day."

He glanced up at me while he continued chopping onions. "There are benefits to the way men communicate. Jade has a big mouth."

I chuckled. The two of them bickered endlessly. "Jade was right about telling me. I need to know about these things." I peeked at my watch. Noah and my dad were just over an hour into their trip. "I hope Noah gets my dad to the airport in time for his flight."

"That's what lights and sirens are for. *Sis.*"

I watched as he chopped yet another onion and didn't shed a single tear. "How do you not cry while you cut onions?" An all-too fresh memory infiltrated my mind from a decade ago when I was cutting an onion and wiped my tearing eyes with my hand. I never made that mistake again.

"The trick is to not slice off the root of the onion before cutting it up."

"I'll have to remember that." Probably not something I'd have to clutter my brain with since I avoided onions with all my might. Including now. I stood and shoved the stool back underneath the counter. "I'm going to collect my partner and go upstairs to my apartment for a minute."

"Collect him from where?"

"Jade."

He nodded.

"Let me know if you want my help when you're done with the onions."

"No. But now I know how to keep you away. Like garlic to a vampire."

We both laughed, and it felt good. A dose of Tony was good for my soul.

Aspen and I had just reached our apartment when my phone buzzed in my back pocket. I slipped it out and looked at the display.

"Noah? Is everything okay with my dad?"

"Chandler's fine. As soon as we left for the airport, I called Terry, who said he was just going to call me. He found out Fawn is dead. Apparently, she died from suspicious circumstances."

I gasped. "That's horrible."

"I had someone else check into it. He just called me back, and it turns out she died shortly after she joined the commune."

"Which means it was shortly after the broken engagement." My mind began spinning theories.

"Exactly what came to my mind."

"How did she die?"

"I don't know yet. Like I said, suspicious death, but doesn't sound like the police thoroughly investigated it. It doesn't surprise me, though. Sometimes those communities want nothing to do with the outside world until they need something," he muttered. "Fact of the matter is, I'm surprised someone reported it at all."

I drew a deep breath and exhaled. "Do you think Terry could have a record?"

"I can't answer that. We do a thorough investigation on police employees, so I wouldn't think so, but nothing or no one is infallible."

"If Terry did something to Fawn, maybe Beau and Sara found out and Terry silenced them."

"We can't jump to conclusions. I don't even know what kind of commune it was. Pretty much anything could have happened to her there. And if they don't believe in medical intervention, she could have died from natural causes." He took a deep breath. "Anyway, I wanted to let you know the chief put Terry on leave. Since Chandler was staying at Tony's, let him know. And if Terry shows up at the inn, let me know immediately. And do *not* go looking for him, Andie Rose."

"Is that a unique spin on *Stay out of my investigation, Andie Rose?*" I tried my best to mimic his voice.

He gave a dry chuckle. "Consider it so."

I hung up, my mind heavy with theories spinning faster than rumors spread in a small town. I had to find out if Terry had a connection with anyone who had access to Dad's yet-unpublished manuscript. But I didn't know how I would find out without talking with Terry himself. Noah told me not to go looking for him and to call him immediately if he showed up at the inn. But if I'm in town and I run into him, well…It wouldn't be nice not to at least acknowledge someone you know. I sighed. That meant another trip into town. Unless I could ask Sister Alice and Quinn to keep an eye out for him and let me know if they see him. Spirit Lake proper was only a mile and a half from the inn. It would only take five minutes to jump in my car and zip into town. And when I went there, I could stop by The Raven Motel and talk with Stan Price. It was one thing to be a super fan, but quite another to get inside information on an unpublished manuscript.

My day was filling in for tomorrow.

Chapter 18

After leaving my dad another voicemail, I fetched the remote control for my long-ignored tiny twenty-four-inch television, and pouting, plopped onto the sofa for the evening news. I'd never felt so far away from him, even when he was here in town. This whole thing robbed us of much needed time together.

Aspen lapped from his water bowl and then jumped up beside me as I flipped through the channels. I watched for at least twenty minutes, puzzled there had been no mention of Spirit Lake before we reached the weather report. Could I have missed it? I glanced at my watch. Eight forty-nine. Spirit Lake wasn't a big city, but we were still newsworthy. Maybe murder doesn't rank as high as paranormal activity in the media world.

I clicked the power button and tossed the remote. I'd tune back in for the ten o'clock news. I leaned back and pulled a flannel blanket around me and Aspen, who snuggled in like a giant lap dog. And that was the last I remembered until I woke to Aspen's wet nose against my cheek.

I stretched and winced at muscles cramped from staying in one position for far too long. Yesterday had been a crazy busy day, for both my body and my mind, but it felt like I'd tied one on last night. I worked a few kinks out of my neck and shoulders and groaned.

Aspen stared at me, head cocked to the side, and

whimpered.

"I hear ya, Aspen." I stood and looked around the apartment, still dark though it was six o'clock. When the events of the prior day came rushing back, it was like my brain had absorbed a triple shot of caffeine.

I slipped into a pair of sweatpants, a hoodie, and a jacket, stepped into my slipper mini boots, and opened the door to take Aspen outside. The predicted storm for yesterday narrowly missed Spirit Lake, only drizzling a thin layer of sleet on us for a short period. The air was pleasantly warmer than I'd expected, so the moisture would be gone by the end of the day. We always say if you don't like Minnesota weather, wait a minute, because it will change. Dad said Coloradans say that too, but I'd insisted we started it. Not competitive or stubborn at all, no sirree.

Wanting to unravel the events of yesterday from a rested mindset, I led Aspen on a path in the woods so he could do his thing with the squirrels, rabbits, and mark anything and everything while I took advantage of the silence. I attempted to stay alert to bear, newly awakened from hibernation.

I recalled each of the events yesterday from both Winston and Shirley's odd departures, not to mention Shirley's claim she had information for Noah but didn't go to the police department. But that only brought to mind Shirley's gross infatuation with my dad. I grimaced. And what about Dad's fan mail, particularly from Simone Holloway? I pondered Sara's death and the odd circumstances surrounding it from the method, location, and the weird headstone. If one could even call it that. *Backstabber*. Who had she upset enough to kill her? Was there a connection between Simone and Sara none of us had discovered yet? And since Noah couldn't find anything on Tina Cartwright, could she actually be Simone Holloway? Or maybe Sara was simply collateral damage from Simone's hatred of Beau. They say it's all about who you know, and Sara not only knew Beau, they'd been married, divorced, and recently business partners.

Aspen darted away from me, hot on the trail of a squirrel who'd been taunting him from a tree branch before scurrying down the tree trunk and into the forest. I followed after him, but after what felt like too long without catching up to him, I stopped and glanced around me. I'd been so wrapped up in my thoughts I hadn't been paying attention to where I was. I knew eventually I would either reach Whisper Lake, Big or Little Spirit Lake, or Spirit Lake Proper, so in normal circumstances, I would enjoy the detour. But these weren't normal circumstances. There was a killer on the loose, hell-bent on framing my dad for not one murder, but two. But then another thought resurfaced: if it was a deranged fan, I could understand why they'd killed Beau, and maybe even Sara if I stretched it far enough. But they wouldn't try to set up my dad to be the killer. *Would they*?

I called out for Aspen and waited a couple of minutes. When he didn't come, the thought of Aspen becoming a casualty, or even a target, in the killer's plan caused the familiar symptoms of impending panic to descend on me, gripping me in its unyielding claws— quickened breathing, tunnel vision, tingling fingers.

I scanned the surrounding area and came up empty. Blood pulsed in my ears, limiting my ability to hear much, and the symptoms intensified. I cupped my hands around my mouth and called Aspen's name. Finally, I spotted him from over a hill, running toward me in the graceful way I'd always admired. He must have detected the anxiety in my voice, because he came right up to me, sat at my feet, and looked up at me, tail sweeping the forest floor. I stooped next to him, wrapped my arms around his neck, and rested my cheek there until my panic subsided. I blew relief through my lips.

"Come on, buddy. Lead the way home."

Aspen nudged my cheek with his nose before I stood and started back for the inn, my lifesaver staying close by my side.

As we walked, I tried to recall anything I might have missed yesterday, whether Gemmalee had mentioned anything about Stan or whether Terry Finne had mentioned something I didn't pick up on at the time. But nothing more came to mind. I had to be missing something. We all did. And what about my dad? Why hasn't he answered his phone or called me back yet? Despite there being a time difference between here and Colorado, it was only one hour. Not enough to make a difference. For the first time I can remember, I was irritated with him. I shrugged it off like the unwanted guest it was, before it grew into something more, like a resentment—the kiss of death to one with a propensity to drink, no matter how much time one had been sober.

By the time we reached the inn, an hour had passed, and it was late enough to call Quinn. When she didn't answer, I left her a voicemail, then showered in record time, whipped my red curls into its usual ponytail, applied the typical black eyeliner and blackest black mascara, and a touch of lip gloss. I snatched up my phone to check for missed calls. Like I wouldn't have heard it ring. So when I saw I had indeed missed one, I frowned.

Had I been so engrossed in my own thoughts while in the woods I hadn't even heard the phone? Talk about a walking target for a deranged killer.

But my heart skipped a juvenile beat when I saw it was from Max. I listened to it and grinned. Looked like things were moving forward with his purchase of the pharmacy in town. I took a moment to entertain the idea. He wouldn't live here, but owning the pharmacy would mean more frequent visits to Spirit Lake. I had no plans in dating, but I sure wouldn't mind getting to know him better. I caught my lip between my teeth and grinned at what the future might look like. Quinn came to mind. Maybe she was more interested than she was letting on. Thoughts kept chasing each other in the playground of my mind until I laughed. Max might not have any interest in either of us. As far as I knew, he might be involved in a relationship with someone in Birch Haven. "Stop trying to control the future, Andie," I muttered.

I called Sister Alice, who answered on the first ring.

"What's up, kiddo?"

I filled her in on Noah's call yesterday. "So I was wondering if you could let me know if you see Terry in town today. Or Stan Price."

"That might be difficult."

"Why?"

"Because I haven't the foggiest idea what either of them looks like."

I sighed. "I'm so used to sleuthing together it hasn't even crossed my mind you weren't with me for some of it this past week."

"Okay," she said, sounding a bit weary. "That puts things in perspective, doesn't it?"

"Meaning?"

"That you've grown accustomed to us solving crimes together. How, oh how, has it come to that?"

"You know what I was thinking?" I asked, ignoring her rhetorical question.

"Is it safe for me to know that?"

Again, I ignored her question. "If Fawn was murdered, that would be an entire family wiped off the face of the earth, all in brutal ways. *Poof*! Gone." Aspen lifted his head and glanced my way, then rolled over onto his side. "What are the chances of that happening? Talk about bad luck."

"Hmm," she said, distracted.

"While Terry and Stan are high on my list of suspects, especially Terry, after finding out the lies he told about Fawn, it doesn't make sense how either of them knew the details of my dad's book. That's why I really need to talk to him. I guess to be fair, Terry didn't lie so much as leave out critical information. But lie by omission is also critical here. I haven't been able to find any photos of Stan, but if I can find a picture of Terry from the police department's website and send it to you, would that help?"

"Obviously. And what will you tell Noah? I can't imagine he'd be happy about you getting involved. Again."

I'd neglected to tell her about Noah's warning. Okay, not necessarily neglected, but conveniently left out. I sighed. "Until Noah checks things out and rules Terry out as a suspect, he told me not to go looking for Terry and to call him immediately if Terry shows up at the inn."

"What part of that confused you?"

I explained my logic.

"For the love of all things holy, Andie Rose, if there's a loophole, you'll find it."

"So you'll let me know if you see him? I left a voicemail for Quinn, too. She met Terry when we were at the coffee bar. He's supposedly dating Cindy." I gasped. "Oh no. I need to talk with her."

"And tell her what?"

"That she can't go away with him for the weekend as planned. What if he's dangerous?"

"Dear God, child." I pictured her displaying the sign of the cross and sending an SOS to the Big Guy. "What if he's not? Don't assume and openly say things like this you can't prove. It could ruin lives."

"Well then, what do I do? I can't just sit here and knowingly let her go away with him if he's a killer."

"Take a breath. You've jumped from withholding information to murder in under a minute. Everyone deserves the benefit of the doubt. Innocent until proven guilty. You're a life coach, for goodness' sake. You should know that."

"I agree with that a hundred percent. Except the wellbeing of someone I know could be in danger."

"And if you tell Cindy something that could destroy how she sees Terry, making her run away from him, it may destroy Terry in the process. Two people's lives destroyed because of baseless suspicions."

"*Destroy* is kind of a strong word, don't you think?"

"You're looking for arguments against doing the right thing."

"Well, if I don't say anything, it could *end* her life, not only destroy it."

"Make sure and hit up the meeting tonight, yeah? I think you're forgetting some of the core things we're to do. Like keep your own side of the street clean and do the next right thing."

"You'll still tell me if you see Terry, right?"

"Text me a picture. *If* I see him, I'll let you know."

"Spending less time with me this past week for work has taken the spark out of you."

She laughed. "Being your sponsor has been hazardous to my health and to my life."

"But you love it, right?"

"From my lips to God's ears, yes, I do."

I grinned. "You just made the sign of the cross, didn't you?"

"Affirmative."

The smile came across the line, loud and clear. I think Aspen even sensed it because he rolled onto his stomach and looked at me.

After I hung up, I sat cross-legged on the floor beside Aspen. I tossed around some thoughts, creating nothing more than a tangled mess like that of Christmas lights after haphazard storage. I'd never asked my dad who the killer was in his book. *Duh*! I smacked my palm against my forehead and sat up straight. Aspen lifted his head quickly and studied the rude interruption of his morning nap before deciding the nap took priority.

Some detective I was. Noah had to have asked my dad that, right? I mean, how elementary was it to follow up with that specific question when the placement of the body and the cause of death were the same as in the book?

I called Noah, but as has been my luck with everyone else except Sister Alice, his phone rolled into voicemail. Just as I opened my mouth to leave a message asking him to call me back, Quinn called through, so I clicked over.

"Hey, Quinn! Thanks for calling me back. Have you seen Terry Finne around town yesterday afternoon, evening, or this morning?"

"Gosh, no, but I haven't been out on the street either. I've been inside covered in dust, organizing and unpacking crates. I wasn't patient enough to leave my things in boxes until the guys are completely done in here. I'm too anxious to get out of Noah's house." She sighed. "I'm sorry, that's not what you called to hear about. He's just driving me crazy."

I snickered. "Understood. If you skip out for a walk or an errand and you spot Terry, could you give me a call and let me know? I want to ask him something."

"Why not just go to his office?"

I exhaled slowly. "Oh, where to start? Noah told me Terry wasn't truthful or forthcoming with critical information related to the murders. Chief Romero put him on leave."

"Wait a minute; does my brother think Terry is somehow involved in the murders? What about your barista? Isn't she going on a weekender with him?"

"Exactly. Which is why it would make me feel so much better if I could talk with him. But I have to do it under the radar."

"Let me guess; my brother has asked you to stay away from Terry and the case."

I clamped my lips tight. No way was I getting in the middle of brother and sisterly love.

"He means well, Andie Rose. He just takes his job very seriously. Not to mention protecting those most important to him."

"Well, that makes sense for you, but I don't qualify

in that category. I've been a worm in his tequila since he moved here."

Now she laughed, though quietly. "Okay. Keep telling yourself that."

"What is that supposed to mean?" I pinched my eyebrows together, hand on my hip. But I'd be lying if I said flutters didn't occur in my stomach before I reminded myself—again—that I'm not interested in a relationship. Was I? Max came back to mind, but I quickly pushed it away.

"Tell you what, I'll take a stroll through town, up one side of the street and down the other. If I spot Terry, I'll call you."

"Thanks, Quinn. You're the best. And guess what? Max has started the paperwork on the pharmacy in town." Okay, not *completely* out of mind, apparently.

"Hmm," she said in a nondescript tone.

I couldn't tell if she was interested or not. I also couldn't tell for sure if I would be pleased if she wasn't. I had some serious issues to work through. This relationship coach needs a relationship coach. I rolled my eyes at the irony of it all.

"I'll let you know what I find out."

"Likewise about Terry."

I thought more about the creepy fan mail my dad mentioned. He couldn't remember getting anything from Stan Price, but maybe my mother would find something. The ones he mentioned were horrific, but they weren't in Spirit Lake during the murders. Or were they?

I shivered and let out a puff of air through tense lips. *Darn it, Shirley*. She had me so hung up on this dangerous fan theory I couldn't even think about anything else. And it was probably only to take the spotlight off herself. Maybe it had nothing to do with my dad at all and everything to do with some kind of family drama of which Beau and Sara found themselves fatal targets. Maybe they got on the wrong side of the wrong family member. Or even the commune Fawn was once a part of.

But I knew that wasn't the truth given the murder eerily followed my dad's manuscript. And it was because of that reason I was still betting on either Winston, Shirley, or even Terry. And that both Winston and Shirley were here in Spirit Lake at all was odd. Sure, Winston said it was because he'd invited Shirley, but could I trust him? If he was a killer, then no. Winston didn't exactly make it a secret he couldn't stand Beau. But why Sara? Even though it came out Sara was the one scheduling Beau's releases, it's not like she would have anything to release with Beau dead. Same for Shirley. And Shirley wouldn't get herself dirty by doing any of the heavy lifting. Maybe they were in on it together. And where does Terry fit in? Why was he concealing information critical to the case? Had he known Fawn was dead long before this and left that out, too, knowing the focus would then be on him? Or did he really *not* know Fawn was dead until now?

I checked my phone to be sure I hadn't inadvertently silenced it. I needed to talk with Noah, Dad, and Terry. But staring at my phone wouldn't get me anywhere. The only thing guaranteed to help was to put my hand to the plow and do some work. I loved working around the inn. My favorites were helping Frank with the gardening, Tony or Izzy in the kitchen, and even cleaning the common areas. I loved making it sparkle. Today, with Frank picking up the maintenance duties, he could probably use my help.

****

Unfortunately, Frank insisted he wasn't overloaded with work since it was still too early to be tied up with the gardening. So I spent the next blissful hour chatting with guests, having fun with the rest of my staff, and helping in the kitchen and dining area. I even skipped away for two minutes to admire the baby grand in the parlor, willing it to play. But no luck. Apparently, ghosts don't perform on demand.

I sat gingerly on the piano bench, lightly running my palms over the velvety fabric on the cushions, then placed my fingers on the cool, smooth keys, imagining Honey in this very position. I drew a sharp inhale when the keys depressed on their own, softly playing Enchanted Moonlight. The surprise quickly turned to basking in the comfortable warmth of feeling so close to Honey. I kept my fingers on the keys, pretending to play. I wondered if Honey had asked Lady Lucy to visit me.

"Lady Lucy," I whispered, "I have a feeling you've been in touch with Honey. I promise you, after this mess with my dad is over, I am going to find out what happened to you so you can finally be at peace."

Suddenly, the music stopped, and the fallboard slammed shut. I'd jerked my hands out in the nick of time, shuddered, and rubbed my fingers. Aspen let out a quick yelp as he sprung to a sitting position. He looked around as if trying to figure out what had just happened until he stared into the empty space on top of the piano. I looked from him to what held his focus and back to him again. He stood and trotted toward Jade, who zipped around the corner and into the parlor, Lily and Noah behind her.

"What happened?" Lily asked.

"Did you get hurt?" asked Noah as he strode across the room to inspect my fingers I continued to rub.

"I didn't even know you played," said Jade.

Jade and Lily looked at me expectantly while Noah inspected my fingers. I pulled them back and said, "It's okay. I'm fine. Really." One glance at Jade, though, and I knew we were both on the same page. Either Lady Lucy didn't enjoy the idea of moving on or we had a second less-than-friendly ghost here. If that was the case, suffice it to say, I wouldn't be naming him anything nice.

"Did you accidentally knock the cover down?" Lily asked.

I nodded. "Yeah, I must've." I knew both she and Jade were believers in the spirit world. But since I wasn't sure where Noah stood on the issue, I didn't fancy having a conversation about it in front of him. He already thought I was a little crazy. I offered a shaky smile. "Clumsy me."

"You never said you could play the piano," Noah said.

I can't. "You never asked. My dad got to the airport on time, right?"

"Of course." He looked at me like I was an idiot for doubting it. "You got a minute?"

"Sure. I wanted to talk to you about something, too." I looked at Jade and Lily, who both excused themselves.

"Ladies first," he said.

I dipped my chin and looked up. "You seriously think I'm going to fall for that?"

"Okay, caught me. I need to know what you've done so I can prepare for disaster mitigation."

Though still shaken, I chuckled, then grew serious.

"Did you ask my dad who the murderer was in his book? How he was connected to the murder victim."

He frowned. "What do you take me for, an amateur?"

"Well?" He didn't say anything, so I went on. "You might as well tell me because I'll find out from him, anyway."

"Let's just say there's a reason I'm zeroing in on the bizarre mail he's gotten and why I need copies of those letters to get names. Not so much for the mentally unstable inmates, but for those on this side of the bars. I need to do background searches on them. Although I'm not dismissing the notion that someone behind bars doesn't have someone on the outside."

I blew a long breath through pursed lips. "I feel so much better now."

He exhaled and ran his hand over his hair. "The department called me back with some of their histories."

"And?" I rolled my hand in an out-with-it gesture.

"All but one name I collected from social media has come back either clean or nonexistent."

"What do you mean, nonexistent? Like Tina Cartwright? Everybody has a so-called footprint, don't they?"

"First of all, I found out Tina Cartwright's real name is Suzanne Miller. She uses an alias because of her business. She doesn't want her family to know what she does as a side hustle. The whole ghost hunting thing. She's legit and cleared from the suspect list. Second, as for the rest of the non-existent people, it's social media, Andie Rose. Even I know it's not uncommon for people to create a fake identity, especially if they're doing something unfavorable."

"Okay, yeah, I get it. You said all but one. Who was that?"

"Simone Holloway. She served time for cyber-criminal activity. She found her way back behind bars for leaving the country."

"Why is that criminal?"

"Part of her parole was to stay in the country and to stay in contact with her parole officer if she had to go anywhere outside of the state."

I held my breath a moment before I asked, "What state, Noah?"

He held my gaze. "Colorado."

I rubbed my biceps. "Do you think that's who has been following my mother?"

He nodded. "It's possible. I have—"

My eyes grew wide. "Oh, my God. If Simone Holloway is so infatuated with my dad, she might do something to my mother. To get my mother out of the way so she has clear access to my dad."

Noah put up a hand. "Don't get ahead of things, Andie Rose. She served time for cybercriminal activity. That's a far cry from murder."

I locked my gaze on his, wondering if I wanted to know the answer to the question burning my tongue. I had to.

"What country had she gone to?"

Noah chewed the inside of his cheek a moment and said, "Colombia."

Chapter 19

"Holy wicked whiskey," I breathed as I walked on trembling legs to one of the wingback chairs in front of the fireplace. I plunged into it; the piano incident was a distant memory.

Noah sat in the chair opposite me, perched on the edge. "I think we may have found our killer," he said gently.

"What happened to cybercriminal activity being a far cry from murder?"

He ran his hand slowly over his face and grumbled. "Yeah, well...I think we both know I misspoke about that in this particular case. But once we nab her, and we will, your dad won't have to worry about it anymore."

I frowned. "Yeah, *after* you get her. But until then, he'll have to worry about my mother's life, and maybe even his own. Neither of them is safe until this woman is behind bars."

"We'll get her before anything happens." He reached over and laid a hand on my arm. "Promise. The Colorado police are looking for her as we speak."

I leaned back in the chair and stared, seeing nothing at all. I had so many questions.

"How could Simone Holloway know about my dad's book? No one has read it yet except Shirley, Winston, and anyone else at the publishing house. Unless she has someone on the inside there. And I don't even know if others at the publishing house have access to it. I can't imagine they wouldn't have, though." I caught my breath and sat on the edge of my chair, my muscles rigid. "Oh, my hell! This woman has been in Spirit Lake with none of us knowing who she was or that she was a killer. I've probably passed her on the street. Worse, she might have even been inside the inn. A guest at the coffee bar or worse, checked into a room under a false identity." My brain became the piste as the possibilities began a multi-player fencing competition. "How could this woman get the frog back here? How could she get it through customs?" I bolted a finger in the air, feeling as though I might hyperventilate. Aspen quickly sat up, and front two paws on my thighs, crawled up onto my lap like a small lapdog would. He'd never done that before. I didn't know what to make of that. Had I freaked him out, or could he sense something else in the room that freaked *him* out?

I encircled him with my arms and leaned to the left to look around Aspen so I could see Noah. "How could she have gotten out of the country? Wouldn't they have known about it from her paperwork? I would hope our nation's security is tighter and smarter than that of a criminal."

"Don't get me started on that one," Noah grumbled. "But like I said, nothing or no one is infallible. People have gotten through security with things before that they shouldn't have. And if she's a cybercriminal, she most likely has exceptional computer skills. She could have produced counterfeit documents. Or know someone who can. These people rarely work alone."

I shook my head slowly and Aspen, deciding the threat was over, sprawled across my lap, his right-side legs hanging over the edge. I gently nudged him, lowering him onto the floor.

"Even if she didn't work alone, it doesn't explain how she could have gotten the frog over here."

"We'll find all that out in due time. Right now, we just need to focus on apprehending her."

I nodded and looked into nothingness again. "I can't help but be hung up on the problem of how she got the inside information from my dad's book." I looked at him, holding his gaze. "What if everyone is so focused on Simone no one's paying attention to Shirley or Winston?" I shot to my feet. "Wait! Maybe Simone doesn't only know someone at the publishing house, maybe she actually works there." I chewed on my lower lip a minute as I tossed the ideas around, making one heck of a salad. "Have you checked on that? If she somehow has ties to the publisher?"

He raised his eyebrows and reached for his phone. "I'll do it now. Maybe we should hire you on the roster as a consultant. No," he blurted when I gave him a pleading, hopeful look.

I shared a small smile and mumbled, "You'll come around."

When he hung up from the department, he said, "I could do the checking myself, but it'd be quicker with a computer." He put his hands up. "Of which I don't have right now. I'll let you know when they get back to me."

"How about I find out? All it would take is a call to Shirley."

"How about you don't. Until Simone Holloway is officially charged, I don't want you talking to *any* of the suspects."

"Except my dad. You can't keep me from talking

with my dad."

He grinned. "Yeah, I know. I don't think anyone can keep you from anything."

"How about a little credit? I'm so much better now than I used to be back in the day."

"So I've heard."

I gave him a sidelong glance. "What, exactly, have you heard?"

He smirked. "Let's just say Chandler and I had plenty of time to talk on the way to the airport."

"Is that so?" I pressed my lips together, narrowed my eyes, and nodded. "Yeah, I'll definitely be talking to my dad. Have you checked if Simone Holloway checked into a hotel anywhere in the surrounding area? Or look into flight plans?"

He made a face that asked me if I thought he'd just been born. "Again, impressive. But not enough to be a *trained* detective." He leveled his gaze on mine for a hot minute before he answered. "Yes, I checked on the flight plans and yes, on the hotels, too. And no on both. But that doesn't necessarily mean much. Especially if she doesn't want her parole officer to know she left the state. Especially the country. She's apparently back there now—in Colorado—that's our primary concern for obvious reasons."

I took a deep breath and stood. "Okay. I'll call you if I have any more suggestions."

He stood and started for the doorway. "Oh, I'll be waiting."

"Sarcasm noted," I said.

When Noah left, Aspen roused and followed me to my office where, once again, I called my dad. And, again, it went to voicemail. Except for our difficulty in connecting when he was just here, it wasn't like him not to answer or call me back within minutes if he wasn't writing. And he wouldn't be writing, given his and my mother's lives were in danger. I had a sinking feeling something was going on, and it wasn't good. I sat cross-legged on the floor beside Aspen, trying to halt the shallowing breaths, then dialed Mother's number. She also didn't answer.

I stood and dropped into my chair, set my phone down, and drummed my fingers on my desktop while tapping the lead of a pencil with the other hand. *Hmm.* Maybe Mother had talked Dad into leaving town for a while. Maybe even into the mountains where there was no cell phone coverage. But what about the inn?

I stood and said to the empty room, "Worrying does no good," and tried redirecting my thoughts like I teach my coaching clients to do. It usually garnered miraculous results. Except this time it didn't. I needed to get out of this room and *do* something.

Before I reached the door, Aspen right by my side, Sister Alice came in.

"Where you off to, Ant?"

"Why does it feel like a demotion to go from *Grasshopper* to *Ant*?"

"It depends on how you look at it. Ants are small, but they're smart and hard workers."

"Aww," I crooned and swept in for a hug. "I'll take that as a compliment."

She chuckled and pushed her glasses—cobalt blue frames today, my favorites—further onto her nose with her pointer finger, then teased, "Like I said, it depends how you look at it."

"I need to move around. It feels like I'm about to

jump out of my skin. Let's go out there." I gestured toward the hallway. "I'll fill you in on everything you've missed. Trust me when I tell you it's a lot."

She frowned. "Andie Rose, I have been away from you for mere hours. How much could I have missed?"

I screwed up my mouth. "Like I said, a lot." I shot out my hand. "But in my defense, it's not because of what I *did*, it's what I found out."

She exhaled her relief. "Thank the good Lord. Let's go grab a coffee and enlighten me." I turned toward the coffee bar, and she grasped my elbow. "On second thought, maybe the coffee bar isn't a good idea."

"Why not?" Before she could answer, I said, "Oh, I get it. You're afraid I'll tell Cindy my concerns about Terry."

"Remember, the next right thing, a step at a time. How about we make those right steps toward the parlor?"

"Fine. But let me at least get a cup of coffee first."

"How about we get that from the kitchen?"

I scowled. "Cindy's not even working this morning. She's gone, remember? Possibly with a murderer, because you wouldn't let me clue her in."

"If you had even an ounce of proof, I wouldn't be so adamant about it. But you can't just go around accusing people of things on a whim."

I gave her a deadpan stare. "A whim?"

"Do you have anything other than a hunch?"

I continued to stare at her. "Fine, I know how this looks. But if it makes a difference, I would have done it in a calm, non-accusing manner."

She shook her head and clucked her tongue on the roof of her mouth. "How do you see that to have played out? What would you have said? Have fun on your trip, but don't let the nice man murder you?"

Despite the seriousness of the issue, I laughed. "Yeah, that would have worked." I turned toward the kitchen. "But fine, to make you happy, we'll stop off at the kitchen and then go to the parlor. But stay away from the piano," I warned.

"Pshaw! I'm not going to spill anything on it, for goodness' sake."

"That's not what I'm afraid of. Although it's a valid concern." Neatness wasn't her forte. She narrowed her eyes, and I snickered. "Kidding."

"Then why the compulsion to warn me away from the piano?"

"Such strong language. Warn? Compulsion?" I winked at her and wrapped an arm around her shoulder in a side squeeze as we reached the kitchen. "Go on ahead into the parlor. I'll fetch our coffee, a biscuit for Aspen, and meet you in there."

"Tea for me today, thank you. Come with me, Aspen." She patted her leg, but Aspen didn't look like he thought it was so great an idea. He stayed planted beside me and merely looked at her as an object of curiosity. "What does that dog have against me? He likes Jade, for goodness' sake."

"Hey," Jade objected, "I heard that."

Jade has held a grudge against Sister Alice since a comment she'd made a while back about Jade's sweater cut too low. She might have said something to the effect of "Tuck in the twins, honey. This isn't that kind of establishment." Okay, that's *exactly* what she said. Sister Alice has never been one to speak eloquently, but Jade hadn't forgotten it and apparently clutched that grudge with a death grip.

"It's because you take Aspen's front seat in the car," I told Sister Alice. "And you call him a dog." She scowled, and I shrugged. "What? That's the God's honest truth."

Sister Alice turned for the parlor, shook her head, and mumbled, "Calling a spade a spade has never been wrong before."

Rather than wait for me by the kitchen doorway, Aspen trotted over to Jade. She reached for her bottom drawer. "I'll give him a biscuit from my stash,"

The inn has become famous for our specialty dog biscuits alone. Granddad and Honey made quite a reputation by selling them to the businesses in town. Even surrounding locales placed their orders and picked them up weekly. It made me happy we were such a dog-friendly town. And now, with Lord Watson, maybe I'd have to see about expanding our services to cat treats as well.

"Hey, Kaz," Izzy called over the loud whir of the blender.

"Hi, Iz." I headed toward the tea bags and reached for two cups. "What'cha making?"

"Lavender milkshakes. Want one?"

"Ooh, yeah." I put the tea bags and cups away and snagged a couple of aqua blue sea glass mason jars. I brought them to her, and she filled them up. "Thanks. Hey, let's think about adding cat treats to our animal menu and promote them along with the dog biscuits."

She wrinkled her nose. "Like tuna or something? Disgusting."

"Well, since you wouldn't be the one eating them, it's not an issue, right?"

"Yeah, but I'd have to smell it." She stuck her

tongue out.

I laughed. "Tony?"

"Can't say as I'm a fan, but I'll do it."

I grinned. "Because it's for Quinn?"

"Quinn is hot, but if she's going to be dining on cat treats, that's a deal breaker."

I laughed, snatched up the two glasses of the lavender milkshake, and waltzed my way to the parlor.

Sister Alice stared at the glass I handed her.

"Well, take it. It won't bite."

She reached for the glass. "I was trying to figure out what kind of tea this is."

"It's a lavender milkshake."

She wrinkled her nose. "Lavender is a scent, not a flavor."

"Just try it. If you don't like it, I'll go get you something else."

She put it hesitantly up to her nose, sniffed, and sipped. Her eyebrows shot up. "Ooh, this is good."

"Right? And there's not even any alcohol involved."

"Who'da thought." She licked the remnants from her upper lip. "Now tell me about your command to stay away from the piano."

"And I thought Sister Eunice was the dramatic one." Sister Eunice lived in the same house as Sister Alice and Sister Ida. She jumped in to help in the kitchen as the need arose.

"Heh." She grinned. "Go on, now. What's this all about?"

"I think we might have another ghost on the premises."

The hand holding the glass up to her lips as she prepared for another drink froze, and she looked at me over the rim. "Come again? I thought you said there was no alcohol involved."

"I'm serious," I said. "Hand to God." I filled her in on Tony's knife incident in the kitchen and Jade's experience with the stapler.

"And?"

I shrugged and squinched my eyebrows together. "And what?"

"What's that got to do with my going near the piano?"

I proceeded to tell her about that as well and watched as she appeared to process the information while slowly bringing her glass down to her lap.

"It appears you might have stirred something up," she mumbled.

I reached over and poked my pointer finger in her arm but squirmed at the look she gave me over the rims of her eyewear.

"How might I have done that?"

"Your grandpa and Honey were smart to leave well enough alone. You've been talking about wanting to help the present ghost—"

"Lady Lucy."

She rolled her eyes and shook her head. "Anywho, as I was saying, by disturbing the quiet nature of things, you might have unearthed something else. One must be careful when it pertains to ghosts, in case it's something more sinister."

I scrunched my face. "Sinister?"

She nodded. "A demon."

My jaw dropped as I processed her warning. But then I shook my head before tilting it from side to side. "There's probably a perfectly logical reason for each of the three incidents."

"Yes, there could be. But obviously you don't think so or you wouldn't be concerned about my safety near the piano. The other world is nothing to mess around with, Andie Rose."

Her serious tone caused me to shift in my chair. "I haven't done anything. Yet." She quirked an eyebrow. "I haven't!" I averted my gaze from hers. *Geez!* "So about that new football team?"

"Football season is long over."

"Yeah, but talk of the new minor league team is recent." She leveled her gaze on me. I pressed my lips together to stifle a grin and sat back in my chair, crossing my legs at the knee. "I heard you loud and clear. Now, getting back to the murder, what will happen to Beau and Sara's bodies if there are no family members?"

She frowned and swallowed hard. "What made you think of that?"

"With Fawn dead, what if there isn't anyone else?"

"They'll expand their reach for any next of kin."

"And if there isn't any?"

She pushed her glasses higher on the bridge of her nose with her forefinger. "They don't have any next of kin? Brothers, sisters, nothing?"

I shrugged. "I don't know. Just curious."

"Oh, of course you are. I believe in most cases, the body is cremated and stored for a set time in case someone comes forward."

"Hmm. And what happens to the property?"

"If there is no will and no next of kin, I think the estate goes to the state. But that would be something to ask Noah. Why the questions? Other than your insatiable curiosity."

"Takes my mind off other stuff for a bit." I drank my milkshake in momentary silence, my taste buds throwing a party.

"Tell me what else you learned besides Fawn's death, bless her soul."

I checked my phone in case I'd missed any calls before I filled her in on the news from Noah about the criminal histories, or lack thereof, of the names he found from social media channels, as well as his guess that the ones who don't come up at all are probably fake names. And then I told her about Simone Holloway, her criminal history in cybercrime, her recent travel to Colombia, and her home state of Colorado. I finished up with the hangup calls my mom has received and the person following her, leading to my dad's quick departure.

I looked at my phone again as if I wouldn't have heard the ringtone over my voice. "And now I'm getting a little concerned. Neither my dad nor Mother are answering their phone or calling me back."

Sister Alice took a drink of her milkshake, again leaving a white mustache rimming her upper lip. She licked it off with a quick swipe of her tongue, reminding me of Lord Watson. "Okay, so listening to everything and trying to fit the pieces, if Simone Holloway is such a computer genius, capable of creating counterfeit documents that could fool the government, who's to say she couldn't have hacked into your dad's computer and read the manuscript."

My eyes popped open, and I sprang forward in my chair; the half-full glass nearly slipped from my hand.

"Holy wicked whiskey! Sister Alice, you're a genius." I processed the full extent of what she said when another thing popped into my head. "Anything anyone does online leaves an electronic footprint. We should be able to find out where Simone is by her comments, right? I mean, I don't know how to look at that or how it works, but I bet Matt would." Matt was a computer nerd from our recovery group and had helped us both in the past on occasion.

"We'll talk to him at the meeting tonight." She glanced at the clock on the wall. "It's already after two. I need to get a move on for a home visit before the meeting. If I'm late, no one gets coffee or treats."

"Trust me. If you're late, everyone will find them anyway."

"Not true. Old Mother Hubbard's cupboards are bare. It's my turn to pick them up and I haven't yet." She drained the rest of her milkshake, stood, and said, "Tell Izzy good job. She just gave me a new favorite. And Andie Rose?"

"Yeah?" I followed her, Aspen sticking close.

"If Matt says what you want done is illegal, you don't do it. Clear?"

"As vodka."

Planning to go check in with Frank, I grabbed a light jacket and stepped outside behind her, Aspen in tow. I watched as she strode toward her contraption. A moped with a sidecar. Her helmet hung from a handlebar.

"Want a ride?" she asked as she smashed the helmet over her short, spiked hair.

"Um, thanks, but no thanks. Even if you had an extra helmet, it would still be a hard pass."

She chuckled. "Thought I'd offer."

"When are you going to get something more practical? And safe."

"It's in the works."

228

My eyes popped wide. "What? Are you serious?"

"Yep. The heater went out in my car again, and the estimate to fix everything else is more than the car is worth. I need something I can drive year-round."

I was speechless. There's a first for everything.

She slipped her goggles over her glasses, revved the machine to life, and started off with a jerk. I watched until she turned the corner of the long driveway when my phone rang. Dad.

"Are you okay?" My voice hitched.

But as I listened, I breathed a sigh of relief, and my body visibly relaxed. As I'd hoped, he and Mother went for a drive in the mountains to get away from reality for a while. A friend was watching the inn. That Mother agreed to go into the *wilderness* with all the *man-eating wild animals*—talk about drama—told me just how worried she was about Dad.

Aspen and I hung out with Frank in the shed by the greenhouse for a bit, absorbing all the good feels from his Southern gentlemanly charm, then left for the meeting early, with plans to stop at The Raven Motel to talk to Stan Price before he left the next day. If they hadn't left already.

The owner was perched behind the front desk, reading a magazine. When he saw me, he scrambled to shove it beneath the counter. It fell onto the floor, centerfold up. *Uffda*! As Honey would say. Aspen stayed by the door. Couldn't blame the guy.

"Hi, Jim. Can you tell me if Stan Price is in his room? I'm here to talk with him."

He kicked at the magazine, flipping it closed with the toe of his boot.

"You know I can't reveal who's staying at my

establishment, Ms. Kaczmarek. Maybe you do that at yours, but not me. I run a professional business here."

I swallowed a chortle, embarrassed when the sound escaped from my nose. "Sorry." I cleared my throat and said, "Can you at least tell him I stopped by to see him?" I slid a business card across the scarred, dark wood countertop. "Tell him I'd like to talk with him."

He snatched it, held it up to the light, and examined it.

"It's a business card, Jim. Not a fake hundred-dollar bill."

He tossed the card onto the desk. "Too bad. A hundred spot could get you a lot of information."

I lifted my eyebrows. "Are you asking for a bribe, Jim?"

He scoffed. "Course not. Like I said, I run a professional business here."

"Um-hm." I nodded toward the floor. "Might want to get some professional magazines when you're behind the counter. Seems to have opened up again."

"Don't judge. These women are professionals."

I rolled my eyes and turned for the door. I wasn't sure who was more relieved to leave, me or Aspen.

Chapter 20

The meeting was exactly what I needed. The laughs, the sarcastic quips, the jokes no one but those of us with addictions could ever understand—let alone find humor in—the awful coffee, all of it. I was a self-professed coffee snob since sobriety, and the coffee in this room was among the worst I'd ever had, yet one of my favorites. And Aspen here with me was the cherry on top. The group doesn't allow animals at meetings unless they're service animals. And while Aspen isn't a certified service animal (thanks to the changes in law regarding emotional support animals—yeah, I'm a little upset about that if you couldn't tell), the group had no problem with me bringing him here. In fact, I think they preferred him over me. Except Wes and Scooter. We three bonded right out of the gate.

After helping clean up the room, Aspen and I headed back to the inn.

"Hey, Jade," I said as we walked through the door. Aspen, my poor attention-starved canine, trotted toward her for his dose of attention.

Jade nodded toward the parlor and whispered, "Gemmalee Price is waiting for you. She's hoping to get a last-ditch coaching session."

I frowned and glanced at the grandfather clock. "At this time?" On the bright side, that meant they hadn't left yet, and I had more time to catch up with Stan.

"She said her husband up and left without warning."
Bummer. "I guess he left a note that said he did something stupid, you were onto him, and he'd be in touch with her when and if he could. She doesn't know what to do."

Oh my hell! It sounded like Stan might be the killer, not Simone Holloway. That this information fell into my lap when I least expected it was as much a surprise as the fact that Gemmalee revealed so much information to Jade, but I was glad she did. Obviously, she was desperate for help and willing to say anything to get it. And I was desperate to find out more about where Stan might have gone and what she thought he meant when he said he did something stupid. I had a good hunch, but I wanted to hear it.

Gemmalee was staring, wide-eyed, into the fireplace when I entered the parlor. She glanced at me and then back at the fireplace, pointing at it.

"That sucker just came on by itself. I know it's gas-fueled, but a spark crashed against the glass door."

A sudden cold draft breezed our way, and the flames flickered. But just like that, the flame once again became warm and mesmerizing.

Her eyes became giant pools of questions. "What the hell was that?"

She looked at me again, her eyes pools of questions.

I tucked my lower lip between my teeth. *What was that indeed*? The cool breeze from the fireplace was new. Aspen appeared unsettled, his focus intent on the fireplace. Before long, he turned a few circles and curled up on the rug in front of it. I breathed my relief. Mentioning the ghost to Gemmalee when she already wound up might set her over the edge. And I needed information about Stan's *stupid* behavior he believed I *was onto*.

Finding my voice, I said, "You're under a lot of stress, Gemmalee. Having anxiety is completely understandable and normal."

"Oh, I get it," she said and chuckled.

"Get what?"

"The fireplace. It's on one of those timer thingies." She turned toward me. "Did you know it's possible to operate those by apps on your phone these days? You don't even have to use a timer. Of course there's programming involved, but nothing I couldn't do. If you ever want me to install that for you, let me know."

I nodded and stopped a knowing smile.

"I will. Thanks. Weren't you guys leaving today?"

"Originally, yeah. But since the Raven had plenty of vacancies, we decided to take advantage of it and stay for a couple more days. Until Stan—well, did the gal at the front desk tell you what happened?"

I nodded. "She did."

"Can we maybe talk in your office? I know it's late, but I'll pay double for the session."

"Of course. Follow me," I said over my shoulder. "But you won't pay double. I don't work that way. But remember, a life coach is not a therapist, so if it's not something I can help with as a coach, there's no payment." Getting some answers would be more valuable than any dollar amount. Plus, I was ashamed to admit it, but if it wasn't a professional paid-for appointment, I wouldn't feel bad about asking questions.

I bit my tongue to keep from asking questions before we reached my office, not wanting to appear too desperate. But the minute we each took our seats, I jumped right in.

"So, what's this about Stan leaving?"

"His note said he'd done something stupid and had to leave because you were on to him."

"On to him about what?" I watched her carefully, trying to read anything unspoken.

"That's what I was hoping you could tell me. The only thing I could think he referred to was the murders. Do you know anything about those that implicate Stan?"

"I'm sorry, but I don't."

"Then why would he think you did?" She shrugged and blew a long exhale. "I'm sorry. I didn't mean for that to come out so harsh."

I bit the inside of my cheek and took a moment to choose my words carefully. "Gemmalee, do you think Stan is capable of murder? Does he have a history of violence?"

She shook her head. "No. That's why it confused me. He's a kind man, but he's also the most loyal man I've ever known. So if he believed someone he liked was being mistreated or cheated in any way, I don't know what he'd do to mitigate that. You know how men are. They're fixers."

My eyebrows shot up. Was she justifying murder because someone was a *fixer?* "Gemmalee, can you vouch for his presence in the motel room on the nights of the murders?"

She nodded. "Yes. Unequivocally. Which is another reason I'm so confused."

I shrugged. "I wish I had some answers for you."

She leaned back in her chair as if defeated, resembling one of those old Raggedy Ann dolls. "He sounded so convinced you knew something, Andie Rose.

If you do, you have to tell me. Please."

I took a moment to study her to see if I could spot any signs of battered woman's syndrome. Maybe Stan hadn't left of his own accord at all. Maybe he was snuffed and stuffed under the bed in the hotel room. I shivered and released a breath. *Who's the one close to the edge now, Andie Rose?*

"I know absolutely nothing, Gemmalee. He was mistaken."

Aspen, who'd stayed with Jade, scratched on the outside of the door. I stood to let him in, closed the door after him, and sat back down. I scooped up a pencil and toyed with it between my forefinger and middle finger, a nervous habit.

"Have you reported this to the police?"

She shook her head quickly and swallowed. "No! I don't want him to get in trouble. But I don't know what to do, which is why I'm here."

"Gemmalee, if he *is* responsible for murder—or even suspected of murder—" or ultimately the one *murdered*, "we have to tell the police. My dad's innocence, his future, is at stake here. In fact, his *and* my mother's safety."

She frowned and shook her head again, her hair swinging from side to side. "There's no way the police will think your dad could have done this. They'll for sure figure it out. Chandler Langston is an icon in the thriller genre. Who would want to hurt him and your mom?"

I opened my mouth, but no words came out. Finally, I said, "I just need to find the actual murderer, so suspicion isn't hanging over my dad's head. Do you know what that would do to his career?"

She inhaled sharply. "If Stan *did* do it, that would

make more sense." She shot her hand out. "I'm not saying he did, just that it would make more sense. To a thriller author, this kind of publicity has the potential to blow up his career. In the best possible way. This kind of publicity could set Chandler's career on fire."

Her statement was disturbing, to say the least. I watched her closely for a moment. "The why doesn't justify murder."

"If Stan gets arrested, it wouldn't help anything or anyone. Beau and Sara would still be dead."

This conversation took a dark, uncomfortable twist. I shifted in my chair.

"But to err on the side of caution, let's put our heads together. Is there anything at all that could suggest Stan wasn't referring to the murders? I mean, the wife's cause of death wasn't unusual; nothing you don't see in the news every day. It wouldn't take anyone special to do that. But what a horrific way for Beau to die. Not to mention unique." She shuddered. "I've never heard of anyone dying from a frog before. Someone had to have access and know something no one else did. It doesn't even seem possible." She grimaced and clenched her teeth.

I caught my breath, met her gaze, and frowned. Aspen, who sat beside my chair, looked up at me.

"Gemmalee, did Stan mention that information in his note? Because that's not public knowledge. If he has confidential information, we need to find him immediately."

My cell phone rang and, tempted as I was to let it go to voicemail, I saw it was Noah and answered.

"Hey. Can I call you back in just a few minutes? I'm in my office talking with Gemmalee."

"Do not hang up," he blurted. "I'm calling about Stan Price, but don't let Gemmalee know you're talking with me, okay?"

Holy wicked whiskey! Had they found his body?

I stared at Gemmalee, engrossed in her phone, now appearing calm as could be. Almost relieved. My pulse rocketed.

"Andie Rose?" Noah said, a note of panic in his tone.

"I'm here. That sounds good."

Gemmalee glanced up at me, then back to her phone.

"Andie Rose, there is no one by the name of Stan Price that fits with the Stan Price supposedly at The Raven Motel."

He may as well have said Stan Price is a cat or a dog. I shook my head, clearing the confusion. "Well then, who was it? A fake name?"

Gemmalee's head snapped up to look at me. She set her phone on the edge of my desk. "What happened?" she mouthed.

I pointed a finger in the air, indicating I needed her to hold on for just a minute.

"I was working on the case just now when Quinn came to see me. She spotted a picture of Simone Holloway on my computer. Simone Holloway is Gemmalee Price." I gasped and tried to conceal it with a cough. "You need to get out of your office. Now. But stay on the phone with me until I get there. I'm on my way."

My gaze darted to Gemmalee, her arm pulled back, poised to throw what appeared to be a small arrow at me.

"Hang up, Andie Rose." Her tone held no emotion, her eyes were cold. She nodded at the dart. "You don't want this. Hang up."

I punched the button on my phone and laid it on my desk. She relaxed the dart enough to give me a pinch of hope.

"Detective Parker knows you're in my office. If anything happens to me, he'll know it was you."

"And I care, why? By the time this dart hits you, you'll have an agonizing three minutes before you die. The most beautiful things are deadly, aren't they? Not only did I make some loyal companions in Colombia, but we help each other out. If you catch my drift. And the good thing about prison is you have ample time to, shall we say, *network*."

"That's how you got Beau's body to the cemetery," I said, worried about my fate before Noah could get here.

"I was the brain of the operation; they were the brawn."

"Who are they? *Where* are they?"

Her lips curled. "Long gone by now. Back in Colombia."

"Why Beau?"

"He was damaging Chandler's career, Andie Rose. You're his daughter. I shouldn't have had to take care of the matter. You should have. You don't deserve him."

"But why Sara?"

"Because after I killed Beau, I discovered she was actually the one behind the evil plan to thwart your dad's career. Beau was too much of a wimp to stand up to her." A small smile crossed her lips, her face softening. "Your dad's main character in his series is about me. Did you know that? He loves me. There's no room for your mother in mine and Chandler's life together. Or you. Not anymore. Neither of you deserves him."

238

Her eyes appeared like hard gray stones, and her jaw twitched. I desperately searched for my options, a means of escape, of which there were none. If I went through the window, she'd get me with the dart before I could get it open, much less get through it. If I attempted to get out the door, I'd be too close, and she'd for sure ram the dart into me. I only prayed she didn't get to Aspen.

She started toward my side of the desk, drew the dart back, ready to plunge me to my death, when the large picture of Granddad and Honey fell from the wall and crashed to the floor. Miraculously, the glass remained intact without even a crack. With her focus on me broken, I took advantage and lunged for the door before she shot her arm out in front of me, bringing me to a dead stop.

She raised her arm, held the dart above me, and prepared to slice it through the air toward my neck when it flew from her grasp and across my desk, hitting the window through which I'd just recently considered escaping. The dart fell to the floor, the window opened, and a chilly wind blew across the room.

Gemmalee froze, her eyes and mouth equally large circles. "What the hell is going on in this place?" Her gaze flicked around the room before she attempted to jump over my desk to where the dart still lay. In yet another move I could only attribute to Lady Lucy, Gemmalee's legs flipped out from under her. She screamed, then groaned in pain as she lay on the floor. I winced, my teeth clenched. I'd suspected Lady Lucy of helping me in the past, but never with such aggression. Until now, I'd thought of her as gentle. But there were no other explanations. Was Lady Lucy the menacing ghost Jade and Tony experienced?

The window slammed shut and with an obscenity or two, Gemmalee scrambled off the floor and toward the door where Aspen stepped in front of her, sending her toppling headfirst, thumping into the unyielding wood.

Dazed, she pulled herself to a sitting position right as the door flew open and knocked her down yet again. This time, it was Noah.

"Andie Rose?" He looked behind the door at Gemmalee, momentarily incapacitated. She was out cold.

"Get her checked out," Noah ordered an officer while pointing to Gemmalee.

The officer kneeled beside her, and Noah scurried behind my desk, nearly tripping over Aspen, who'd planted himself firmly by my feet. I stooped beside him and wrapped my arms around his neck.

"Good boy, Aspen," I mumbled into his fur. I took a deep breath, inhaling his comforting presence before I stood. But Noah swept me into an embrace that squeezed the breath from me. Finally, he released his grip and held me at arm's length, his hands firm on my biceps as he looked me over.

"Are you okay?" I nodded and exhaled a long breath. "Thank God we got here in time."

I glanced at Gemmalee, who had regained consciousness, groaning and writhing on the floor, making a fuss as the attending officer slapped cuffs on her wrists.

"This would be a lot less painful and easier on you if you'd be still," the officer warned.

"Easier on *you*," Gemmalee said between clenched teeth.

I licked my lips and released a long exhale. Turning

to Noah, I said, "I'm so grateful you got here when you did. And thank God for Lady Lucy and Aspen, too. I'da been a goner."

He pulled back and drew his eyebrows together. "Did you hit your head, too, Red?" After another second, he let go of my biceps, shook his head, and said, "Sounds like a story I need to hear. But first, I want to take this crazy woman off the street personally and put her behind bars so I know it's done. No question about it."

I nodded and stooped beside Aspen again, lying my head against the silken red fur of his neck.

Chapter 21

Sister Alice dropped by the next morning at eleven. Apparently, Noah called her when he left the inn, asking her to check in with me in the morning. Instead, she immediately called to be sure I was okay and promised she'd come by in the morning after mass. "It'll serve as a trifecta: a home visit, a sponsor visit, and a friendly visit. A triple-play," she'd said.

Today she sported sunny yellow frames, and her usual silver crucifix hung around her neck.

I hugged her. "Coffee shop? I drank two soup-bowl sized coffees Tony made, but today calls for double that."

She raised her eyebrows. "How about a nap? I think you're entitled to one after what you've been through."

"Too much I want to do to celebrate life and my dad's freedom. Both from jail and from a deranged fan. Not to mention my mother's life. Besides, there's time to sleep when I'm dead. Which isn't yet."

"The way you're headed, that time'll be here sooner rather than later. Without you, I would have no fodder for my upcoming bestseller."

I heaved a sigh, smiled, and turned toward the coffee shop. "Let's go to the coffee bar. You no longer have to worry about me telling Cindy anything about Terry."

"Why? Now that you know he's not the killer, he's in your good graces again?"

"No. Because I don't staff the coffee bar on Sundays. Which means Cindy's not working today. Besides, until Fawn's cause of death is revealed, if it ever is, we don't know Terry's not a killer."

She chuckled. "Oh, Ant. What am I going to do with you?"

"What?" I lifted my shoulders and let them drop again. "I don't dislike him. But his lack of honesty and failure to come forth with information in a murder investigation tarnishes his character a wee bit." We turned into the coffee bar, where I went behind the counter to make our drinks.

"Dark roast?"

"With—"

"A gallon of cream and sugar. Of course."

She snickered. "Your spunk is still thriving, so that's a good sign."

I grinned, made our coffees—a giant lavender latte for me—and made my way back to the table Sister Alice chose. The one smack dab in the middle of the room.

"Have you never told a lie?" she asked me when I settled in.

I narrowed my eyes. "Is that a setup question?"

"You're holding a grudge against Terry for—for what, exactly?"

I frowned. "I'm not holding a grudge; I just don't trust the man. And it's not for a poor reason, either. How do we know he wasn't somehow responsible for Fawn's death?"

"What evidence do you have to think he was?"

"Well—I don't have anything concrete. But with the cause of death suspicious and not thoroughly investigated, how do we know for sure?" She opened her mouth to speak, but I pushed my hand out. "The last thing I want to do is judge, but—"

"But you are."

I sat back and stared out the window for a moment before I nodded slowly and looked back at her. "I'm a terrible human."

"No, dear. You're not terrible, but you *are* human. Be thankful we're the fortunate ones who have the tools to be better than that." I gave her a blank look. "Everyone on this earth is human, but those of us in the Program are fortunate in that we have a blueprint to follow."

I nodded.

"Just because Terry lied by omission—which I'm not excusing—that doesn't mean he's a murderer, too. Don't judge others because they—"

"Sin differently than you," I finished the advice she often dished out. "I know, I know. It's just that—"

"We're all a drink away from a drunk, Ant, and you're trudging dangerously close to the ledge." She touched her forehead, chest, and shoulder to shoulder in a cross and pushed her glasses further on her nose with her knuckle.

I slid a napkin across the table. "For the love, will you clean those lenses, please?"

She shook her head and smiled. "No. Because this makes me truthful when I tell you how good you look after all the events of last night."

I laughed and smoothed a hand over my hair. "You are so ornery."

"Hey, boss." I turned toward Tony's voice. "You have company."

Noah and Quinn followed behind him. Aspen pushed himself up to greet an unenthused Lord Watson, and I stood to grab two more chairs. Tony snagged another from across the room and straddled it backwards, his arms crossed and resting on the back of the chair. I gave him a quizzical look.

"What? I'm taking a coffee break."

"During lunch?"

"Izzy popped in to grab some stuff from the walk-in cooler, so she said she'd hold the fort for a few minutes."

Tony sneaked a look at Quinn. It was quick and subtle, but I definitely saw it. I didn't know whether to be happy for him or afraid. Happy because I knew Tony has been lying low, waiting for the right person to catch his attention. But afraid because of—well, she was Noah's sister, after all. And I know how he was with Max.

"Andie Rose?"

At Tony's voice, I shook my head back to the moment. "Yeah?"

"You've got a goofy grin on your face."

"Just happy you've joined us, is all. It's all you, my friend." I looked at Quinn and then back at him, smiled, and stood. Aspen pushed himself to a stand as well. "Noah and Quinn, what do the two of you want to drink?" I giggled when I glanced down at Aspen, now completely disinterested in Lord Watson. He had his priorities in order. "Yes, buddy, you can have a pup cup."

"Personalized service," Noah said. "Even for Aspen. Impressive."

"What can I say? We have a full-service inn." Noah asked for a black coffee and Quinn passed. "Tony?"

He shook his head. "Nothing for me. My boss will take it out of my paycheck, and I get peanuts the way it is."

A round of laughter erupted.

"Poor baby. But I've seen your house. You're not living in poverty."

Another round of laughter before Noah stood and followed me to the coffee bar.

"How are you feeling after last night, Red? Any nightmares?"

I reached for a mug from the shelf and prepared a single coffee for him.

"No. I'm good."

"You don't have to be so tough all the time, you know. It's okay to—"

"No. I'm good. Truly." I hoped to discourage anything more about it. I was tired, emotional, and needed more time to process it all before talking it through with anyone else besides Sister Alice. And my dad.

"So we're even?"

I handed him a ceramic cup, the steam rising deliciously. "Even?"

"Yeah. You keep saying I owe you after last winter. I'd say we're even."

I chuckled. "Let me think about it."

I lowered Aspen's pup cup to him. He grasped it between both paws, and in no time at all, it was nearly gone.

"Geez, buddy. You're going to make everyone think I never feed you." I took a drink of my latte, set it down on the table and shook my head.

"How'd you sleep last night, Andie?" Tony asked.

My gaze flicked from him to Noah and back to Tony. "Are you two ganging up on me or what? It seems Noah is concerned how I slept too. With my eyes closed." A discreet look exchanged between the two caused a wave of shame.

"I'm sorry, guys. I suck." I hung my head. Noah touched my arm on one side; Quinn rested her hand on my arm on the other side. Twin responses. Except Noah released his so quickly I wondered if he'd touched me at all. "I thought I crashed, but my mood would state otherwise. And I'm still emotionally raw." I reached down for Aspen, licking the remnants of the whipped cream from his schnoz. Calm washed through me at the feel of his fur. "Aspen will take care of that, though. He's the best medicine ever."

Tony scoffed. "He's great in every way except how much he admires Jade."

Noah and Sister Alice gave an amused smile, but I shot him a playful dagger.

"The two of you get on each other's nerves like siblings," I told him.

He laughed softly, another furtive glance at Quinn. This time she saw and returned the glance with a shy smile.

I said to no one in particular, "I was shocked the glass on the window hadn't cracked when it slammed shut. Nor did the glass break on Granddad and Honey's picture when it fell."

"Nothing is impossible in the supernatural world, is it?" Tony said.

Sister Alice glanced from Tony to me. I knew her well enough to know she was pondering the news about the second ghost I'd flippantly mentioned. Her silence surprised me, though. Instead, she drained the last of her coffee and set the mug on the table, her fingers remaining around the handle.

I shrugged. "Beats me about the paranormal stuff. I'm still learning as I go." I looked toward Noah and then Quinn. "Sorry if you guys aren't believers, but the rest of us are." I looked at Sister Alice, still pondering. I said to Tony, "Here's where I'm unsure, though. Lady Lucy has helped me in the past, but never so aggressively."

Tony gave me a sidelong look. "She kept you alive. Who cares how she did it?"

"I'm just saying, with the less-than-nice occurrences that have happened with you and Jade, was it Lady Lucy or was it—another?" I ventured a look at Sister Alice, whose eyes narrowed ever so slightly.

Noah leaned back in his chair. "I have to admit, you're right. I'm not sold on this whole woo-woo stuff."

"You will be," I said and looked at Quinn. "After the other day with Max in the library, you must believe, don't you, Quinn?"

She raised her eyebrows. "Are you kidding me? I'm a creative by nature. I love a good mystery."

Noah tipped his head back and groaned. "Great. But more importantly, what happened with Max in the library?"

There was the stern, protective brother again.

I looked between her and Noah, failing to see any similarity other than their own unique, extremely good looks. Noah with his prematurely white hair and Quinn's petite frame, her round glasses and long hair. But both had fair complexions. My cheeks warmed with embarrassment when Noah caught me looking.

Quinn waved a dismissive hand through the air. "Nothing. Just because you're my brother doesn't mean—"

Noah's gaze was glued on his twin. "What happened

with Max, Quinn?"

I laughed. "No wonder she wants to get into her own place."

Sister Alice said, "What about the person who was following your mom in Colorado? Who was that if Gemmalee—or Simone—whatever we're calling her, was here?"

"I can think of a few things to call her," Noah grumbled. "And none of them are Gemmalee or Simone."

"I talked to Dad this morning. He said Mother discovered the person in question was a visitor of one of the inn's guests."

"And the hangups?" Sister Alice asked.

I lifted my hands. "I don't have an answer to that question. We don't know. They've stopped, though, which is a little suspicious." I looked at Noah. "Speaking of unanswered questions, why did Gemmalee want Beau in Spirit Lake, much less the cemetery? She said her criminal buddies got him here, but why *here*?"

"She knew about Chandler's ties to Spirit Lake. She hacked into your dad's computer and read the manuscript, then sent an email from his computer to Beau's computer, asking to meet him in Spirit Lake. That it was a matter of life and death. Little did he know he was walking into *his* death."

"I knew it!" Sister Alice said as she slapped her hand on the table. Quinn and I jumped. "Didn't I tell you, Andie Rose?" To Noah, she said, "Anytime you have a slush fund, I'm available for hire to help solve cases."

Noah groaned. "That won't be necessary."

"Wait." I frowned. "So her pals didn't bring Beau here at all?"

"We're still too early in the investigation to know much, but from what I've been able to piece together so far, Beau came here because of Chandler's email. From there it was all the other guys."

"She must have promised them worthwhile favors in return. Eww." I wrinkled my nose. "But why wouldn't my dad have seen the email to Beau?"

"She wiped it from his computer after she sent it. From what I've gathered, she made it pretty convincing to get Beau, a recluse, out of his apartment. Like I said, telling Beau it was a matter of life and death. One of her criminal buddies from Colombia owed her a huge favor. He provided the poisoned darts. I don't yet know exactly who the brawn was. The one who staged Beau at the cemetery."

I shuddered. "That just freaks me out to think of being buried alive. Even if it was on top of the ground. Just being shut inside of a coffin."

Aspen, who'd been lying on the floor nose to nose with Lord Watson, both napping, pushed himself up and strolled to my side. He rested his nose on my thigh.

"He was dead before they put him in the coffin," Noah said.

"Thank God," I whispered. "And Sara?"

"Gemmalee lured her to the spot where Beau's body was and took care of Sara herself."

"Sick people." After a beat, I said, "So Shirley and Winston's weird behavior was only that—weird. Nothing more."

Quinn pushed her chair back and stood. "Not that I don't find this interesting and all, but I'm going back to town to check up on my store. It's supposed to be finished next week. Including my living quarters. And

I'm dying to get out of Noah's house." She looked at him. "No offense, brother, but you're suffocating me. I need my space."

At that, Tony stood. "I'll walk you out. I need to get back to work anyway, so Izzy can beat it. Not to mention my boss is a slave-driver." He winked at me.

I laughed. "You have no idea."

After they left, I said to Noah, "I think there's a connection between those two."

Sister Alice chuckled. "I caught that, too. It appears Tony's coming out of relationship hibernation."

Noah narrowed his eyes, his lips a thin line. "What does that mean?"

I grinned. "Exactly what she said. He's claimed to have stopped playing the field. He wanted to, quote, hold out for someone special, unquote. He might have found her."

His lips relaxed, and he nodded slowly. "Hmm. I guess he seems like a good man. Better than that Max character. But you can bet I'll be doing a background check on Mr. Valentino."

I dropped my chin and looked at him. "I'm not saying you'll find anything, but everyone has a history, Noah. And everyone deserves the right to change."

Sister Alice dipped her chin and looked at me over her glasses. "Do you hear yourself?"

Knowing she referenced Terry, I ignored her. Kind of. "I can vouch for Tony."

"Like I said," Noah said, "she could do a lot worse. Max." The name was more a grumble.

"What is it you have against Max?" I asked. "You don't even know him."

"Which is why I don't trust him."

"You're a hard a—"

"A hard man to please," Sister Alice interrupted.

Jade waltzed up to our table and slapped a folded piece of paper on the surface in front of me.

"A message from Max Winters. The quick version is he's coming back to Spirit Lake in a couple of weeks and wants you to call him back."

Noah's head snapped from Jade to me, where his gaze heavily settled. So heavy, in fact, it squeezed the breath from me. I averted my eyes and slipped the note in my pants pocket. Sister Alice smiled and toyed with a sugar packet.

Noah lifted his eyebrows. "You're not going to read it?"

A bead of sweat ran down the center of my back from the intense heat of his stare.

"Later," I said, then turned my focus on Sister Alice. "How about helping me assist Lady Lucy to cross over and determine if we have a new spirit who's moved in?"

"I can't get on board with your careless methods."

"If I'm careful?" I wiggled my eyebrows. "I have a contact, who turned out not to be the killer, who said she'd help should I decide to look into things. Tina Cartwright."

"I want in on this endeavor," Noah said. "Here's your chance to turn me into a believer. I bet you can't do it."

Butterflies flitted between my stomach and my chest. I lifted my cup in a toast. "Game on."

A word about the author...

Rhonda is a retired paralegal and victim witness specialist, an exercise enthusiast, avid reader, lover of words, and coffee and dark chocolate connoisseur. She is the author of The Inheritance, a contemporary womens' fiction novel; seven books in the Melanie Hogan cozy mystery series; Finding Abby and Abby's Redemption, a romantic suspense duology. Her nonfiction book, Finding Peace Through Gratitude, is published under pen name Alexandra Benn. She is also an indie author consultant and was awarded the 2022 Master of Literary Arts Award from the Brighton Chamber. She can be found at her online home at www.rhondablackhurst.com.
www.rhondablackhurst.com